A *New York Times Book Review* Editor's Choice

An NPR Best Book of 2015

Long-listed for the Chautauqua Prize

Praise for *Not on Fire, but Burning*

"Hrbek's prose is sharp and trenchant, his voice remarkably complex yet assured, and this novel is an impressive achievement: a narrative that is changing even as it is still taking place, still being reshaped by the news, by our collective and individual memories, and by the very consequences still unfolding from the event itself."
— CHARLES YU, *The New York Times Book Review*

"Masterful . . . A strong, suspenseful novel, rich in its language, clear eyed in its characters and propulsive in its plotting. Full of ambiguity, yet precise in its construction, *Not on Fire, but Burning* is a shining example of post-9/11, pre-next-disaster storytelling."
— MICHAEL BERRY, *San Francisco Chronicle*

"*Not on Fire, but Burning* reads like a fever dream—spectacular, seductive, eerie, and surreal . . . Hrbek's prose is hypnotic, his abrupt POV pivots are both dizzying and delightful, and his overarching meta-speculative style is utterly entrancing. Fans of Delillo, Atwood, or just great, innovative fiction—this one's for you."
— ADAM DAVIS, *Buzzfeed*

"Brilliantly uncanny and read-it-under-your-desk-at-work suspenseful . . . You can approach the book as an allegory for the long-term aftermath of 9/11, or as a good, creepy read—it holds up beautifully on both fronts."
— LAUREN LARSON, *GQ*

"With *Not on Fire, but Burning*, Hrbek has crafted something audacious: A novel that operates simultaneously as apocalyptic alarmism, brain-bending quantum fiction, character-driven drama and gripping mystery. It's as poignant as it is perplexing and profound." — JASON HELLER, NPR

"*Not on Fire, but Burning* is simultaneously a dark look at our possible near future and a hopeful one. The book had me in tears by the end."
— JOANNE KELLY, *CBC News*

"A strange and beautiful genre-busting novel about danger and memory."
—ELIZABETH MCCRACKEN, *The Miami Herald*

"As [Hrbek's] characters uneasily navigate each other and their new world, they grapple with the same issues and prejudices of our current post-9/11 instability." —SHELBY POPE, KQED, 10 Fall Books to Anticipate

"Hrbek beautifully depicts the very human longing for a better reality."
—MATTHEW FAY, *PopMatters*

"Like the best speculative fiction, [Hrbek's] 2038 America could serve as a warped reflection of our own time, probing post-9/11 anxieties."
—MICAH MERTES, *Omaha World-Herald*, 8 Must-Read Books

"Hrbek . . . may be poised to be the next indie breakout."
—*The Millions*, Most Anticipated Books of 2015

"Hrbek's engagement with themes of loss and recovery and his vibrantly lyrical prose style reach a peak in this dark, allusive fantasy, which seems intended as a metaphor for the anxieties still lurking in our post-9/11 universe." —*Kirkus Reviews* (starred review)

"A profound cautionary tale, a vivid and often deeply unnerving reminder that our choices carry real and lasting consequences."
—*Publishers Weekly*

"Hrbek delivers a captivating story filled with nuance. Every chapter brings a surprise, and Hrbek has real knack for stunning, unforgettable images and turns of phrase. *Not on Fire, but Burning* boldly questions America's moral standing since 9/11, and brings to life the horrific consequences of ignorance, fear and hate." —*Bookpage*

"Brilliant . . . It's troubling and beautiful, bold and compelling, a brainy, heartfelt page-turner." —ELIZABETH MCCRACKEN

"Audacious, masterful, fresh, and compelling. I couldn't stop reading, and I couldn't stop questioning what I knew."
—V. V. GANESHANANTHAN, author of *Love Marriage*

"*Not on Fire, but Burning* is a mystery, a thriller, a sharp critique of contemporary culture, and an explosive family drama all in one. Hrbek gives us that greatest of literary gifts: the inability to do anything but keep turning pages." —RON CURRIE, JR., author of *Everything Mattters*

NOT

ON

FIRE,

BUT

BURNING

Also by Greg Hrbek

The Hindenburg Crashes Nightly

Destroy All Monsters

NOT
ON
FIRE,
BUT
BURNING

A NOVEL

GREG HRBEK

MELVILLE HOUSE
BROOKLYN • LONDON

NOT ON FIRE, BUT BURNING

Copyright © 2015 by Greg Hrbek

First Melville House hardcover printing: September 2015

First Melville House paperback printing: October 2016

Melville House Publishing   8 Blackstock Mews
46 John Street   and   Islington
Brooklyn, NY 11201   London M4 2BT

mhpbooks.com   facebook.com/mhpbooks   @melvillehouse

Paperback ISBN: 978-1-61219-606-0

The Library of Congress has cataloged the hardcover as follows:

Hrbek, Greg.
  Not on fire, but burning : a novel / Greg Hrbek. — First edition.
    pages ; cm
  ISBN 978-1-61219-453-0 (hardcover)
  ISBN 978-1-61219-454-7 (ebook)
  1. Boys—Fiction. 2. Brothers and sisters—Fiction.
  3. Muslims—United States—Fiction. 4. Terrorism—Fiction.
  5. Culture conflict—Fiction. I. Title.

PS3558.R47N68 2015
813'.54—dc23

2015017984

Design by Adly Elewa

Printed in the United States of America

1 3 5 7 9 10 8 6 4 2

NOT

ON

FIRE,

BUT

BURNING

PROLOGUE

She saw the impact. But Noah must have seen the object coming. From the next room, where he had been playing Monopoly by himself, he said:

"Skyler, look."

"What."

"Skyler, look."

He was five years old and Skyler Wakefield had been his babysitter since she'd started college, a year ago now. In a few weeks, classes again. She was ready to declare her major. She was going to be a fiction writer, like her father. This is what she had been thinking in the moments before it happened. *Like my father.* Then she looked. The house, set on one of the city's hills, had views of San Francisco Bay and the Golden Gate Bridge and the Marin Headlands on the far side of the bay. What Skyler saw through the window confused her: A plane. But not a plane. It was too bright. Like something cosmic come at high speed through the atmosphere, a star falling in broad daylight, but now decelerating strangely, like a machine, as if to land in the water of the bay. Then not landing. Slowing and lifting—all of this happening very quickly—as it approached the bridge, seeming to shrug its wings like some impossible dragon, though there were no wings, and yet something, metal or fire or a bolt of electromagnetism, was severing the suspension cables; and as each red cable lashed whiplike into the air, the roadway fell by stages to the pure morning blue of the water.

More than a crash. Not an accident. Get away from the window. Knowing what was coming now. Skyler put her back to the wall— shut her eyes, hard—and tried to shout to Noah. But her voice was gone from the terror of knowing. Even with eyes closed, she could see the flash of light.

If he's looking, he'll be blind.

A moment later, a shock of wind hit the house and the sound of every window breaking, of flying glass, of glass shards being rifled into walls and furniture, chiming against objects held together by metallic bonds, was like the music of the world please no glass plane dream help now Mom Dad Dorian . . .

When Skyler woke up, smoke was flooding the room. The door— the one leading to the hallway and the adjoining room where Noah was—she could not see. She tried to feel her way to it, but objects blocked her way, and she crawled in circles. She stopped. She pressed her cheek to the floor, trying to hear, afraid that the membranes in her ears must be slashed, because the only sound now was a pure and constant tone, like the hum of a tuning fork. She reached in her pocket for the phone vibrating against her thigh. On the glowing screen, she saw the numbers and the name. Noah's mother. She pushed ACCEPT and held the device to her ear, and was able to hear the voice, just barely:

"Skyler."

"I'm here," she said.

Of course, the mother wanted to know if Noah was there. "Are you still with him?" "I'm with him and he's all right," Skyler said, not knowing if this was true. The mother gave her very clear directions. Take Noah out of the house and go three blocks south and one block

4

west to a school with a fallout shelter. Being told what to do made Skyler angry. Take him out. Take him out how. Then the voice was lost. The call had dropped. The network collapsing under the weight of attempted connections.

In the hallway, there was less smoke. Here, she could breathe, though breathing only thickened a sooty residue in the flue of her throat. She made it to the room he was in. The window hung in the dark like a painting of orange fog. She did not want to go in. If she went in, she might not come out. She took off her shirt, pulled it inside out, and wrapped it around her mouth and nose. She found him under the window. After saying his name close to his face and not hearing a response, Skyler took him by the wrists and pulled him toward the door. He was not heavy: because he was small. He looked younger than five years old; it made him crazy how people were always low when guessing his age. I should be running, she thought, then remembered a way outdoors through a south-facing room at the end of the hall. She would take him, but first she would find the door and open it.

She felt the door, the knob. Decided there was no fire on the other side. Turned the knob and pushed. To the left, steps up to the street; to the right, a dark cloud lit from below and within. She got Noah onto her back. His arms dangled over her shoulders, and his lips, when his head moved, seemed to be kissing her neck. Skyler took him straight up to the street, worried if she put him down she wouldn't pick him up again. There was no one else nearby. One person, a block away, running south. At the crest of a street, beyond the enclave of opulent homes, Skyler looked down to the burning neighborhoods along the bay. What she saw down there recalled a medieval painting of hell she had studied in Art History. Innumerable scenes of crazy torture, some brightly lit by fire, others in shadow, all of them under a sky impastoed with sun and ash. The street leading down was so sharply pitched that steps had been built into the sidewalk on one side. People were climbing towards her, climbing the steps on their hands and knees. Skyler felt a surge inside. Up here, the metal posts of street signs might be twisted into the shape of palsied limbs and the trees along the streets defoliated, but the buildings were still standing; and so was she, and she had the boy. She shrugged the boy higher onto her back. Three blocks south and one block west. Not far. She told herself that the worst was over and she had lived through it and she could keep living if she did everything correctly. The boy weighed nothing now. With every step: easier to carry. Skyler imagined she was carrying her brother, who would turn three in a few weeks. She felt like she was carrying Dorian.

After a couple more blocks, she saw the school on the far side of a public park she'd visited before with Noah. From a half block away, she could make out the sign with the symbol of three inverted triangles nailed above an entrance to the building; but not until she got to the doors could Skyler read the message, handwritten in magic marker on a sheet of looseleaf paper and fixed to the inside of a window. The shelter was filled to capacity. Steadying him, she tried the door handle, though she knew it wouldn't move. The strength went out of her. Going down to one knee, she laid Noah on the concrete, supporting his head as she had her brother's when he was an infant.

"Locked," a voice said.

She looked up.

"I tried every door."

The man was standing right over them. A kind of rain had begun to fall, black and oily. The man held the boy under the arms, and Skyler took his feet and they moved him under a portico out of the rain.

"Your phone," the man said. "Is it working?"

"No."

"Honey," the man said. "About your boy."

"He's not mine."

"Whoever's he is. You've got to get him to a hospital."

She didn't answer.

"Honey."

"Don't call me that," she said.

"Look at him."

She looked at him. He was a boy, a few years older than her brother, though not much heavier. She wasn't sure what else the man wanted her to see.

Skyler had been sixteen when her parents had Dorian. Her mother on the cusp of forty. Skyler knew they weren't planning more family. It had been six years since the last child (her other brother); and a whole decade separated her from Clifford. The truth was, every single one of them had been an accident. Her father had told her, one time, that accidents could change your life for the best. Which is exactly how Skyler felt about Dorian. Back when she was sixteen, when it seemed she would soon lose her family forever, slip out of their reach and beyond their power as through a hole in the fabric of space—there he was: covered in blood and fluid and trying to express something with his tiny lungs while her mother came out of the violent trance of childbirth and her father smoothed her mother's hair and Skyler guided the curved tangs of the scissors to the umbilical cord and cut the mooring.

On the note fixed to the door of the school, the location of another shelter had been written. The man told Skyler he would help her carry the boy there, though he didn't think it was a good idea for anyone. He knelt there, waiting. The rain was more like tar than oil. Then the man suggested that maybe she wasn't thinking clearly and the thing for her to do was leave the boy here and go with him to the next shelter.

"Leave him where?"

"Here."

Skyler didn't answer. She closed her eyes and wished the man would disappear. When she opened her eyes, he was gone.

City wireless was still working. She did a search for hospitals. The nearest one, by chance a children's hospital, was close enough. But the rain. A wet toxic shit, not falling hard, but after a few minutes they would be covered. *The air, too*, Skyler thought—and they could not but breathe the air. Still, the rain seemed more dangerous. They needed clothes. She left Noah by the school and ran along the sidewalk to a row of houses whose bright colors Skyler could still make out through the cover of ash. She scrambled up a set of stairs. The door was locked, but the panes of glass were gone, as was the glass in every other window. She reached through and turned the knob on the inside. On the floor of the foyer: a scattering of mail. Accruing, Skyler guessed, for a week. They weren't here. They were somewhere else. Clothing hung from hooks on the wall. She pulled on a windbreaker and zipped it to the neck, and took a hooded sweatshirt for him.

What else?

For the second time, she felt a qualm of nausea. Didn't want to eat, but she should take food for later, and there might be filtered water. She got halfway down the hall and retched. It must be in me. She found water in the refrigerator. Rinsed her mouth, and drank. Then she pulled out her phone and sent her parents an e-mail. Subject: I M OK.

She hadn't been there more than five minutes. When Skyler got back to the school and found Noah gone, a spike of panic went into her heart, a feeling from a dream she'd had weeks earlier in which she was her brother's mother, realizing she'd lost her child after dark in an amusement park with attractions made of ice. Someone in the school had taken Noah. Or maybe not. Was he never really here? For a moment, Skyler saw through all the tricks her mind had been playing. Then she looked across the street—and there he was, wandering over the smoking waste of the park.

"Hey," she said, catching up with him. He didn't respond. When Skyler touched his shoulder, still no reaction. She had to get in front of him and stop him with two hands.

He blinked up at her.

She said: "And where do you think you're going?"

He nodded.

The rain was in his hair and dripping down his face and into open wounds she somehow hadn't seen until now.

"This isn't a natural reef," he said.

"What?"

But he didn't say anything more. He just stared at her, though not directly. Eyes open like the eyes of a sleepwalker. Skyler passed a hand before them. The pupils didn't react. The flash, she realized. And Skyler remembered, long before Dorian. Her father had been in Japan, and she and her mother and Cliff had met him there, and they

9

had traveled all through the country (she was six, seven) and arrived finally at the Peace Park in Hiroshima. She hadn't really comprehended. But she had never forgotten, of all the memorials, the one dedicated to the children, and how her mother had lifted her up so she could take hold of the rope and ring the bell.

The hospital. The nearer they came, the more people they encountered streaming in the same direction. Some were bleeding and soaked with blood; others seemed completely untouched, and Skyler wondered what they were doing, not sheltering in. Since opening his eyes, the boy had not wanted to be carried. He insisted on doing his own walking, though his vision was gone; as was some of his hearing; and, Skyler guessed, a good part of his memory. He wasn't saying a word about parents or home, nor asking a single question about what had happened. Now she swept him up and tried to run the rest of the way, an activity that made her stomach sicker. The entrance in view at last was for the emergency room. When she saw the crowd outside, Skyler stopped and set him down and heard herself sob. All confusion: no help here. Then she caught sight of someone wearing a protective parka with a respirator mask. Heard instructions knifing out of the chaos. She picked up the boy. Around the corner, at a different entrance: pulsing lights of a police cruiser; fewer refugees; more responders in hazard suits and masks, turning the childless away and directing anyone with a boy or girl toward the doors.

Inside, there was nothing as organized as a triage station or a line. Women and men in blue scrubs were moving through the crowd, examining patients and then directing them, as if they were a form of traffic. The room—the smell of burnt skin, the sight of so many hurting children—made Skyler want to vomit. She thought she could feel it in her system now, the poison: a slow burn along the fuses of arteries and veins. A woman in scrubs took one look at Noah and checked the yellow box on a color-coded tag.

"Tie this to his arm," she said. "Over there. Yellow."

"What does that mean?"

"It means yellow."

Skyler felt stupid for asking the question, and selfish. She tried to thank the woman, the nurse or doctor or medical student; but her voice got lost in the whirling flock of voices, and the woman was already checking the next tag—red—and securing it to the wrist of a girl whose body hung on her father's arms like a deserted cocoon. Skyler took Noah's hand. Affixed the tag and went with the other yellows. Wounded and lost forever, but not in danger of dying. That, she thought, is what it must mean.

"Is he your brother?"

"What?"

It was a man speaking to her. They'd been pushed close to one another on the way through doors that were painted like barn doors and gave onto a ward whose walls were bright murals of farmland.

"No," Skyler finally answered. "No, he isn't."

She sat on a chair with the boy in her lap, waiting, mind and pulse finally slowing. People around her talking about where they had been and what they'd been doing when it happened. Skyler had been writing. Working on a short story while Noah played Monopoly. She tried now to recall. Couldn't. What was the story? Something about . . . She had been writing it for weeks, but couldn't remember anything now about the plot or the characters. When it happened, she had been writing a story. Noah had said look; and as she ducked away from the window, the computer, still on the table with the file open and a sentence unfinished on the screen, must have been hurled melting through the air. And her story must have gone with it.

They had been waiting for one of two doctors in blue scrubs, neither much older than Skyler. Finally, the young man came. Detached the lower tab from the triage tag and took the boy's wrist. Took his pulse and wrote on the next tab and only then gave her a kind of smile. He put a hand on Noah's chest and said into his ear:

"Breathe now."

The boy kept breathing.

"What's your name," the doctor said.

"Skyler."

"Him?"

"Noah. He's my— I mean, I babysit him."

"Mother?"

"She's out of town," Skyler said.

"Father?"

"They're divorced."

The doctor withdrew his hand from the boy's chest and wrote again on the tag. Then asked Noah firmly: his name, where he lived, where he was now. The boy's answers made no sense. Again, the doctor looked at Skyler, and asked: "Do you know what happened out there?"

"No . . ."

He nodded. "Where were you when it hit—indoors or outdoors?"

"In."

"Where? What neighborhood?"

"Presidio Heights."

"So you sheltered in for a while."

"No."

He didn't seem to understand. "Well, what've you been doing the last two hours?"

She couldn't speak.

"Look," he said. "Tell me your name again."

"Skyler."

"Skyler. You've been under the plume for two hours—"

"It wasn't that long."

"It's been two hours," he said. The words sounded so final, Skyler thought he would move on to the next wounded kid and not look back at them. But he stayed long enough to change the status on Noah's triage tag from yellow to red—and to look at her once again. Never had she seen eyes so transparent. The one pale comparison Skyler's mind would make was to a boyfriend from the previous semester. The way he'd looked at her when she dared tell him one night: I think I love you. As if there was nothing he could say and nothing to be done for her.

They took Noah in one direction and led Skyler in another. Down the hallway of an evacuated ward. Windows blown out. The young cancer and leukemia patients had gone to the fallout shelter or acute care; and now here Skyler was, with other parents and guardians from the red group, walking over broken glass and smeared blood. She held a towel and a gown. Every shower on the ward was streaming water. She went into a bathroom and shut the door behind her; removed her clothes and added them to a pile of contaminated clothes; then stepped into the warm flow. Bowing her head, she shampooed the tar out of her hair. She went down on her hands and knees and tried to vomit directly into the drain. She had seen a land line telephone in the outer room. If it worked, she had to call them. She wanted to talk to them. But from the very beginning, blindly and whole-heartedly, like someone under the spell of ageless superstitions, she had been afraid to. She laved every inch of her skin with liquid soap and stood beneath the water for a count of sixty.

"Sky. Oh, Sky."

"I'm okay."

"Where are you?" her mother asked.

"I'm at a hospital . . ."

"Skyler."

It was her father now. Just as she had known. Their voices. Each so loving and terrified: she wasn't going to live through this.

"Sky, are you hurt?"

She told him no and that she was safe where she was, but it was a children's hospital and she couldn't stay there.

"Why not, hon."

She was wearing the gown and her tennis sneakers. Standing by an empty bed. In the bathroom a few feet away, the next person was showering and she could hear that person throwing up. She tried to explain to her father what the doctor had explained to her. That given her proximity to the explosion, the time of her exposure, and the presentation of symptoms—

"Slow down," her father said. "Let me talk to a doctor."

"I don't know where they are."

"Sky . . ."

She felt faint all of a sudden and the tears in her eyes seemed very hot. Her father was talking. Suggesting she do things that made no sense. He was too far away to understand. A hundred miles north— and the bridge between here and there didn't exist anymore, the way from here to the town she'd grown up in, enfolded by hills yellow in summer (the arrow of the wildfire danger sign set to orange) and emerald green in spring; the river beneath the redwoods, flowing west, meeting the ocean at a shore where harbor seals came to pup every spring when the hills greened.

Outside the hospital, Skyler saw that the rain was coming to an end. The black rain, people had been saying, was in fact the water of the bay, drawn up into the cloud and fallen fouled back to earth.

She had heard a lot of things in the hospital.

What was true?

If we decontaminate now, we will probably live. No matter what we do, we have a week at most. There's another plane. Another plane went down in the middle of the country. It wasn't a plane; it couldn't have been, it was too bright. It was on fire. No, not fire, a burning light. Her father said: just walk, walk south, Sky, and we'll meet you, we will find you.

She thought of something she had read in Existential Philosophy. What if a demon came to you in your loneliest moment. Said: this life, just as you have lived it. Would you choose it over and over again for all eternity? Are you strong enough to want nothing more?

She had walked two or three blocks, under a brightening sky, when she suddenly believed herself to be missing something. The boy. She stopped short. As if to go back for him. Then remembered. Not mine anymore. Skyler felt the pocket of the hospital gown for her phone and the two small tablets of morphine.

Overhead: blue of noon.

The wind had changed direction. The plume of darkness sheering east. Away from the city, toward the other cities across the bay. And the university. Most of her schoolmates had gone home for the summer, but not all; and now Skyler thought of the names and faces of the ones who had stayed, as she had stayed, though her mother had not wanted her to. In fact had nixed the idea. If not for her father's intervention, she would've been home for the summer. Would be home now. She felt her lips moving and realized she was speaking aloud, barely aloud. Saying in a whisper: *Mom. Mom. Don't blame Dad. It's isn't his fault. It's not anybody's fault.*

She walked miles that afternoon. Beyond the blast zone into streets where windows were still intact; through a neighborhood where someone had sketched upon forsaken vehicles—traced in the blanket of ash laid over hoods and windows (with a fingertip, she thought)— myriad peace signs; and along a wide commercial boulevard where the pharmacies and markets had been reborn as free medical clinics and food banks. She drank down a bottle of spring water. She passed a chain clothing store with its doors propped open; went in and found jeans that fit and a shirt, and rejoined the current of emigrating people. People. Seeing them at last. Complete with bloodied clothing, burned skin, cindery hair; holding hands; conveying each other in wheelchairs, shopping carts, and red wagons; helping to their feet the ones who fell; lending their phones; saying thanks to each other. So many walking together. Like the marches Skyler had been to and to which her mother had gone when she was young and her grandmother before that. Through the streets as one. Across

16

roadways renamed for martyred leaders into the green world of the park, through the shadows and healing scent of eucalyptus trees, past the great Victorian greenhouse, into the maze of the arboretum where they seemed to hear someone, enfolded by the flora, playing a very old song on a guitar, and where Skyler offered to an elderly woman suffering the torment of beta burns one of the two tablets of morphine allotted to her at the hospital. The sun was going down over the ocean, ionized particles endowing the sky with the beauty of skies painted on the domed ceilings of cathedrals. She felt dizzy and feverish. Just for a little while, she thought, lying down on the grass, skin hurting, thinking that in a few weeks her brother would turn three. She had already made secret birthday plans. To bring him into the city, to a science museum by the bay with exhibits that played tricks on your mind and senses. There was one called the Listening Vessels. A pair of giant parabolic reflectors which focused sound in such a way that the whisper of a person seated in one reflector could be heard fifty feet away by a person seated in the opposite one, and vice versa: like reading minds across space and time.

1

Summer in the future. Third straight to be the hottest on record, and the first since Dorian's birth to coincide with the emergence of the periodical cicadas. Brood X. Also known as the Great Eastern Brood. *Magicicada septendecim*. Dorian knows all about them from Science class. How seventeen years ago, they sang and mated by the millions; and the females, with knife-like ovipositors, scored the bark of tree branches and laid eggs in the slits. About two weeks later (by which time all the adults had died), the newborn nymphs dropped from the trees and burrowed underground—and that's where they grew in secret, waiting for their time to tunnel to the surface . . . It happens one night in June, around sunset. Dorian and his friends are out at the old race track on Union Avenue. For more than a century, the town had been defined and made prosperous by the sport of thoroughbred racing. But that was back before the summers got too hot for horses to be pushed to the limits of speed and stamina. The track is in ruins now. Taken back by nature. The sandy loam and grass a jungle of weeds and brush, though a kind of trail has been forged alongside the running rail—and in the old stables still lay the bones of a racehorse named Strange Victory.

"When are you taking off?"

"6-13."

"Shit, man. Sayonara."

"I wish *I* was going to New France."

"Why."

"Because it isn't a province of America the god damn Beautiful."

"I sympathize, but the camp doesn't allow intersexuals."

"Suck me."

"How about camel-fuckers. Do they let them in?"

"Jesus, look!"

They all stop talking—Dorian, Zebedee (whose real name is Plaxico), Keenan, and Dean—and look to where Dean is pointing. They have been passing around a green; and each boy thinks, for a moment, that the motion before his eyes must be drug-induced, a trick of his own mind, in which case it's strange for the others to be aware of it. Then they realize: The ground really is moving. More precisely, the soil (a sandy clay dried to a pale brown after rainless weeks) is trembling, as if the rocks below are subducting like tectonic plates. But it's not that; it's the cicadas. The nymphs emerging from their underground cells. At first, the boys think they can be counted. But no. They're everywhere. Dozens of little heads rising up from the dirt, forelegs reaching up into the air like the arms of babies reaching for something suspended overhead. This is happening everywhere: in the yards, in the park at the center of town, on the campus of the college, in the woods and the nature preserve. The brood is emerging. Slowly and without sound. All across New York and beyond its borders, up and down the Atlantic coast, from the Province of Massachusetts Bay to the Virginia Colony and even west of the Proclamation Line. Dorian is kneeling and watching one of them struggle out of its burrow. Someone offers him the green and he takes another drag . . . "Just think," Keenan is saying. (He's got one of them in the palm of his hand.) "Seventeen years. Since before we were born this little guy has been growing and waiting and now here he is out of the dark ready to—what did Mrs. D'Angelo call it—'continue the beautiful cycle of nature . . .'" He takes the nymph between two fingers and pinches until the abdomen splits and the gut-snot comes out.

19

•

I am eleven, going on twelve. I am Dorian. Don't get me confused with Keenan. Our names have the same last syllable, but we are nothing like each other. He lives on my street. I was in third grade with him and this last year in fifth. But we were never friends until the thing at the mosque. After that, while half the world was harshing on me, Keenan was on my side. To say he hates Arabs is an understatement. It's like saying Hitler didn't *prefer* the Jews as a people. But what I did at the mosque—

Well, I didn't want to go to the mosque in the first place. What I wanted was for my parents to not sign the consent form. I knew that Keenan's wouldn't. I figured half the class wouldn't be going. "Then you'll be in the open-minded half," my mother said, scribbling her signature.

In the end, twelve of twenty got on the bus. My class had been to Albany before. The provincial museum is there: a windowless maze of passages and galleries with everything from combustion-engine cars a century old to the taxidermied corpses of extinct birds whose archived souls call out from speakers in the ceiling. I remember feeling a cramp of anger when I saw the mosque. The imam was standing at the entrance in his long white robe. I was not angry at the imam. He wasn't very tall and his voice was soft and his skin was black. As he led us through the place, showing us all the things we'd read about in our textbook (the wall that faced Mecca and the mimbar from which the khatib delivered the khutbah), I thought about how most Muslims in America were probably like him, even the Arabs. Despite all that, in the bathroom (in a toilet stall that looked like every other toilet stall in the world, containing a toilet that looked like every other toilet), I unzipped my backpack and removed the magic marker and wrote on the metal partition:

FUCK ISLAM

20

•

They live now in the Province of New York, not far from the Procla-mation Line and Crossing No. 6. Every morning, Kathryn commutes by electric car from their small suburban town to the provincial capital. Albany is a city that appears to her, in these globally warmed days, to be a scale model of itself enclosed in a transparent sphere aswirl with photochemical smog. She takes the exit for the govern-ment buildings and brakes at the security scanner of the subter-ranean garage. Clearance is indicated by a green glow that floods the interior of the car like alien moonlight. Her office is on the twelfth floor of Agency Building 3. A window overlooks the plaza. Down there, she can see the sky, clear as a painting of the sky, in the rectangular surface of the reflecting pool. Once, last winter, she had been staring down into that sky and saw a jet plane crossing the blue, a tiny unreal thing, and she'd been filled with a terror she didn't understand.

What was it?

San Francisco. Of course. Because a lot of people believe it was a plane. Though others believe very different things. And yet that trag-edy was not the source of the fear. The source was harder to trace. Something about a reflection of a thing very far away. The sky facing up. Things turned upside down or inside out . . . Summer now. Only June, but already very hot. Kathryn plays her voice mails; and while listening, stares down at that mirror of water (upward-facing sky the hazy gray of amnesia) and thinks about her son, the younger one, Dorian, whom she and her husband have been worrying about for months—who, all of a sudden, just when they've begun to think that maybe the whole weird thing is finally fading away, comes down-stairs at seven-thirty, sits at the counter in the kitchen, fills a bowl with dry cereal, and, while adding milk, as if challenging all of them, her and Mitch and Cliff, to a duel with pistols, says:

21

"I had a dream about her."

Her . . .

Kathryn can remember very clearly where she was, what she was doing, when she heard. Eight years ago now, but like yesterday in memory. They lived in California then. In the Russian River Valley about a hundred miles north of the city, a few miles inland from the Pacific. Dorian three years old. Cliff nine. Dorian at preschool. Cliff at camp, just down the mountain, and Kathryn was home working on a brief in the study when she got an alert on her breaking news app. Something had crashed into San Francisco Bay and exploded. The bridge had been destroyed. The Marina District was on fire. For some reason, she hurried through the house to a door that gave onto a small brick patio: a trellis threaded with bougainvillea; a bird bath; and then a wooden gate that opened onto a side yard windbroken by a line of eucalyptus trees. She went into the grass and stopped. Like she was looking for something and had suddenly forgotten what. She stood there. On the distant hills, the cattle stood motionless, too. Hills the color of straw. Sun. The fog bank melting overhead like a polar cap. Great shelves of fog falling into the sky and fading into the blue. Next thing, she was in the car driving down the mountain and into town. She passed the firehouse and saw that the dial on the wildfire sign was set to orange. On the radio, they were saying intercontinental missile. So she was thinking about where to go, where to take the kids, where to hide. She didn't know. Because no one had thought about this for many years, much less prepared for it. Nuclear war. Words from a language she didn't speak, because she hadn't learned it growing up. No one in her generation had learned it. As she drove, she tried to remember where in town she had seen the sign—yellow and black, three inverted triangles: **FALLOUT SHELTER**—the kind of thing you'd buy in an antique store, evocative of another time and irrelevant to your own.

When the phone rang, it was not her husband, who was up in Mendocino at a cabin in the forest beyond the reach of wireless signals. There wasn't even a land line. She touched the answer button.

"Kate," her mother said. "Do you know what's happening?"

"Yes."

"You're in the car."

"I'm getting the boys."

"They're saying there's another plane."

"Plane?"

Kathryn told her mother what she'd heard and her mother said she hadn't heard that. What she'd heard was a passenger plane with the words AIR ARABIA on the fuselage—and that every airborne flight in the country had been grounded, but there was one not responding to air traffic control. And then she was at the camp and Cliff was running to her under the redwoods by the river, teary-eyed, smartphone in hand, saying an asteroid had hit the city and soon a cloud of dust would encircle the planet and cause our extinction. By the time they got to Dorian's daycare, Kathryn had convinced him that his online source was not reliable: No one knew yet what had happened. It was about eleven o'clock. The little parking lot was full of cars; parents were carrying children in their arms or securing them in safety seats. Inside, she found Dorian in the story corner listening to *Danny and the Dinosaur*. It seemed to Kathryn that she was watching the sun of his childhood going down. She didn't want him to see her until the story was over. Didn't want the story to end for him.

"Kathryn."

Beside her stood the director of the center, a woman, maybe fifty, whom the children called Miss Izzy. She asked Kathryn:

"Do you have family in the city?"

"No, not family."

Dorian turned as if he had heard her voice, though she'd spoken in a whisper. He got to his feet, slowly. Before coming to her, he glanced once more at the open book.

"He doesn't know?" Kathryn asked.

Miss Izzy shook her head. "We haven't told the children anything."

Dorian says he had a dream about her; and then he waits, like someone shipwrecked and marooned who has fired a flare into a dark sky. The colors of distress light up the room. His parents make believe they don't see. "I have to get to work," his mother says, and hurries upstairs. Cliff is earphoned. As for his father: It's summer, classes have been over for weeks, and he is in between writing projects, lost and miserable, convinced he will never conceive another fiction. He has nowhere in particular to be, but he turns to the stove clock as if the sight of the time will create an imminent deadline. 8:02. Dorian eases a spoonful of granola and milk into his mouth. His father removes his eyeglasses and holds them with the silver arms folded into an X. It is hip to wear glasses, to look like you come from another century, but no one actually has prescription lenses in the frames. There isn't a pair of eyes in the world whose imperfections haven't been corrected by laser beam—except for those of his father. When Mitchell Wakefield takes his glasses off, he literally can't see more than a foot in front of himself.

"Are you trying to upset her?"

"No."

"But you know you are."

"The reason why—"

"Don't start that again," his father says. "We've been through all of this. You promised, Dorian."

"All I said is, I had a dream."

His father stares at him. Not seeing him clearly, Dorian knows. Seeing a blur; general shape of a son. Then he puts the glasses back on, takes a deep breath, and says: "All right, tell me the dream." And Dorian realizes he doesn't want to tell it. Hasn't brought it up for any good (or, as Dr. Beltran would put it, "forwarding") purpose. He knows perfectly well that his desire is to move the family backwards, back to the time, last autumn, when he had accused his mother and father and brother of hiding everything from him, *everything*—and, after they'd responded with a show of ignorance and confusion, had felt justified in going totally nuclear on them. That's what he wants to do now. Because when he had shouted and cried and demanded they tell him the truth, the pressure, wherever it was coming from, had lightened a little.

Now his father says: "Tell me. I want to hear."

"No, you don't."

"I do. I want to help, Dodo."

"I don't need *help*."

But he does. He does need help. Just not the kind they are offering. *If I keep this up, I'll wind up in that doctor's office again.* So he says he's sorry, there was no dream. "I don't know what my problem is. I'll say sorry to Mom." And he walks upstairs. The bathroom door is open a crack and his mother stands before the mirror drawing a dark line along the ledge of her lower eyelid. Faint scent of perfume in the air. He says nothing. He goes into his room and clicks the door shut. Sits on his bed and turns on his pad and waits for her to at least knock, poke her head in and say goodbye so he can ignore the farewell, or make a sound indicating that her departure means nothing to him. But she doesn't knock. He can see the end of the driveway from his window: the car turning onto the curve of the cul-de-sac and arcing out of sight.

———

25

He has fitted the pieces they've hidden from him, the ones he has found in dreams, to the open spaces in the pictures he knows. They left California when Dorian was three: six months after the attack. No one denies this. But they didn't move because his father found a new teaching position and they were afraid of radiation blown on the winds and settled into the soil. They moved because she had died. Because his parents couldn't bear to live in the same place where she had been born and had grown up. The way he remembers it is— Well, he doesn't. He was only three and you don't really remember anything from that early time. You hear stories and you look at pictures and become convinced over time that things retold and recorded are your own true memories. What if no stories are told and all images are deleted? When they left California, what happened is: They stopped talking about her. Gave away her old toys and her clothes, school notebooks and artwork. Purged her from the photo folders on the family desktop. He has been through them many times: no image of her; nor any image *within* an image, such as a photograph in a frame on a shelf in the background, or a grade-school collage on the refrigerator with her name printed in a corner. He had zoomed such pictures and found nothing. Yes, they had done a very thorough job. Left absolutely no evidence. Allowed a silence to grow up around her death, unnatural and supernaturally dense, like fairy-tale brambles around a castle in which she slept under the power of an evil spell. He must have asked about her at first—but after a time (say, a year), stopped asking, wondering if perhaps all she'd ever been was an imaginary friend beyond whom the time had come to move. Then he must have started to forget. But you never really forget, do you? It's always there, deep down. But that's not where it is. These memories are very high up, saved in a kind of cloud that moves across the sky in your dreams.

———

Evening of the emergence. After sunset. Dorian is with Plaxico at the park downtown. Of all his friends, this is the only one who knows about his sister. They've been best friends since kindergarten. This past year, in the course of a school geneaolgy project, Plaxico learned of a lynching in a distant branch of his family tree—after which he decided he wanted to change his name in honor of that murdered forefather, and his parents let him. So his name is legally Zebedee. But Dorian (and only Dorian) still calls him Plaxico.

"I dreamed about her the other night."

"Her . . . ?"

While they sit against the black slab of the war memorial, the cicada nymphs advance in the twilight to the trunks of trees and crawl up to the leafy branches, making a sound like faraway whispers.

"I thought that was over," Plaxico says.

"No."

"It never was?"

Dorian shakes his head. "I just said that to get out of therapy."

"Now what."

"Yeah, now what."

"You have to figure out her name," Plaxico says. "If you knew her name—"

"I think I do actually."

"You do?"

"Skyler."

"What happened . . . when you searched it?"

"I found two Skyler Wakefields. One was a flute player in a orchestra in Boston fifty years ago. The other is a eight-year-old boy who had a art project displayed last year in a county fair in Indiana."

"Okay, so that's obviously not her name, bro."

Dorian shrugs.

"How would they do that," Plaxico says. "Erase everything."

"I dunno."

"Look, D. I'm trying to be open-minded over here. But you can't erase *every*thing."

"Yes, you can."

"No, you can't."

"The attack," Dorian says. "The whole truth about the attack got erased."

"That's different."

"How."

Plaxico says: "You know how."

They sit in what is now the total gray of twilight against the memorial and the carved names of murdered civilians. In the sky, no evidence of sunset remains. No star strong enough to show itself. The announcement comes on, broadcast from the top of the civic center. Fifteen minutes to curfew. Plaxico gets up, a rule-bound kid who has a streak of three straight years without a tardy on his report card, much less a curfew violation.

"In the new day," Plaxico says.

"Later."

From the park to his driveway by bike takes seven minutes. Only when the clock on his phone reads 8:54 does Dorian start home.

Your friend has a point. It isn't possible, is it, to completely strike a person out. Certain hyperlinks can be purposely broken, certain pages removed, but not all. If it really is her name, you would've found some trace. Words spoken to a reporter at a protest march (*Seventeen-year-old Skyler Wakefield from Sebastopol, California, said she was concerned about . . .*); or an announcement of a prize won for creative writing (SHORT STORY, FIRST PRIZE: "THE LISTENING VESSELS," Skyler Wakefield, Laguna High School), or Sonoma Valley Academy, or one of a score of other private schools within an hour's drive of the old house, every one of which Dorian had already contacted long ago to ask if there had been any female students between the years X and Y with the surname Wakefield. There had been twelve. None of whom turned out to be her. Although it had seemed briefly that one, a Maya Wakefield, might be—because the reply from the headmaster of the school mentioned a tragic death, and included a link to a memorial website; and as Dorian clicked, the feeling that came over him was of a door about to be thrown open. Then the page appeared. And he saw a girl who looked nothing like the one in his dreams, from a family not his own. She had drowned in the ocean, taken from a beach by a sleeper wave . . .

Plaxico is right. San Francisco is one thing, your sister is another. A hacker working for jihadists or domestic anarchists, or a cyber-specialist under orders from the government—someone like that could erase everything: every video taken from the ground that had clearly shown a passenger plane being steered into the bridge, a plane with the words AIR ARABIA on the fuselage crashing into the bridge and then exploding. But your parents . . . When he gets home, Dorian types the name in again. SKYLER WAKEFIELD. And combs through the results. And finds nothing more than he did before. A dead flautist from the Boston Symphony and a third-grader from Indiana. Can't be the right name. But he knows it is. Her name is Skyler. Dorian saw it very clearly at the end of the dream:

He was in a windmill and there was a kind of door and a fog swirling in the doorway through which he could see another place, a different room, where a little boy was bent over a board game.

What's your name?

Noah.

The boy rolled two red dice and one came up a four and one came up a one and he moved the old-fashioned race car five spaces to Luxury Tax. Through a window, Dorian could see what he understood to be the Golden Gate Bridge, though in the dream it was not a thing made of iron painted blood red, but a kind of drawing made of innumerable iron shavings that seemed to be trembling under the power of an atmospheric magnet.

I'm looking for my sister, Dorian said.

Skyler?

Where is she?

As he counted out make-believe money, the boy named Noah pointed; and Dorian crossed into the next room. Thinking: Skyler, Skyler. A laptop computer was asleep on a table; a chair was empty. Dorian waved a finger over the touchpad. The computer woke up and the document came to life—and when he saw the title (THE LISTENING VESSELS) and the name (SKYLER WAKEFIELD), what was happening did not feel like a dream anymore. It felt like something else.

The next morning, Dorian can't remember having any dream about her. He had gone to bed feeling on the verge of new and damning proof. Her name was like a key brought into sleep. *Skyler*. His mind would fit it into a lock, the door to a palace inside of which he would find one truth after another. In fact, he did dream about a palace (images downloading all of a sudden from subconsciousness), but his sister had not been inside it. The dream had nothing at all to do with her. Something about an Arabian palace. One of those opulent superstructures from the Second Abbasid Caliphate that the Coalition wasted in Gulf War III. Though Dorian understood, as he walked through it—a labyrinth of halls, chambers, rotundas, and grand staircases overspread with rubble and glass—that he wasn't in Arabia, but somewhere in the Territories: Nebraska or Montana. In one room, a huge throne room, there was the weirdest thing—one entire wall was a mural of Mount Rushmore made from ears of dyed corn. Trying to remember: *Where is Mount Rushmore? Dakota?*

He gets out of bed.

Has to pee, but it's summer and he sleeps in tighty-whiteys, and recently he's become self-conscious about his morning erections. He could put on pants but he's too lazy. So he paces the room waiting for the thing to go away, which it won't, because there seems to be a direct correlation between the fullness of a bladder and the duration of a boner. It's 7:47. Strong possibility his mother will be in the main bathroom, blow-drying her hair, and his father will be in bed reading . . .

He cracks his door.

The door to his parents' room is open. He peers around the jamb. Sure enough, here is his father (a man who literally wears pajamas), drinking coffee with a book in one hand, a pencil perched in the crook of his ear.

"Who's in your bathroom?" Dorian asks.

"M-O-M."

"Cliff's in the other one?"

"What do I look like," his father says, "a surveillance narc?"

He goes down the hall and tries the knob.

"Morning, nitwit."

"I have to pee."

"Uh-huh," his brother says. "And I have to shit out half a Chinese buffet."

He returns to his room, pulls on cut-off jeans and walks outside, planning to take a leak in the little woods behind the gazebo. Barefoot across the dewy grass. He is already going, the pee slapping into last autumn's leaves, when he realizes they are all around him, on the trunks and branches of the trees. The Great Eastern Brood. Each insect perfectly motionless; as if glued to the bark. But each one also moving. Dorian shakes off the last drops and zips. Overhead, the leaf canopy shifts in the wind and there's a pulse of morning sunlight. There must be hundreds of them on each and every tree, every cicada both still and not—or maybe the way to describe it is: each moving within its own stillness. He studied this in school. The insect is molting. Shedding an outer layer: the nymphal exoskeleton. But what he's watching here is less like science than magic. What's happening is: They are coming out of themselves. They are freeing themselves from themselves. Old self splits apart, dehisces down the back, a divide so clean it looks like the work of a surgeon; and a new one—white and waxen and winged—pushes through the gap. The head breaks open next. Dead eyes diverge. The new eyes, the living sighted ones, are blood red and wide with astonishment, as if the creature itself can't believe the change.

2

A drive this long. Couldn't make it without music. I am into the old, old stuff. I'm talking the Prophets of Grunge. The things you loved as a boy, you want them around you when you're an old man. The Marvins, Black River, Dreamgarden. There was a lot of genius in that sound before it became the ear candy of the masses, and my pod is crammed full of it. Enough to get me all the way to Dakota.

I was out here once. I was probably eight or nine. Way before any of this shit came to pass, back when the interstates were free and open roads, my grandpa took me to the Badlands and the Black Hills to see Mount Rushmore. Along the way, we got off the highway and drove a frontage road and turned onto a rural route and there in the middle of a flat green plain was this thing like an empty lot surrounded by a chain-link fence with a sign: NO TRESPASSING—USE OF DEADLY FORCE AUTHORIZED. We walked right up to the fence.

"There's nobody here," I said.

"They're underground. Maybe two members of the USAF."

"Can they see us?"

"Dunno."

"What's that," I said, pointing to a metal dome that looked like the access hatch of a submarine.

"That slides open," my grandpa said. "Before launch."

"So the missile is under there."

"Correct."

He had a book with maps that showed where all of them were. In the car, on the way west, I paged through it. The black spots symbolizing the silos were everywhere, spread all over the Territories; and in each of those places, buried under the ground and waiting for a time to emerge, was a weapon powerful enough to set an entire city on fire. That day, we made it to Mount Rushmore in time to see them turn on the lights. It was dusk. In the gray-shaded distance, you could just barely make out the outlines of the monument. Then the spotlights came on and the four faces on the mountain took on the complexions of gods.

He is about four hundred miles shy of Dakota, just west of the Quad Cities when a National Guard Humvee overtakes him. He pulls patiently to the shoulder of westbound I-80 and turns down the music and waits while a soldier in desert camouflage approaches the window, cradling his M-16 like a newborn . . .

"Where you going, sir?"

"Dakota Reservation." He hands the passport, last stamped at Crossing No. 6, through the window.

"Dakota Res."

"Yes."

"Now why the fuck would you wanna go there?"

"I'm adopting a detainee."

The reservist looks at him. "William Banfelder," he says, reading from the passport.

"That's me."

"You're seventy years old."

"Seventy-one."

"I'm going to have to run you through the system."

Will smiles.

"Something funny about that?"

"Third time since yesterday. But it's all right, I understand. I ran convoys in Gulf War III."

The soldier's eyes go skeptical. But then he asks Will, in a tone of respect, to sit tight for a minute. Recedes in the side view mirror. On either side of the highway: post-harvest Iowan fields; flat as the world was once believed to be; no less brown and bleak than the deserts of the Middle East. Here and now, on this highway, the sun is ahead of him, lowering in the west, as it often had been on those highways, there and then—when you would blink as you drove into the fire of it, flipping down the tinted lenses of the sunglasses that every merc in-country swore by but seemed only to obscure and blur detail, like an advent of glaucoma, so you felt you weren't seeing as sharply as necessary, like the time in the Forbidden Zone when you missed something at your ten o'clock which, only after the rocket had buzzed over the port bow of the Suburban, did you realize had been jihadists behind a berm with a shoulder launcher. So if you had been driving one mile per hour faster, if the berm had been ten meters closer . . . which is why later, drunk in that shithole of a base on the edge of the Zone, you had left that message ("I almost died today, Emm"), knowing she wouldn't pick up and yet believing that she would call back; and when, day after day, she didn't, your imagination supposed, *The grenade actually hit us and you're dead and hell is being in this war forever and thinking you can leave whenever you want and in truth you never will* . . .

"Sir, you're good."

"Thanks," Will says, taking his passport.

"You have a weapon?"

Will pulls back the curtain of his jacket. The Glock is holstered left of his heart. The reservist nods, and says: "You be careful out here."

"I shall."

"Don't drive over anything."

"Roger that."

"Including roadkill. Other day, at the off-ramp for Iowa City, we found an old TS-50 in a prairie dog."

And then he's on his way again. North by northwest. Into the middle of nothing, through the dusty buttes that look so much like that Middle Eastern desert across which, forty years ago, he escorted the supply trucks of the coalition. He has thought long and hard about those days. About what happened over there and about his original intentions, which *had* been good; and yet what had come to pass—the things he got involved in, the things he did . . . *Well, I have another chance now. Not that I'm trying to erase the past. No, that's not the point. You hurt people, okay. The point is, can you bring things into balance before time runs out* . . . Sun setting. On the passenger seat lie the papers, approved by Homeland Security and the Internment Authority. The boy's photo is clipped to one corner. His name is Karim. Twelve years old. Hurricane of black hair; angry accent mark eyebrows. Born in Kerkook, Arabia. Family emigrated legally when he was three. A year later, the attack; and a few months after the attack, after the formal declaration of war, he became one of the million relocated to the wastes of the Territories: Nebraska and Montana and here, Dakota. His family was Sunni, and each member thereof—mother, father, sister—is listed as a casualty of sectarian conflict. *Bullshit. A hundred thousand people dead on the reservations in the last seven years. A hundred thousand! Don't tell me a hundred thousand dead by car bombs and suicide bombs and blood feuds. The whole thing has been systematic. Drone strikes and who knows what else. American government killing its own citizens* . . . He has been eating sandwiches out of a cooler since the

Proclamation Line, because highway food gives him the runs. But when he hits Sioux City, what does he see a sign for? A druggie-force craving hits him. Tendersweet Fried Clams and an Orange Sherbet. He curves along the exit, turns at the light, and there it is, all lit up in the gloaming, roof as orange as sherbet, perfect as a mirage: Howard Johnson's.

Two days before the man arrived to take him away from the camp, six months after his mother and father and sister had been killed when a government drone launched two air-to-surface missiles into his block in the Sunni half of what had once been Mitchell, South Dakota, Karim got high for the last time with Hazem and Yassim in the ruins of the old abandoned palace on North Main. Carefully, he stabbed a needle into the last pea-size ball of opium they'd bought at the souk.

"Faster, Karim."

"Chill out."

"You chill out, mozlem."

He picks up the disposable lighter. Flicks the striking wheel. Holds it a couple of inches below the drug.

The palace is made of corn. Well, not *made* of it exactly. But covered, outside and in, with multicolored ears of corn. It used to be a tourist attraction. The city would change the corn on the outside every year, make different patterns and patriotic pictures. That was before the government moved the people of Mitchell and built an electrified fence and put people like Karim inside it. By now, the corn has all been pecked away by birds or shot out with bullets. Not much left but bare cobs turned brownish-green. But the letters above the main entrance—MITCHELL CORN PALACE—have not completely faded; and the domes and minarets, painted green and yellow, still reach toward the sky over the plains, giving the building the look of a mosque from the old country.

The drug has grown soft.

Yassim holds the pipe and Karim smears the flower-sweet goo on the curved sides of the bowl. The boys pass the pipe, heating the drug until they can draw it into their mouths as smoke; once the process has been repeated until there's nothing left but a gray ghost of resin, Karim says:

"Thazzit."

"It."

"Opeem," he says. "Thizshithole. I cant bleeve izallover."

"Cant bleeve it."

"Cant bleeve it."

"I wish," Yassim says, "youka come withuss."

"Me too."

"Leeme seet."

"Kikt," Karim says, and hands the pipe to Hazem. Then, tearfully: "I wanna come widjuguys."

Hazem says: "You are cominwidjuss. Juzza matturahtime."

The three orphans lie back on the cool tile floor; and as each one feels his soul levitating just above his physical self, he thinks of the sheikh, Abdul-Aziz, who has said to them, "You may be going your separate ways now, my sons, but very soon you will be together in the highest gardens of heaven. It is just a matter of time." Each boy contemplating the same thing in his state of flotation: That for which he is destined. Paradise. And wondering. Will Paradise feel as good as this? But thinking also of what must come first. Is it true what the sheikh says? That if we lay our life down in the path of God, we will feel nothing when our body explodes. Can dying be so easy? But even if it's hard, even if dying hurts very much. To feel like *this* after. Forever. Matter of time to feel like this foreverafter. To float above the physical world and dream. To be with your family again . . . Karim reaches into the pocket of his short pants. Touches the eyeglasses. The lenses are gone—the ovals of curved glass which helped her see clearly have cracked and broken into tiny pieces (scattered now, who knows where)—and one of the temple arms has broken off. But what remains, the shape of the plastic frame, helps Karim remember his mother's face.

Hold it before your eyes. Remember her eyes. Then fold down the temple arm and return it to your pocket. The only memento.

Two days later, dressed in new donated clothes given him by the nuns (a pair of corduroys worn smooth at the knees; a collared shirt, bright red, with an alligator stitched onto the left breast; a pair of tennis sneakers), he sits in a bus painted the blue of a bruise and rides out of the camp and onto a road so straight it might have been drawn on the plains with a ruler. The window of his seat is pushed up. A breeze comes through. On the horizon, he can see a rainstorm: a dark cataract of water plunging from a thunderhead as massive as an intergalactic mothership. The camp, that divided city, is already out of sight. And Hazem and Yassim. Won't ever see them again in this world. Next week, they leave for the Michigan Territory. A shelter for Muslim-American youth where they can surely score Dream and probably play soccer all the live-long day while you, in some heathen suburb, are getting the agonies and the shit kicked out of you. Karim shuts his eyes and rests his left temple against the window sash. The wind goes right up his nose; it's like drowning. Like that time a couple years back when they were playing war and he was the terrorist and they tipped him back on a board and poured water into his breathing passages. One of his friend's mothers found out about that episode and told the other parents and he and his crew got the tongue-lashing of a lifetime. You think torture is a game and so on.

Well, yeah. They did, actually. Though looking back now, Karim can sort of see their point. When you're seven, eight, you make plastic explosives from Play-Doh and fill up matchboxes with rusty nails and tape it all onto a belt and it's a fucking breeze to kill yourself. Then, one day, you're eleven, twelve, and you're a part of something real, more important than childhood, and more important than yourself.

•

"Him?"

"Yes," the nun says. "The boy in the red shirt."

"Jesus Christ Christian . . ."

They are standing at a window looking out on a fenced, razor-wired area, like the exercise yard of a prison. His adopted son has just walked off a bus. A kid at least ten pounds underweight. Whose flesh looks mildewed. Who's hugging himself around the midriff as if to keep his guts from spilling out.

"I thought you knew," the nun asks.

"Yeah, but."

"But he's just a boy, I know. Come, I'll introduce you."

Out of the building and across the dirt lot. When they get close, the kid sees them and forces himself to stand straighter.

Will has had a lengthy inner debate about conduct in this moment. It's about the kid, not you. Empathy. Big picture. Imagine you're three years old and you and your family get packed onto a cattle car and shipped off to a slum with no exit; eight years later, you're the only one left, and some old white guy comes out of nowhere and expects you to call him father. Be cool and take it slow.

The nun says, "Hello, Karim."

"Hi, Sister."

"Karim, this is Mr. Banfelder."

The kid looks up at Will with eyes big and tear-filled. Not crying, exactly. It's a symptom of withdrawal.

Will kneels down in front of him and says: "You're a Dream addict."

"Yessir."

"How'd you get the stuff."

He shrugs and hugs himself harder.

Will reaches into the breast pocket of his coat and takes out a pack of greens. He shakes one out and hands it to the kid, then produces a disposable lighter, and the nun says:

"Mr. Banfelder . . ."

"Sister, I've seen this before. I knew a guy once, back when I served, who got into this shit. Said he never coulda kicked if it wasn't for grass."

He lights the cigarette.

The kid sucks and exhales. Shivers. Wipes his eyes.

"How long?"

"Five months, I guess."

Will nods and lets the kid take a few more drags. "Feel any better?"

"A little."

"Mr. Banfelder, I don't think—"

"Opinion noted, Sister. But Karim is my responsibility now. Legal guardianship and all that jazz."

The nun gives a kind of smile. Then she says her goodbye to the kid, a hug and a kiss on the cheek; then she shakes Will's hand and is off to her next good deed. Which leaves the two of them.

"You called me 'sir,'" Will says.

"Yessir."

"Don't do that."

"Okay," says Karim. "So, what then?"

"You know Arabic?"

He nods.

"How about 'jaddi.'"

The kid looks at him and wipes his eyes again. "*You* speak Arabic?"

"Na'am."

"Jaddi," the kid says. "Like, grandfather."

"That make sense?"

"Sure."

"Okay, then. Jaddi it is. Finish the smoke and let's go. It's an hour to Sioux City. We'll get you some vitamins and a milkshake."

•

The trip to New York is hell. Although Karim has been through this before (several times since he started using), every other time he's had the agonies he lay still on the mattress in the half-light of the lean-to—Hazem and Yassim with him, all of them on the twin mattress like a litter of whining dogs—until withdrawal had become a state of suspended animation. You sort of forget you're alive. But this time. The world racing past the window at impossible speed, the glare of the sun, the heat of the sun and the chill of the air conditioning, the stink of a cattle farm. (How can something possibly smell worse than that open sewer by the lean-tos?) But the speed is the worst part. Even when he closes his eyes, he can't rid himself of the sense that nothing outside the window is staying still. Somewhere on the first day, they get pulled over by soldiers in desert camo—and even though the old guy has got stamped papers, they search the car. They pull up the false floor of the trunk and take out the spare tire. Then they make Karim remove all his clothes right there by the side of the highway. Though he is finally stationary, the motion of the car won't leave his head and he pukes up the milkshake from Sioux City. That night, they stay in a motel with two beds, where Karim,

42

curled fetally in the clean sheets, feels like he's adrift on a lifeboat. He drifts off and has a dream in which the camp hospital is heaven. His mother, wearing the jilbab she died in, looks as though she has waded waist-deep into a river of blood. Yet her eyes are open, and she's squinting—and saying: Karim, is that you? Where have you been, habibi? You have my eyeglasses. He wakes up and it takes him a long space to understand where he is. Not heaven, not yet. Not the lean-to. Then he hears the old guy in the other bed, making a sound in his sleep like a flooded car engine. After this, he can't sleep. Feels like there's something inside him, clawing at the dead shell of his self, trying to split him apart and get out. Perhaps this is your soul. He lies awake, thinking of the sheikh. Dark beard with twisting hairs, a beard of thorns.

3

By the next day, the insects have changed once again. The eyes are still red but the body has gone from white to black; the veins on the wings from pale yellow to brown. And the males have found their voices. The world is full of the noise: a dizzy trilling that gets trapped like a greenhouse gas below the dome of the sky and echoes as endlessly as surf in the helixes of a conch shell. Dorian and his friends are outdoors, playing a kind of game. Each boy has captured a fully matured cicada and pinned it, alive, to one of the four corners of a cork board. Each of them has a magnifying glass from a science kit and is using it to concentrate the energy of the sun into a single point on his insect. Whoever's catches fire first wins. But the whole thing is a bust: All that happens is, they burn a smoking hole through the poor things. The lack of a dramatic conflagration leaves an emptiness where there might have been a thrill; and other feelings, annoyance and pity, for example, claim the hollow space. The dizzy echoing noise, the chorusing, which comes not from screaming mouths but from vibrating abdominal membranes, seems to get louder.

"Whose bright fuckin idea was this?"

"Keenan."

"Brilliant, dude."

"We did prove something," Dean points out. "They're not flammable."

"Idiot," Keenan says.

"What."

"It's just not enough heat is all. Phase two, we need a medicine dropper. Everybody gets two drops of lighter fluid . . ."

This is when the car comes up the curve of the road. Mr. Banfelder's Argo Electric, which has not been sighted for a week. He sees the boys and gives two friendly taps on the horn. There's someone in the backseat.

A kid.

They all see him. And the window is down, so they see him pretty well. They see shaggy black hair squalling in the slipstream. Skin that isn't black or white, but an unmistakable in-between brown.

"It's a haji," Keenan says.

"Jeezuss."

"Am I right?"

"You're right," Dean says.

"Zeb?"

"I didn't really see him."

"Dorian?"

But Dorian doesn't answer. He watches the car follow the curve of the cul-de-sac and pull into the driveway of the house with maroon shutters and the old lawn jockey statuette on the grass. Car stops. Passengers disembark. It's a kid, all right. A boy. Judging from his size relative to that of the car: eleven, twelve years old. He's looking up at the air, at the trees. (*That sound.*) Then he crouches down and picks something off the blacktop of the driveway. Holds it in front of his eyes. (*What the fuck is this?*) . . . As a finger whistle whipcracks across the subdivision.

"He wants us."

"Us?"

"To go over there," Dean says.

Dorian sets his magnifying glass down on the corkboard where the four insects lay impaled and scorched, and starts walking toward the Banfelder house. One at a time, his friends fall in behind him.

Will has been anxious about this moment ever since committing to the adoption. He knows these boys well. He's known them for years. The Wakefield boy in particular. All good kids. Except for the one who dressed up like a Jew from the Holocaust last Halloween. Actually shaved his head. Keenan. But other than him, they are as good as you can expect. Still, is it too much to ask of them? To befriend a Muslim. No, not that. Just accept him. Understand him and let him be.

"Karim."

The kid doesn't respond or move. He's in a crouch, holding a cicada by the wing, though not looking at the insect. Watching the posse approach. Four kids: three white, one black. Will says, in Arabic:

"Stand up, Karim. And give a proper greeting."

For the first time, Will has spoken to him in what you could call a fatherly tone of voice. And the kid obeys. Though first he looks up—with eyes to make an old man think of a past that won't let go. (Like a time we were at one of the old palaces, where we weren't supposed to be, but in the early days everyone was: We'd ride into these fallen citadels in our up-armored sport-utility vehicles, firing in the air like Yosemite Sam and any towelhead who didn't put his hairy face in the dirt wasn't alive for evening prayers, which is how it went on this one day in Samara or Babylon or Tikrit, who can remember anymore, all incidents and settings seem interchangeable now, but wherever it was, there was a haji in a dishdasha with a camel; and even when the team leader, an ex-Marine named Brainard, walked directly toward them with the sawed-off Winchester

46

1887 he'd brought from Toad Suck, Arkansas, herder and animal just stood there, staring us down. It was not surprising when Brainard put the muzzle of the shotgun to the patella of the camel's left foreleg. Shot. All at once, the lower half of the leg was dangling from a bloody cord of muscle and fur. The guy came next. Same place. In the kneecap. Brainard ejected the spent shells and started toward the palace; and as usual, because the suffering didn't seem to unduly concern anyone else on the team, you were the one to clean up the mess and put each thing out of its misery. The man didn't bother you so much, the way he swore and spat at you. But the animal. Which had stood for a few moments on three legs before collapsing suddenly onto the road. Kneeling beside it, you thought: Odd animal. The hump and the two-toed hoof. As you knelt beside it, the head on the long neck craned strangely. Eyes searching, for what?) Back then, what Will Banfelder did was: He stroked the smooth fur of the head, once, twice, then pressed a gun to the top of the skull. What he does now is: Puts an arm around his new son's shoulders (think *son*, use the word in your mind), and says, "It's all right. You're going to like them."

The boys have a superstition with the lawn jockey. Every time they cross to the Banfelder property, they slap him five. He's one of the old ones with skin painted the color of a charcoal briquette and big red lips. The Negro, they call him. To slap The Negro five is cool. To not do so is to dis The Negro. Dorian walks right by the statue and Plaxico says: "Bro, you dissed The Negro." He doesn't give a shit. His mind is otherwise engaged by the idea of walking right up to this kid and clocking him without saying a word. The feeling is terrible. He knows nothing about him yet. Nonetheless, Dorian's body is cramping with anger. Hating . . . not him exactly, but the idea of him, or the idea of people *like* him—and though he has been taught to not believe in the sameness of all such persons, a logic as inborn as the structure of his DNA connects each and every one of them . . .

Mr. B says: "Whazzup, boyz?"

"Hey."

"Someone I'd like you to meet. This is Karim. Karim, this is Dean, Plaxico—I mean, Zebedee—Keenan, and Dorian."

"What does *that* mean?" Keenan asks.

"It's called an introduction, pal."

"No, that." He points to the rear of the Argo Electric. The bumper sticker says: **WHERE THE HECK IS WALL DRUG.**

"Wall Drug," Dean says. "Must be a hash bar."

"Good guess. But no. It's a tourist trap in the Dakota Territory."

"Dakota," Dorian says.

"Which is where we just came from."

Dorian looks at the kid and speaks to him directly: "That's where you live . . ."

"Sort of," Karim says.

"*Used* to live," Mr. B specifies.

"Used to."

"Where does he live now?" Keenan asks.

"You're lookin at it. Thirteen Poospatuck Circle. Christ, it's hot out here. And these bugs, it's a like a goddamn Bible plague."

"I don't get it," Keenan says.

"Don't get what."

"Thirteen is your house."

"Correctamundo," says Mr. B. "Thirteen is my house. It's now also Karim's house. That's why I called you guys over. Introduce you. Let you know there's gonna be a new kid in the hood."

"For how long?" Keenan says.

"Indefinitely, son."

All at once, everything freezes like streaming video when there's a dearth of bandwidth at the point of reception.

Finally, Dorian says: "You're from the camps."

"No," the kid says.

"Where, then."

"I'm from the Jamestown Colony."

"What Karim means," Mr. B says, "is that before his family was interned, they lived in Jamestown."

"And where's his family now?" Dean asks.

"They're deceased."

While Keenan answers his ringing phone and wanders off, talking and glancing back as if someone might be sneaking up on him with a lead pipe, Dorian thinks (flash of cicadas dead on corkboard): *I'm sorry about your family. It sucks and I can relate. Can even imagine, What if I was you. Reverse everything. This is an empathy exercise I learned at school: Imagine I'm the orphan and some old guy in a turban adopts me and makes me meet a bunch of camel-fucker kids who clearly hate my guts, of whom you are one. I'd be looking at you, wanting to stomp your goddamn brains into the ground. And like you wouldn't be wondering what the hell your old neighbor is thinking, bringing someone like me into your sandbox. Indefinitely. Because let me tell you about this street. There's Black, White, Vietnamese, Indian from India, Catholic, Unitarian, African Methodist, Jewish, Hindu, Free Will Baptist, and Agnostic. Notice what's missing? Over on Mohegan and Onondaga, there are some of you, and there's exactly one day out of the year they come over here, and that's Halloween* . . . Such is the path of his thoughts as the pow-wow awkwardly breaks up. Pretty phased, Mr. B is saying. Long-ass drive. Et cetera. Keenan still standing a good thirty feet away, with zero intention of rejoining the group. "See you around," Plaxico says. But the new kid already has his back turned. In some kind of pain, judging from the weird twist in his spine. Maybe holding a shit since Ohio, Dorian thinks

49

as he walks down the driveway. By the road, The Negro, in his white shirt and pants, red vest, and red-and-white cap, is bent forward (he doesn't look so comfortable either), one hand pocketed, the other thrust forth for a reason long forgotten. Slap him five. The summer of your eleventh year is in motion.

4

They can't understand where the idea could have come from. A sister. Eighteen years old at the time the bomb exploded, or the meteor hit, or whatever happened happened. Kathryn and Mitch have spent hundreds of hours, literally hundreds in the past six months, trying to figure out a source. A story he read, a movie. They started seeing a psychologist (the two of them with Dorian, then Dorian alone, then all four of them), a man who talked in private with Kathryn and Mitch about paracosms. Imaginary worlds created in childhood. The doctor made the phenomenon sound harmless, even propitious. A phase of intellectually gifted children. But at the worst point, in the icebound days of January, with their son shouting at them almost daily, accusing them of familial conspiracy (some of the episodes so irrational and paranoid, they thought with terror of schizophrenia), Mitch had said: "We need to be completely honest and consider every possibility."

"I know."

"Well, think. According to Dorian's story, she would've been born in, what . . . '09. So, '09. The summer of '09."

"What about it."

"Don't act stupid, Kate. Please. This is too serious."

"I know what you're talking about," she said, making a great effort to keep her voice steady. "But I can't imagine why you'd bring it up."

"Look—"

"Now of all times. Like we don't have enough going on here."

"There could be a connection."

"Like this isn't crazy enough without throwing that in."

"I'm not throwing it in."

"I mean, what are you thinking?"

"I'm thinking it's the same year. '09. And that's weird, Kate. It's a very weird coincidence. What I'm thinking is, the whole fantasy could be coming out of that. If you'd had the baby—"

"Just stop it," she said.

And he did stop. And hasn't mentioned it since, though Kathryn has thought about it plenty. The conversation comes back to her in these sorts of moments: alone in the car, backed up on the Northway while the sun capsizes in a sea of tropospheric aerosols, another day ending with the colors of holocaust. What happened in '09 was, she was with Griffin and then she was also with Mitch. When she got pregnant, the question of *whose* could only have been answered in one way—and what would be the point of having such a test if not to choose one man or the other based on its results. One fate or the other. *Maybe some people can make a decision that way, but not me. Is the future all mine to shape? What am I going to do, award myself to one of them like a prize? I can't start a life that way.* Thus went her reasoning all those years ago, twenty-six years ago now, when what she did was, she let it go, all by herself. Didn't tell either one of them. Believing there was purity in this. Knowing, not much later, that abortion had been a way to protect herself against what she'd thought of as total loss. What if you lose both of them *and* the baby. In the end, she had told Mitch (and can see even now the way he had squinted his eyes, as if trying to see through a swirling fog), but the truth is, by then, what was this admission but itself a kind of test. If you love me.

Exit 8.

She calls home and leaves a message saying she'll be late (what's new) and is anyone working on dinner.

52

She turns on public radio.

The news is: There are elected officials out there, governors and senators, saying that their provinces and colonies, in defiance of the recent court ruling, will close their borders to all former internees. Turn it off. Can't take it. These poor people. How many different ways must you prove your hate for them. She wonders what Dorian is thinking about all this. End of the camps; the renaturalizations. *Should have talked to him weeks ago. It's your own fault he's backsliding. Of course the news is setting him off. He sees these people as criminals. They're set free and, abracadabra, this bizarre projection of his reappears. This symbol. There's nothing mysterious about it at all. You studied psychology in college. It's not complicated. He sees her in dreams and she is nothing but fear given form in a dream. Stop thinking about what your husband said that time. Which he only said for his own selfish reasons. A weird coincidence, yeah. But Dorian cannot know anything about that. Still. If you'd had the baby, it might have been a girl. She would've been conceived in '09. Would've been eighteen when he was three. And she could have been in the city when it happened*—and when you step into this current of imagination, you lose your balance, emotion passes between you and rationality like a moon between planet and sun. Shadow over your heart. There's something feasible here. If you had done one thing different.

•

One of the first things the old guy does is get him a smartphone; and once Karim has it, he starts thinking about what Abdul-Aziz instructed him to do. Call the number. Not immediately calling the number does not mean he's not *going* to call the number. Karim will do as he was told by the sheikh (which is the rightful thing to do in the eyes of God, and which he wants to do), he just can't seem to bring himself to do it today. *Tomorrow*, he tells himself. Same thing he told himself yesterday after the old guy had taken him to the mall and bought the compact device in its red metallic casing, giving Karim the power to access the Internet, take pictures still and moving, download and play games, and make unlimited audio and video calls. He had never used one of these before. In the camp, they were contraband. Somehow, though, the sheikh possessed one; and once, after dark, Karim had held it in his hands, Hazem and Yassim on either side of him, and the boys watched the glowing screen, blinking like moths winging at a flame. "Don't be afraid," said Abdul-Aziz, as the boy in the video was prepared by men in dark hoods, as plastified explosives and tubes filled with nails and steel balls were taped to his skin and bones. But fuck were they afraid, all three of them terror-filled, expecting that at any moment, by design or accident, the boy might burst on the screen before their eyes into a cloud of blood, flesh, bone, and guts. Which he did not. Though he did no less suddenly burst into tears; and when a voice asked him why he was crying, he sobbed, "*Because I am so happy. I am going to see my mother in the highest gardens of heaven . . .*"

June 22.

Only three days past Dakota. But the camp and his friends, the lean-to they'd built out of scrounged cardboard, sheet metal, and particle board: all just disappeared. And now *this* house. Soft carpeting, gentle gusts of cool air, staircase leading to a second floor and a room all for him (with a futon whose plush makes him feel like he's remembering something from before the encoding of memories), and in the back yard, get this, a pool, a real swimming pool filled with clean water and covered by a transparent dome. He can't swim. But the depth is only four feet from end to end. He can lunge around, make some attempts at the rudimentary strokes, and float on a giant yellow smiley face with holes for eyes. You put your ass in one of the holes and let your head rest on the big happy mouth, and eventually Satan will ask a question of you: Is it possible you've already laid down your life—a painless passage, as the sheikh promised—and this is Paradise?

It could be ten minutes, could be a century later that he hears a muezzin chanting the azan.

"*Allahu Akbar . . .*"

"*Allahu Akbar . . .*"

The voice is not coming from a minaret, not from a loudspeaker (as it did at the camp); it's coming from the smartphone. Karim paddles over to the ladder and pulls himself off the float. He drapes a towel over his shoulders. Picks up the phone. "*Come to prayer . . . Come to prayer . . .*" He exits the dome. A few steps on soft grass, a few more across flat stones that burn the soles of his feet. Sliding glass door. Stepping inside is a dream-change. You are now in a subzero dimension: molecules of chlorinated water freeze into crystals on your skin. Across the room, there's a magic machine. Push one button, you get jewels of ice; push another, a cascade of perfectly tasteless water. Karim drinks until his brain aches. As he puts the glass down, the old guy says from the doorway:

"Time for salat?"

"Mm."

"Good, good. You look good today. You feel good?"

"Pretty good," Karim says.

"Good."

"*God is greatest,*" chants the muezzin.

"I was thinking," the old guy says. "Around sunset, how about some mini-golf."

"Some what?"

The old guy joins two fists and makes a funny knocking motion. "You don't know? It's a game."

"Oh . . ."

Down in the basement, the old guy has made a place for him to pray. Persian rug. On the wall, a framed picture of the Grand

Mosque. Karim stands on the rug and faces Mecca. As he recites the first sura, he raises up his hands. Folds his hands on his chest. Bows. Sits. Kneels. Lowers forehead. Touches forehead to rug. Asks for protection from the torture of hellfire. When he's done, he picks up his phone.

Tomorrow.

Tomorrow, you will call the number.

•

Dorian thinks of the dream he had a few nights ago. About the Arabian palace with the mural of Mount Rushmore. Now that Dorian has met the kid, it has an unnerving relevance. Hanging out alone in his room, he thinks: *I had that dream, and then a couple days later a haji from Dakota appears. But a mural made of corn. That's just random.* When he types DAKOTA CORN into the search engine, he isn't really expecting anything to come up. But he gets pages and pages of images. Of a building. He clicks on the first one . . . In the dream, he never saw the palace from the outside, but this first picture is such a perfect match for what the outside *would have been* that he instantly feels this is the building he was in, in the dream. Some kind of weird mosque. Two minarets with pointed green tops like giant, perfectly sharpened crayons; and three curving domes, yellow and green with red pinnacles, like giant heavenward-pointing boobs with flags coming out of the nipples. The highest flying flag is the Stars and Stripes. Above the entrance, letters spell: AMERICA'S DESTINATIONS. Then white columns support a bigger fancier sign: MITCHELL CORN PALACE. The exterior walls are all muraled—and, there, to one side of the doors is the same mural from the dream. The heads of Washington, Jefferson, Lincoln, and Edmonds. Mount Rushmore. Made of ears of multicolored corn.

56

Via videocall, he explains it all to Plaxico, who has his tablet at such an angle that Dorian can only see one quarter of his face as he plays *PGA Tour* on his dad's old console: software so prehistoric you can practically hear, while you're teeing off, archaeopteryxes screeching in the computer-generated trees.

"What do you call that," Dorian says.

"What."

"When a dream comes true, what's that called."

"A dream come true."

He ends the call and walks out of his bedroom, down the hall, downstairs, out of the house, into the meltdown of afternoon sun and the crashing sound waves of the seventeen-year cicadas, over his family's uncut dandelion-filled grass and onto the neighboring lawn (closely cropped and weedless), to the sliding glass door under the deck through which he can see his best friend holding a remote like a Neanderthal boy with a bone weapon. As Plaxico drives a stupendous tee shot over a virtual fjord, Dorian sits in the chair that looks like the amputated hand of a storybook giant.

"Is it déjà vu?"

"That's something else," Plaxico says. "That's when something happens and you know it happened in another life."

The brown-skinned, khaki-trousered, polo-shirted avatar waits patiently on the fairway while Plaxico disappears into the utility room and reappears with two chilled cans of Tahitian Treat.

"Saw the kid last night," he says.

"Where."

"Funplex."

Dorian pops the tab on the soda and gives him a look.

"Sorry, it was Family Night."

"I am family."

"You're *like* family," Plaxico says. "If we start a *Like* Family Night, you're there."

"Whatever."

"Anyway, I saw the kid. First time in his life playing mini-golf, he finished two over par with a hole-in-one."

"So, buy him a green blazer."

"Precog."

"What'd you say?"

"That's what it's called. When you dream of the future, you're a precog. But you didn't see the future."

"Yes, I did."

"You didn't see the kid. You didn't dream a kid was coming."

"I saw the mural."

"So?"

Dorian isn't sure how to explain it. Plaxico picks up his tablet and after a few seconds of surfing says: "Any plans Saturday?"

"Not really."

"Just got a invite. To a pool party."

He reports the news in a tone of dramatic offhandedness that sets Dorian's mind in motion. Must be from a girl. Maybe Hanna Hyashi or Isabel Ambrose. More and more, he is thinking in these terms, in terms of girls and what might happen with them: for almost a year now, a feeling in him—or the desire for a feeling—like when a thunderstorm foments in the summer atmosphere day after day, and you know the rain is coming though it seems it never will, until finally, maybe at *this* very party (*I need cooler cargo trunks*, he starts thinking, *and, I swear, if my mother makes me wear a sun-protective shirt*) . . . But none of these mental projections are relevant, because when Plaxico passes him the tablet, Dorian sees that the e-vite—the maw of a great white shark rising out of a kiddie pool—isn't from Hanna or Emily or any other girl. It's from Karim Hassad-Banfelder.

•

All four boys receive this invitation. For the coming Saturday at eleven o'clock. When Dean opens the message, he is getting stoned on real shit from Indochina with a sixth-grader who goes by the nickname Landru. Dean clicks on the link and he thinks it's funny (the shark that can't possibly fit in the space it is depicted as being in, suggesting a disregard for physical laws, or maybe a change therein, some dimensional passageway at the bottom of the kiddie pool, a wormhole to oceanic depths), but he deletes the e-mail without giving a moment's consideration to the question of attendance as the hands of Landru proffer a water bong the size of a shoulder grenade launcher . . . When Keenan opens it, he is in the in-law apartment where his grandmother aged gracefully until cortical dementia infected her mind like spyware. Now she lives in a community for the memory-impaired while her grandson uses her old quarters as a love shack where he and Amber Kakizaki, a thirteen-year-old girl met on a hike for kids with nature deficit disorder, have tortuous outercourse under the grandfather clock that plays Westminster Chimes every half hour. He clicks on the link and doesn't think there's anything funny about a shark in a kiddie pool (though he does see the potential for humor if one were to add some towelhead kids jumping out of the pool with their eyeballs bugging out of their faces). Far from amused, the thought of being in a swimming pool with one of them, the idea of immersion half-naked in the same water, makes his guts squirm and burn with a furious nausea . . . And Dorian and Plaxico are together when they open it, in the basement of the Hightower home, drinking carbonated fruit punch while on the flatscreen television the facsimile of a long-dead golf pro waits to take his second shot on fourteen. Dorian is not so much angry as afraid—and when he says, "Like we're gonna play Marco Polo with Jig-Abdul of Arabia," Zebedee can see through the show of rancor to the fear inside, which he guesses isn't so different from the fear we all harbor. Still. In this best friend (better known than his own brother), it's something else, too. It's like Dorian is afraid of himself, of the one thing in life you can know in full: more afraid of himself than of any uncertainty or unknowable. It seems to Zebedee that his friend might start crying, and he's trying to think about what to say, even as his own mind is distracted by a series of deep links that range through language and history: Jig-Abdul. Jigaboo. The lawn jockey you call The Negro. Your great uncle dragged by rope, by truck, over a dusty southern road to the field with the hanging tree: He to whose name you have changed your name.

5

On the drive home from work, think of Dorian. The baby he once was; the boy he is now; and the person you are frightened he will soon become. It seems you spend half your waking life these days on the Northway, backed up in traffic, worrying about the person your son might become. A hateful one who will pay hate forward.

Hate.

A strong word. But isn't it an accurate one? What he did on that school trip, at the mosque. Heart hurts at the memory of reading those words written in a hand undeniably his: FUCK ISLAM. What is that, if not hate? When all you've ever preached is love and respect for others, not through religion (you are not religious, though there was, when you first moved east, a brief flirtation with a Presbyterianism so open-minded it bordered on the agnostic), but in the socially progressive terms found in the messages of good books and the enlightened lessons of history. You cannot understand it, any more than you can understand why he sees a sister who never was; and though the two things—the emotion and the illusion—are surely interconnected, the question of which caused which is all but impossible to answer . . . Now this: A new boy across the street. When you heard the news, that your neighbor has adopted an orphan from the camps, you thought: That's strange. Because it isn't a thing you would expect from that man, whom you know and like well enough, but about whom you have heard . . . Well, nothing specific or definite;

only that he was one of those men who went to the war for money, and who, regardless of any crimes he might commit there, was guaranteed through the corruptions of occupying power to never see the inside of an indigenous courtroom. That was three decades ago. Must be seventy years old now. A widower with no children. A man getting old alone—and now, suddenly, a guardian, a father, who in giving this boy a home will put a stop to the wrongs done him. Is this really so strange? If it seems so, it's merely because the world has become so warped that any act of kindness makes us look automatically for some counterwork of cruelty. The more you think about it, the more brightly a feeling sparkles in you; it's like a star appearing strong in a dark sky . . . Which brings us back to your son, who did not, in your opinion, learn anything from what happened back in the fall. After admitting to an act of vandalism, he served a two-day suspension from school. On the first day, you took him back to the mosque, where he apologized to the imam and then covered over what he'd written with a fresh coat of paint. On the second day, he attended a half-day tolerance workshop for tweens sponsored by the hate crimes unit of the police department. And it was just a few days later, in the course of a conversation intended to bring some closure to the incident, that Dorian lost his temper and said he knew he once had a sister, and though he had forgotten for a long time, just as you all had wanted him to, she was coming back to him in dreams, and you couldn't hide it anymore. It had taken you quite a while to understand what in the world he was talking about—but as you absorbed the shock of the idea, you were thinking (not in words, but in a wave of feeling faster than words and more complete) that this claim was a deliberate invention, a way to deny responsibility and reflect blame back at you, as if *you* were the reason for his bad behavior and also the source of his prejudice. So he had learned nothing. In fact, he was only entrenching himself more completely in the kind of thinking that had to change.

———

Dorian has been at Plaxico's all afternoon and now, at about six forty-five, he's sitting at the dinner table with the Hightowers eating Mrs. H's pulled pork and mashed potatoes when he gets a text from his father, which reminds him that tonight is family dinner. "Shit," he says. Mr. and Mrs. H both look at him. "Sorry," he says, pushing back his chair, "I'm supposed to be home." "Don't you leave those dishes just sitting there," Mrs. H says. He clears his plate and glass and utensils and shouts out a thanks as he exits through the front door. Into a sun that is knifing through the day's last quadrant of sky. He sees his mother's car in the driveway. *Good*, he thinks—or maybe he is wishing it wasn't there. Was he trying to upset her? No. That was not the intention. All he'd said was: I had a dream about her. Is it his fault if a simple statement of fact is so upsetting? Of course, there is also the how and when of saying. But Dorian was not thinking of that when he spoke the other morning, and he isn't thinking of such things now. He isn't planning what to say—or how to speak—at the dinner table when the subject of the new kid is brought up. Instead, as he walks (under the two oaks whose green boughs are as heavy with insects as summer thunderheads with rain, the sound downpouring), his mind is thinking what it wants to think, which he doesn't even want to be thinking: *since the thing at the mosque, your mother has scarcely touched you.*

In the kitchen, his father is removing a roasting pan from the oven. Something horrific involving green peppers.

"Where have you been?"

"Next door."

His brother, pushing on a salad spinner as if trying to accelerate lettuce to the speed of light, says: "Set table, pinhead."

A few minutes later, the four are seated equidistantly at the square table; four plates with a stuffed pepper in the center of each.

"What's the problem," his father asks them.

"Nothing," they say.

"So eat."

"It looks like a dead frog," Dorian says.

"Have to agree, Dad. Ixnay on the epperpay."

His mother, as if introducing a mitigating factor, says: "Mine is tofu." She pours wine and Dorian listens to the mouth of the bottle ring against the lip of the glass. "I hear there's a new kid on the block," she says.

Cliff says: "Old news, Mom."

"Well, it's new to me. Why don't you give me a full report."

Cliff says: "Dorian . . ."

"What."

"The general wants a full report."

"I dunno."

"Have you met him?" his mother asks.

"Sort of."

"Meet is kind of vague," Cliff says. "Ask him if there's a pool party for prepubes on Saturday."

"He invited you?"

Dorian nods—and his mother says, in a tone so calm and sincere that he feels compelled to look up at her, "That's great, Dorian." And she looking at him. There's a freeze here. Expression on her face like a phrase written in a foreign language he can almost read. Then the words come out of him:

"I don't like pool parties."

And her eyes blink and the muscles of her face move and the meaning is gone. "Since when," she says.

"Yeah, since when, xenophobe."

"Keenan isn't going. And neither is Dean. And neither am I."

"Your loss," Cliff says. " 'Cause it's gonna be a blast. Do some cannonballs, drink some Kool-Aid, jam to some Arab death metal."

"Could you tell him to shut up."

"Both of you," their father says. "Eat."

His brother picks up his silverware and proceeds to cut along the midline of the vegetable and scoop out the organs.

Through the bay window, west-facing, a crepuscular beam of sun is about to slant into the room: Dorian can see it coming, through the boughs of the elm in the front yard. And as it finds the table— three, two, one, *now*—it makes of the wine in his mother's glass (tapered glass half-full held in both her hands and she staring into it) a living color, sunlight blending with glass and liquid to create a red glow that might be a magic worked by the power of his mother's mind. She is about to say something to you. When she says it, she will not be looking at you, but still into the glass which by then will have gone dead like a fire burned out because the planet will have turned a hundred miles on its axis and the sunbeam will be touching something else far away and until that moment unimagined. Not looking at you—you had that chance at contact and you lost it—and the color going out of the glass and the whole room losing color as she says:

"What's his name, Dorian."

It takes him a moment to contextualize the question. Thinking: Him. The new kid. He thinks the name to himself, but in response to his mother only shrugs his shoulders.

"I thought you met him," she says.

"Yeah."

"So what is his name."

Cliff raises his hand like he's back in high school. "His name," he says, "is Karim Hassad-Banfelder. But Dorian just calls him Camel Fucker."

"You're excused," their mother says.

"What."

"I said, get out."

"I'm being *iron*ic, Mom—"

65

Dorian pushes back his chair. She tells him to sit down. He doesn't. He is walking away and focused on his bike and how much time he's got before curfew when she catches up with him and seizes him by the shirt collar.

"I guess you're not happy about all this," she says. "Maybe you'd prefer it if this boy had been killed along with his family. Then you wouldn't have to be bothered with his existence. Isn't that right."

"No—"

"Your life is one unfair trial after another, isn't it. First you have to go on a school trip, then you have to accept consequences for breaking a law. Now, as if that wasn't enough, you've been invited to go swimming for a couple of hours." (She had let go of his shirt, but she grabs him again now, his arm, the bicep, touching him though not with any gentleness. He almost says, You're hurting me. Starts to say it—) "I promised you last fall I wouldn't let the next thing slide. Now here it is. That boy has lost everything, Dorian. He's reaching out for a friend and I don't care if no other kid on this street responds. You're going to. Show some kindness. Or I will ground you in ways you can't imagine. Do you get me? I will ground you back to the Stone Age."

•

Karim did not want to have a party in a swimming pool or anywhere else for that matter; but the old guy had already conceived the event with such exuberance, to not assent would be to hurt the old guy's feelings—and, for reasons difficult to articulate, Karim did not want to hurt his feelings. "I've got a genius idea," the old guy had announced over dinner on the third day. "Pool party." Which was a thing Karim had never heard of. So the old guy defined it. "First of all, you need a pool, which we've got. Second, you need a hot summer day, of which we have no shortage. You, as the kid with the pool

66

at his house, are known as the host. Now all you need are some other kids . . ."

"What kids," Karim asked.

"Well, mainly some kids from the mosque. I've been talking to a lady over there, Mrs. Mahfouz. She's a volunteer with the local youth foundation. She already told the middle-school group about you, and the boys and girls from the group want to hang with you, so it'll be easy to get some names and e-mail addresses. And then there are the boys you met yesterday, Dorian and Zeb, Dean and Keenan, who of course should also be invited"—and so on about making friends and how a pool party is a perfect way to break the ice until finally Karim said, "All right."

Stupid.

Because the old guy's feelings will only be hurt more later: after you call the phone number the sheikh gave you in Dakota and connect with the cell here in New York, after you have been guided towards your real purpose and have done your duty, at which time the old guy will think back on the pool party and how you went along with the idea and perhaps even seemed to enjoy the day while knowing all along that you never intended to become friends with anybody (you weren't a friend, you were an enemy), and in the end you betrayed the kindness of a well-meaning person in the worst fucking way . . . All this understood by Karim as if in retrospect: as if all of it has happened already. Like he has done his duty and is looking back from the afterlife on his days in the world and contemplating the last thing he ever did—and rather than being proud and joyful, he's full of regret. Of course, none of this has happened yet. It's the night of the fourth day. He is in his new bedroom. The time so late it's early. He was asleep but then he woke up; and now he lies awake, unable to find his way back to sleep. Smelling on his skin the minty soap washed with before bed while the central cooling system breathes down on him like a loving god, thinking all of this even as a voice only he can hear, his own voice but also independent of him, recites the ten digits of the phone number he has not yet called, the numerical code written by the sheikh on a scrap of paper back at the camp and memorized by Karim, an assignment completed without question, because back then, to Karim, everything beyond the camp was a void unknowable and what would he have there, in that empty meaningless darkness, if not the numbers.

The time is one thirty-eight. Across the road, in the house with cream-yellow vinyl siding, Dorian Wakefield is dreaming. His imagination is making him believe he is with that boy who knew his sister. Noah. When the dream begins, Dorian and Noah are playing Monopoly. Aspects of the game not what they really are. Instead of battlefields from old wars, the green properties are named for internment camps: the one that should say Saratoga says Galaga, which Dorian understands to actually mean Dakota.

Is my sister still writing?

Mm-hm.

What's it about?

What happens next, Noah says. But some is what she wished already happened.

View from the doorway that leads to the next room: Skyler at the desk, intently focused on the screen of a laptop, fingers resting on the keyboard. She sees Dorian and smiles. I'm just going to call Mom, he says to her. Stay right there.

Phone already in his hand and he dialing ten strange numbers. Answering voice: *Dorian? It's the middle of the night.* Mom, he says. Come in here. *Dorian, it's the middle of the night, honey.* Her bedroom is right down the hall. If she would just get up and come in here, she would see— As a shock of wind hits the house and the sound of every window breaking, of flying glass, of glass shards being rifled into walls and furniture, chiming against objects held together by metallic bonds, is like the music of the world please no glass god dream help now Mom Dad Cliff Skyler . . .

It is not a nightmare that wakes Kathryn. More like a touch on her shoulder, or the passing of a hand over her face, smoothing of hair; her eyes open peacefully and unconsciousness ebbs. For a moment or two, she is in the old house in California. Confusion with precedent: it happens sometimes; in this unclaimed territory between sleep and waking, she will think she's younger and lying in the four-post bed under the window that looked out on the eastern ridge of hills, until, coming fully to, she feels surprised by how far she and her family have drifted from that other place, that other life, and by how old she really is. The strange thing, tonight, is her aloneness in the room. No husband in the bed; no child standing beside it. Touched by no one. Then she feels that small familiar grasp—inside, at her own crux—like something rooted being pulled. She goes into the bathroom. In the dark, some blood drips out as she pisses. She doesn't need any light. The cabinet just in front of her. Box on the second shelf. She pulls the paper strip and presses the pad into the crotch of her underwear. Still happening, this thing. Forty-five years old, and still the body going through the motions of menstruation. Nothing but an echo in the nerves. Back in bed. The old house echoing in her thoughts—and she, lying in the dark, seeing herself moving through it as she had on that day when she didn't know what else to do but bring the boys home and listen to the news and wait . . . She waited all day for Mitch to call. By the time he'd heard what had happened, packed up, and driven into range of a tower, the shadow of day's end was rising on the hills like the waters of a flood. Soon all the land would be under it. By nightfall, he still wasn't home. While to the south the city burned and smoked and sickened, Kathryn carried Dorian outdoors to look at the stars. Clearest of nights. The galaxy overhead: a river of lights flowing into what some see as heaven . . . Now her eyes are closing and it seems she can feel her son breathing in her arms under that starry sky. In—his chest pushing on her; out—a warm puff on her cheek. Then something moves out by the windbreak.

I heared something, Momma.

Me, too.

I can't know it.

Maybe a deer, she says to him. Unable to tell if he is frightened. She is. Will be, she knows, for a long time to come, perhaps for as long as there is . . .

For a long month he has done nothing but stare at the lines of a notebook, pen unmoving in his hand, or at the computer, on the screen of which a few purposeless lines will dead-end at the blinking cursor that in its appearing and disappearing is almost audible, like the ticking of a clock. Mitchell Wakefield has never been prolific. The words never come easy, and ideas (those worth pursuing and committing to the page) are like creatures that live countless leagues under the sea, rarely seen, and then only after thorough preparation and a long descent into the medium; and even if you make it to that dark quiet place where things luminous can show themselves and reveal forms theretofore unimagined, you might wait and wait and nothing will come visible. This is what he's doing in the basement, in his study—staring at the computer screen in the dark, waiting (ears filled with streaming audio of the crashing of ocean waves and the voices of seagulls)—when suddenly his younger son is standing in the doorway as abruptly as a ghost.

"*Jeezus*, Dorian!"

He says something in response; Mitch removes the canalphones and says, "What?"

"I was talking but you didn't hear me."

"Sorry."

"You have waves on?"

Mitch nods. The sound is audible, though faint as a secret being whispered into a single ear.

"So, you're writing . . ."

"Dodo, do you know what time it is?"

"I've been standing here for about three minutes, so it's probably about one forty-five. Can I sit down?"

As Dorian sits beside him on the couch, Mitch minimizes the document.

"I thought you were writing."

"Not really."

His son picks up the canalphones and inserts them in his own ears. Then leans into Mitch, a childlike thing he rarely does anymore. By the end of the year, he'll be twelve—and one day soon thereafter (just as it happened with his older son), Mitch will understand that the child has gone missing and won't ever be found. He puts an arm around him. Can't hear the ocean any more and yet he can; his ears seem to echo like seashells. *Probably a bad dream*, he thinks. *Dream about her.* Trying to think: *Should I ask. Or just be here quietly . . .* In therapy, Dorian has told about the dreams, which point with the fixation of a compass needle to the same place and time, same landscape of destruction, same fear. "But what is he scared of?" And the psychiatrist had taken a breath and said something like: "In terms of fear, he's afraid that the world is going to end. He thinks a lot about 8-11, and he worries it'll happen again, or something just as

71

bad—chemical, biological—or something even worse. This isn't abnormal. We're all afraid, to differing degrees. At the most extreme, the fear becomes a phobia. Your son," he went on, "isn't phobic. He doesn't have the associated anxiety or the physical symptoms." "But the girl," Mitch and Kathryn said. "Who is not just a dream to him. Who he believes was a real person (isn't that a delusion?) and whom he believes is being hidden from him (isn't that paranoia?), and aren't these signs—? What we mean is, we've read that there's an early-onset form of schizophrenia." To which the doctor replied: "Or perhaps he simply has a highly imaginative mind." He went on to discuss the concept of paracosms: imaginary worlds, fantasy worlds conceived in childhood. Often by gifted children. Usually to process and understand a loss, like the death of a loved one. "In Dorian's case, there hasn't been any loss. But we also might say: There hasn't been one *yet*. He's afraid of what might happen. This we know. Perhaps afraid enough that his mind is reacting ahead of time. The fantasy is helping him process his fears about the future." The explanation sounded conclusive, and Mitch glanced then at Kathryn, whose face was somehow both brightened by faith and lined with skepticism. "That makes sense," Mitch said. The psychiatrist lifted an eyebrow, as if changing his mind, and said: "But we can't rule out every other possibility right now." Then one day, a few weeks later, a few therapy sessions later, Dorian told them that the dreams had stopped. The last two months of the school year passed quietly. Not another accusation, no mention of the girl. Until the other day at breakfast. Now here they are, father and son, at two in the morning, awake, the computer fallen asleep before them, dreaming a slideshow of photos . . .

Autumn past, Dorian at the entrance to a corn maze.

Last month, Cliff in a cap and gown.

Then a long-ago picture Mitch can't quite place. On a beach. He and Kathryn and Cliff. Cliff maybe three. All of them lying in the sand. Faces close up, looking into the camera, chins resting on their hands. All smiles while a blue ocean wave crests in the back-ground—and Kathryn is wearing huge sunglasses he doesn't recall her ever having.

"California," Dorian says.

"Looks like— Yes, must be California."

The picture fades, replaced by another much more recent and recognizable. School play from last year. Dorian, fake-bearded, and Plaxico, wild-wigged: Abraham Lincoln and Frederick Douglass.

"About last night," Mitch says. "I think your mother was a little hard on you."

"A little."

"The thing is, she's basically right. We need to live with people. And not just tolerate them. Be friends with them. Go to their parties once in a while. You know what Lincoln said about the better angels of our nature. This is just one of those times when you have to be a better angel."

"I don't know anything about Lincoln."

"Sure you do."

Pictures form and unform. They are like keys. Every picture opens a lock in the mind. Depending on the image, the room gets somewhat brighter or darker—a slow strobe, conducive to entry into suggestible states.

"Who took that picture," Dorian asks suddenly.

"That one?"

"No, the one on the beach."

"Who took that. I have no idea. Probably some friend I haven't spoken to in ten years. Maybe the Magic Paparazzi."

"I'm too old for that joke," he says.

"Okay."

"It wasn't the timer. You can tell from the angle. Someone was ly-ing down in front of you."

"Didn't notice."

His son breaks from the embrace and sits forward and asks: "Can you go back to it?"

"The saver's on random shuffle."

"Well, let me look through the folder, then, okay?"

"No, not okay."

Dorian turns to him. Against the dim backlight, Mitch can't make out the expression. Not yet thinking: He thinks *she* took it. That thought is buried, hidden below the surface of his confusion about what his son wants with the picture.

"Why not."

"First of all," Mitch says, "it's two in the morning. Second, there are a lot of old pictures in there."

"So?"

"So maybe there are some I don't want you to see."

"Of what," he says. "Of who."

"Of who? Of your mother. And that's not a dis. There really might be naked pictures of her in there. From back in the day."

And Mitchell Wakefield isn't just making excuses. Because recently he has found a flash drive (lost and forgotten until the finding, like an arrowhead unearthed thirty summers ago in the woods in Connecticut), and discovered saved to it a folder of photos. The one on the beach is from that folder, as is another which has already surprised him: of Kathryn before children (after the abortion but before the marriage, in the tweens of the century) on the observation deck of the Space Spire, her hair long and blonde and frenzied by a gust of wind. That picture fit smoothly into the lock it was fashioned for. When Mitch rediscovered it, the cylinder of memory turned, and he saw himself and her, twenty-four or -five, driving north on the coast road of the Oregon Territory, and he could recall how at that time (after she had confessed about *him* and what she'd done about the pregnancy)—how emotions had seemed conjoined, as if love and anger shared a heart . . .

Now, nearly twenty years later, say to your son: "Come on, Dodo." Walk him to his bedroom. At the door, embrace him and tell him you'll talk in the morning. You'll find him the photo in the morning. In your own bedroom, in the bathroom: on the toilet seat, a single drop of blood. Clean it with tissue paper. In the bed, your wife is perfectly still. As she sleeps, think of the photo, the one taken on the beach, which unlocks nothing, as if it's not your key, as if it were made to fit a lock in someone else's mind—and all at once the burrowed thought will break the surface of thinking. *That's why Dorian wants the photo. Because he thinks the person behind the image, lying on the sand, the one holding the camera, is her.*

6

What he did in the third war was vastly different from what he had done in the first. First, second, third. Arbitrary system of numeration. For there was only ever one war, decades ongoing, so long it was hardly surprising if your role, to say nothing of your stance, were to change along with presidential elections and dictatorial regimes and occupational governments from the beginning to what we were promised again and again would be the end. In the third war, when he was forty, forty-one, William Banfelder had been paid by a private American contractor called Securiforce to protect—by any means, necessary or unjustified—cargoes ranging from computer hardware for forward-operating bases in the Forbidden Zone to frozen hamburgers for the fast-food chains in the Diplomatic Bubble. He took the job for the money (several million dinars a week stuffed into a yellow envelope like a ransom payoff), and soon came to understand that one could not do the job without doing violence, and so the making of money had become very quickly and hopelessly equal to the taking of life.

But the first war.

A twenty-, twenty-one-year-old Marine, William Banfelder had been paid by the United States government little better than federal minimum wage (a couple thousand dollars a month direct-deposited into his Armed Forces bank account) to transport food, water, medical supplies, and building materials to about two million refugees who, through the winter, had been starving to death and freezing to death in the Taurus Mountains on the border of Turkish Anatolia and the Islamic Caliphate. He was then a lance corporal. Had served two quiet years in a quiet world. His unit deploying routinely to the Mediterranean then sailing back to the Carolina Colonies across the imitative fallacy of an ocean at peace. Until a breakaway republic within the Caliphate—or a republic sponsored covertly *by* the Caliphate (the whole truth was, and still is, uncertain, though no one disagrees that they were Baathists from Iraq led by an Army general named Saddam Hussein)—crossed the border into British Kuwait and seized the Al Burqan fields of the Kuwait Oil Company. Will Banfelder and the other men of the 24th MEU did not go to the Gulf. When the air war began, they were floating on the USS *Charleston* off the coast of Sardinia—and when the air war ended thirty days later, they were still floating there, and were still floating when the ground war began and a hundred hours later ended. And that, it was proclaimed, was the end. End of a war whose curtain had in truthful reality only just gone up, and onto the stage of which Will would not enter for another month when the *Charleston* would dock at Iskenderun and the humanitarian operation would get under way. Convoys of cargo trucks and Humvees and M934s ring-mounted with .50-caliber machine guns manned by grunts like Will. Four hundred miles overland from the harbor to a forward base in a Turkish village of mud huts and mules called Silopi—and from Silopi, two times daily, over the border into what some called Kurdistan, to a city named Zakho, where an international brigade of soldiers was pitching tents for the people coming down out of the mountains they had fled into when the war had not so much ended as divided like a parent cell to spawn a next generation of fighting, civil and sectarian—and though many had died in the winter, now it was spring in the valley and the people were coming down out of the mountains and not being hurt, they were being helped, and Will Banfelder was helping them.

He was twenty, twenty-one then. He is seventy, seventy-one now. And still, in a ring box furred with velvet, he keeps a thing he earned then, which looks like money though it has no monetary value. A silver medallion: on the heads side is a relief pallet parachuting past an Islamic moon; on tails, an American soldier holding hands with a boy.

●

The kids will arrive at eleven: five boys and a girl. Two of them, Dorian and Zebedee, he has met. The others, from the mosque, he hasn't; and yet he knows them better—not because they're Muslim, but because they have already friended him on Lifebook. Karim has known for a long time about social networking. In the camp, however, he didn't really understand what it was, since there weren't any devices to network with.

One time back before the deaths of loved ones and the addictions of drugs, Hazem had said:

You try to get as many friends as you can.

So it's like a game?

Right. You try to know the most about what all your friends are doing and thinking all the time.

Back then, Karim wasn't so amazed by the idea. His only frame of reference was a pair of walkie-talkies he and Hazem and Yassim had found, still packaged, in a not entirely looted department store: You held a button to speak, pushed another to transmit messages with high-pitched beeps. They were good for playing war: two of the boys with the radios, tracking the third whose mission was to reach undetected, with a dirty bomb fashioned from the viscera of a clock radio, one of two possible targets, like an old barber shop imagined to be a foreign embassy or a dumpy motor inn imagined to be an opulent tourist hotel. But Karim thinks now, with a kind of embarrassment, that all you could do was *talk* on them (or attempt to through a constant crackle of static). Whereas the smartphone is also a television, a camera, a clock. It can show you where you are on a map and the path to where you want to go. Though most incredible to him is that, after only five days in this new place, this new life, he has made fifteen friends without meeting a single one of them.

"Hey, bud. You awake?"

"Yeah."

The door opens; and as the old guy takes one step over the threshold, Karim sets the phone aside and sits up straight on the edge of the bed.

"You know what I forgot?"

"What?"

"Fudge sauce. I got whipped cream and ice cream but I forgot the sauce."

"I think it's okay."

The old guy shakes his head and says a sundae cannot kick ass without fudge sauce. In other words, Karim thinks, get some real clothes on because we're going to the supermarket. But then he says, "But maybe you'd rather hang here." And it takes Karim a moment to understand that he is being asked if he would rather stay for the first time in the house alone. He says, "Yeah, I'll hang here." The old guy nods, almost says something but stops himself, and then departs. As he hears the closing of the front door, Karim can almost see: *It's not that he doesn't trust me; it's something else.* On the way downstairs, he checks his news feed and learns that the girl who's coming to the party later (her name is Khaleela and she's Muslim but not Arabic) is eating Lucky Charms for breakfast. Two people like the post. Karim hasn't liked a post yet, but he decides to like this one—and then he decides to write a comment (*I'm eating Cocoa Pops*), and almost instantly, his comment has two likes, and someone else has written: *I'm eating Corn Crackos.* He smiles. Raises a spoonful of cereal to his mouth. For a few seconds, there's nothing but the conversation thread and the sugary crunch—and then, suddenly, it's like the other day in the swimming pool when he was floating alone, drowsy and content. He wonders if he is being tricked. If the devil is filling his head with illusions.

Think.

What were you just feeling? That the food tastes delicious. That it's nice to know what your friends are eating, too. But this, these brown balls of chocolate, this isn't food. And the names and pictures on the screen . . . It seems a hole has opened up in him and his heart is falling into it. This is not food. Food is the flatbread and honey the sheikh would bring you at night after a day of eating next to nothing—and a friend is someone you ate alongside, with whom you ate flatbread soaked in honey while sitting on a hunk of blasted concrete under a slivered moon while saliva dripped dog-like from your tongues—and a father, a father is not a man with a swimming pool; a father is a man you find in the shadow of a pillar of black smoke after the remote-controlled plane has passed out of sight, skin of his face studded with shrapnel of glass and a dagger of glass set in the neck.

Staring now out of the sliding glass door of this kitchen he is in. Beyond which can be seen a swimming pool and a reflection of morning sun on the dome that covers the pool and strange insects posed here and there on the dome. He signs off from Lifebook. Touches the phone app. He does not have to try to remember the numbers, which a part of his mind has been reciting constantly ever since the learning of them; merely has to touch the symbols on the screen, which correspond to the sounds of the words. One: 1. Five: 5. Three: 3. Nine: 9. Karim is not at all unsure about the next digit. But he sits motionless as if the message has strayed from the path between brain and hand. Four numbers typed, but not a fifth . . . In the camp, there had been no confusion, no paradox. It all made easy sense. *Your family is gone* (the sheikh had told them) *and you have nothing*

80

left on Earth. But if you leave this Earth as a shahid, as a martyr for the sake of Allah: Boys, if you do this, you will have everything . . . But now. What is he afraid of now? What is he *not* afraid of? He is afraid of: the sheikh, the ten numbers, what will begin if he makes the call, what will happen to him if he doesn't, the man he calls jaddi seeing him now talking on the phone, the will of God, defying the will of God, seeing the light shining from the face of God in Paradise, the chance that there is no such thing as Paradise, the belt with its tubes of nitroglycerin and concentrations of nails and screws, the button on the belt, to die, to cause others to die, to live instead of dying, to live forever instead of living . . . These thoughts moving through his mind simultaneously like nails and screws propelled outward in all directions by an explosive charge in a half-moment hardly known before its passing—while beyond the glass door there is not only the pool, but also, nearer to the door, a bird feeder, a little house on a pole where a bird with brilliant red feathers is perched and pecking at the seed; and now another flying into sight to land alongside the first, same kind though gray with a red beak; and then, suddenly, though much later, the birds are gone and the old guy is opening the door. He's got a jar. Not honey, fudge sauce. Holding it up like a trophy newly won until he really sees the boy at the table.

"Karim, what—"

"Nothing."

"Damn. Damnit, son." Then, in Arabic: "I'm sorry." He sits at the table. "I shouldn't have left you alone like that."

"Jaddi . . ."

"Go ahead," he says. "Let it out." (Leaning forward, old hands clasping and unclasping but not daring to touch your hands, which are also on the table, closed around the phone.) "I'm here," the old guy says. (Not understanding at all.) "I'm here," he says. "Damn, I'm sorry, son. I won't do that again. I mean, not until—" (not understanding, not understanding at all) "—not until you're ready . . ."

Keenan gave Mr. B some bullshit about a family crisis: Grandma fractured her femur in a loony bin for the memory-impaired. Dean's excuse was some Calypso Fest at the Civic Center. Come eleven o'clock, it was just me and Plaxico in our cargo trunks and sun-protective shirts and flip-flops heading up the curve of the cul-de-sac. To the party. If you could call it a party: three kids, one of whom was literally an enemy combatant, and a retired mercenary. Then a car rolled by us. Two kids in the back. It slowed down at The Negro, which is when I saw that another car was already parked in the driveway, and there was a woman in a head scarf standing by the open driver's door and a kid was walking from that car to the house. Dressed just like us. Dressed for swimming.

"What is this," I said.

"I dunno."

"Other kids. And they're hajis."

"Yep," Plaxico said.

"Who are they? From Crescent?"

"Crescent, I bet."

Which was a private school in an old crumbling mansion near the abandoned racetrack. We had Muslim kids at our school. But if they could afford it, Muslims sent their kids to Crescent.

"Forget it," I said.

My best friend had a look on his face like maybe he agreed. We just stood there for a few seconds while our sunscreen scattered and absorbed ultraviolet radiation. Hottest day of summer so far. Meanwhile, Mr. Nkondo was coming down his driveway with a garden hose. Washing dead cicadas off the blacktop. Now he closed down the nozzle and I could feel the water wanting to get out.

"Zeb, Dorian. Yo."

"Hi, Mr. N."

He removed his kente hat, ran his wet hand through his wooly hair, and looked at the scene playing out next door. The lady in the head scarf talking to the driver of the car that had passed us; the kids. All of them definitely Arabic.

"Lemme guess. You two are going to a funeral on a beach."

"Pool party," Plaxico said.

Mr. N put the hat back on. "You know those kids?"

We shook our heads.

"Well," Plaxico said. "We know Karim."

"Not really," I said.

"We met him the other day."

"Me, too," Mr. N said. "I met him the other day. Can't say it was love at first sight. The kid's kind of, I don't know."

"Yeah," I said.

"So you got that feeling, too," he said. "Well, let's not rush to judgment. He's been through a lot."

"Do you think it was a drone?" Plaxico asked.

"What?"

"That killed his family."

Mr. N raised the leaking hose to his lips. "You mean, do I think our government has been in the business of killing its own citizens . . . I— Well, I need some proof before I buy into that story."

"Me, too," I said.

"Whatever happened, it left him all alone. I was talking to Ry— Ryder's in Damascus now—and he said, over there, kids who lose everything, they wind up blowing themselves into a million pieces."

"How can kids do that."

"I don't know, Zeb. So maybe it's all good. Help a kid, save some innocent lives. Maybe that's how we get out of this mess. A few lives at a time."

As we walked off, I was thinking about how Mr. N had been an orphan, too. From Nigeria. An American couple adopted him when he was a baby. Growing up, he had been Hendrix Woodworth. Later, he took back his African name. Went to college, got married, had a kid of his own.

Made me wonder.

What if no one had ever helped Mr. N.

As Moses Nkondo opens the nozzle of the garden hose (the water has been surging there like blood behind a clot and now released atomizes against the blacktop, alchemizing into a rainbow-flecked spray), he watches the two boys walk toward the neighboring house. They have, he has noticed, a curious habit of touching the lawn jockey statue every time they go near it. The statue has been there at the foot of that driveway for as long as he can remember. A representation undebatably offensive. The big red lips and the skin not so much black as blackfaced. But one school year, Ryder did a report and discovered that the statues had been used to guide escaped slaves to freedom; and ever since then, he has felt a fondness for the thing, not because of its history, but because of the association with his son, who when he wrote that report was as small and bewildered as the boys seen now through this veil of water . . . He washes the insect death, the exoskeletons and winged bodies, to the foot of the driveway and into the road. Doing this with one hand while manipulating the screen of his smartphone with the other. Checking the countdown timer that tracks the balance of his son's tour of duty. Six months, five days, thirteen hours, twelve minutes, forty-one seconds, forty, thirty-nine . . .

As he slaps The Negro five, Dorian says to Plaxico: "I still say forget it." The sentence is necessary to him, as a bridge is necessary to

84

someone making a crossing. I still say forget it. Meaning that he gets Mr. N's viewpoint—but the viewpoint, sensible though it may be, does not change the facts on the ground. The invitation didn't say anything about other kids; it was therefore extended under false pretenses and accepted based on incomplete information. He is not refusing to go, but he wants it to be sayable later that he went into the whole thing having expressed, out loud and in the hearing of another, a doubt alike to non-consent. On the driveway stand the two adults, the mother in the head scarf and the father from the second car, who stop their talking as the boys approach. The mother, in a tone of pleasant surprise, says good morning. The father, who in sunglasses and Hawaiian shirt looks to Dorian like an Arab general on vacation, gives them a wordless look with implications difficult to divine, as if he has information about them which they don't yet have themselves. An impression shared by both boys, who as a rule move through the world knowing just enough to formulate questions. The answers, it would seem, are always just out of reach. Like: Out in those camps—what's been happening out there? Is it true, what some people say, about drones? Or: That photo from the other night, of my family before I was born. Someone took that picture. Someone is just outside the image. Not there yet there.

Is it *her*?

Dorian hadn't thought this at first. When he first saw the picture, sitting in the darkened den with his father, he had merely thought: California. My brother is two or three. But the image, the angle of its recording had positioned his mind's eye, making him feel he was lying in the sand before his parents and brother, which made him think: the person with the camera was lying in the sand. Then, as the photo faded, he thought suddenly of her (if his brother was two, she would've been eight), and thought also of the other thing he'd noticed: the sunglasses on his mother's face. The lenses were gigantic: two giant convex surfaces in which the reflection of the person in the sand, the person with the camera, might be visible. If he were to zoom the picture to two-fifty, maybe three hundred percent and look into the lenses . . . So Dorian had asked his father for a copy of the photo, and all the following day not receiving one finally wrote him an e-mail, *What about the pic*, to which the reply, *What pic. Oh, that pic. I haven't had time to look for that.* Which is totally bogus because your father has nothing *but* time, does nothing all day but type on a computer after which he will spend the dinner hour moping because he hasn't achieved anything worth shit all day. He knows why you want it. Just because your father is anti-social and self-centered doesn't mean he's not attuned to the action around him. On the contrary. He's a writer. He sees plots everywhere. So why would he give you the photo. When he can remember perfectly well that she is the one who took it. He himself has probably thought about the sunglasses. Has maybe even done what he knows you would do if he gave you the picture; and has seen that you are right, that in the dark lenses (perhaps in one more clearly than the other) it is discernible: the reflection of a girl, eight or nine years old, lying in the sand with a camera.

"The boyz from the hood!"

"Hi, Mr. B."

"Marhaban, marhaban," he says. "That's 'welcome' in Arabic."

At the far end of the patio their neighbor is wearing a cook apron that says GRILL MASTER—THE MAN, THE MYTH, THE LEGEND. The other kids are buds. Hanging close, elbows rubbing. Karim standing off a little, against the house, in a scalene triangle of shade. (*Two of us*, Dorian thinks, *and four of them*.) Then the sliding door opens and a girl steps out: a black girl never before seen by Dorian. She has apparently been in the bathroom checking her phone and applying lip gloss because there's a phone in her hand and her lips have got the luster of hard candy.

"Oh," she says. "Who's this?"

Karim (sort of clearing his throat): "They live here."

"I'm Zeb," Plaxico says.

"Dorian."

"The boyz from the hood," Mr. B reiterates.

"I'm Khaleela."

"Cool name," Plaxico says. "Is it African?"

When she shakes her head, her shoulder-length braids swing with the slow grace of trapezes: "Khaleela was the wife of the prophet."

"You mean," Dorian says, "like a prophet from the Bible."

"Um, no. The Koran."

Once introductions are completed (the boys of Arab descent are named Omar, Tarriq, and Joey), the kids head for the swimming pool while the adoptive father withdraws to the kitchen in his cook apron and readies a banquet of snacks and meats. Under the transparent dome, which covers the entirety of the twenty-foot-long oval pool like a ballistic missile shield, the children do cannonballs, trying to splash the dome and scare cicadas off the outer surface. They have a semblance of a conversation ("How many bugs up there?" "Two hundred, five hundred") while in the kitchen, the old soldier is impaling chunks of lamb and chicken on metal skewers. From this distance, the scene under the dome is one of fun and friendly relations—and the orphan boy, though perhaps on the outskirts, is not outside of it all. It's the girl who won't let him separate or isolate. Showing him something on her phone. Volleying a hot pink beach ball. The girl is like a butterfly, alighting on each male faction in a flight pattern that seems both random and carefully planned . . . She gets on the giant yellow smiley face and floats in the center of everything, sunglassed, head back, counting the insects aloud. "86, 87, 88." The kid named Omar submerges, approaches sea-monstrous from below, and capsizes her. She surfaces, choking and spitting, shaking water from her braids, blinking her huge bright eyes; and cries, "I need mouth to mouth!" When she catches the boy looking at her— the white-skinned one, the only white one, who has a cool cowlick at the front of his hairline—she rolls her eyes and puffs her cheeks out like a blowfish. The boy ducks under the water. Holds his breath and opens his eyes. He can see her legs and feet; toes touching the bottom of the pool, just barely, lifting, touching again; and even under the water, he can hear the cicadas chorusing in the trees above and all around them. Dampened by water, the noise sounds like something other than itself. What is it? Then it comes to him. That tone played on the radio. That cold musical note meaning the next emergency can come at any moment.

I swam underwater to the ladder and climbed out. Plaxico was sitting on a lounge chair, drinking a soda and tapping his feet to that song that goes: *Seasons don't fear the reaper, nor do the wind the sun or the rain* . . . I was going to say, Let's bail. (Because all these Muslims kept looking at me like they knew I was the one, the kid from the public school who'd come to their mosque and written that thing in the boys' bathroom, got suspended, got forced to take a class about hate speech, and then dragged back to the scene of the crime to apologize and paint over the words.) But before I could say anything, the girl was coming with her phone. Her skin wet like with dew. Saying: "Omar, take a picture of us." Then she squeezed between me and Plaxico. Our bare legs were touching, the thighs and calves and even our feet a little, and all of her felt wet and warm.

"Take a couple shots."

"Okay," Omar said. "But you, what's your name again?"

"Dorian."

"Maybe get the booger off your nose."

As soon as I reached up, he pushed the shutter button—and there wasn't any booger there in the first place. He took another with a shit-eating grin on his face, then handed Khaleela the phone. I watched her delete the first picture; and while she was posting the second one, Omar said to me:

"I know you from somewhere. You go to Sacred Heart?"

"No."

"You all go to Crescent?" Plaxico asked.

Omar nodded. Khaleela said no, she went to Dorothy Nolan. Plaxico told them where we went.

"You just look familiar," Omar said. "Do I?"

"Not really."

"I know. You were in *The Wizard of Oz.*"

"Huh?"

"The play. In the park last year. You were the mayor. Of the Munchkins."

"No," I said.

Then he called out to one of the other kids and went off in Arabic. The other one looked at me like I was suddenly in focus and nodded, and Omar took a step closer to me and said: "You do soccer last summer at East Side Rec?"

"Yeah."

"That's it. I knew I knew you from somewhere. Soccer. You were always doing those slide tackles—"

"Karim," Khaleela said. "Your phone."

He picked it up and squinted at the screen. The ringtone was set to OLD TELEPHONE, so it was going off in his hands like an alarm clock from the Great Depression, and Omar was saying, "The green, dude, touch the *green*"—but I think the kid knew what to do, even if he had never gotten a call before. The way he was holding the phone and staring, he didn't look confused. He looked scared.

Back at the internment camp, just for fun, Karim and Hazem and Yassim would sometimes communicate on the two-way radios even if they were all in the same room or walking beside each other on the street. So when a phone started ringing under the dome and the girl, who was holding her own phone, said, "Karim, your phone" (and Karim realized that *his* phone, left on a towel colored like an American flag, was the one ringing), he thought for a moment that it must be her calling him. Then he picked up the device and saw the screen. And everything around him—the pool and its pristine water; the face on the inflatable raft smiling idiotically at heaven; the suburban children in their swim-clothes—all these things seemed to disappear, as if they'd only been aspects of a mirage; while the face on the screen, with its thorny beard and eyes glowing red from camera-flash, was the one and only thing that was undeniably real. The name above the photo, the name was wrong, not the one they called him by in Dakota. But the photo. No doubt about it: It was him.

"Touch the *green*, dude."

Karim moves away from the invited guests. Toward the steps that lead to the ground. The ringing. Like a command shouted again and again. Answer me, answer me. It is impossible to disobey.

Touch the *green*.

Whereupon the picture on the screen will change to a different picture of the same person, this one moving and speaking:

"Abdelkarim Hassad. May peace be upon you."

"Sheikh, I—"

"Karim, greet me properly."

"Na'am. Aasif. And peace upon you, as well as God's mercy and blessings."

"Now, then. Tell me. Are you enjoying the party."

"The what?"

"Those are your new friends I hear in the background? You're very gregarious, Karim. Also disloyal."

90

"Sheikh, I didn't—"

"Scarcely a week and you've already forgotten us."

"I haven't."

"Forgotten your true friendships, the family they murdered, your people, and even God Himself. Or did you simply forget the ten numbers I made quite sure you memorized before leaving?"

"No," he answers. "I didn't forget anything."

"No?"

"No, I didn't."

"Then you have purposely ignored my instructions. Instead of being a warrior for God, you want to make friends on the Internet. You would rather fraternize with infidels in a swimming pool."

"Sheikh, only two are infidels."

"Oh, is that all?"

"Yes, but—"

"Why didn't you say so? Only two. Only one-third of the total number. Why not make it an even half?"

"I will call today."

"It's too late for that, Karim."

The boy has walked a good ten meters away from the pool—into the shade of a hundred-year tree where the insects cry and wail like people mourning the wrongful deaths of loved ones. The boy says: "What do you mean, too late?"

"I mean that your commitment is uncertain and there can be no uncertainty."

"I'm—I'm not uncertain."

"Listen to yourself, Karim. It's a shame. Your parents and your sister, they have been counting on you for the justice no one else can do. I'm sure your mother is greatly pained. That you would rather stay with worthless strangers than be with her and earn her the greatest rewards of Paradise."

"I want to."

"It's not a matter of what you want. It's not your choice—or mine.

91

It's God's choice. God chooses his martyrs. Only God can bestow the honor of martyrdom. He alone bestows the honor or takes it away."

"Sheikh—"

"I'm sorry, Karim. Enjoy your party. I'm sure the water in the pool is refreshing."

"Sheikh, wait."

"And one other thing. About your Lifebook account. I recommend a privacy setting. It won't keep Satan away. But the Internet is full of lesser devils. Beware of them, Karim. Masalama. And good luck."

Back at the pool, in his absence, they are talking while Dorian and Plaxico listen silently on the periphery.

"What a fuckin freak."

"Don't say that," Khaleela says.

"Well, he *is*, isn't he?"

"And what do you think you'd be like?"

"Yeah, that place," Tarriq says.

Omar says: "What about it?"

"No phones allowed and it's totally dark—I mean, what if you were never online."

"I'd be a fuckin freak."

"He's trying to get used to things," Khaleela says.

"What's the score?"

Joey (looking at his phone): "Still one–zero."

"I can't believe we're missing this match."

"What match," Plaxico asks.

"Baghdad United, who else. You like Islamic League?"

"Not really."

"Figures. But your friend likes to slide tackle."

"That wasn't me," Dorian says.

"Who do you think he's talking to anyway?"

"Yeah, who would call him?"

"Not his mom," Tarriq says.

"*What?*" Khaleela says.

"What . . ."

"Is that, like, supposed to be funny?"

"No, I'm just saying."

"You three are assholes."

"Me?" Joey says.

"All of you."

"I didn't say *anything*."

"You don't have to."

"Well—" (pointing to Dorian and Plaxico) "—what about *them*?"

"What about them," Khaleela says.

"They're not saying anything either."

"Yeah," Omar agrees. "Say something."

"We hardly know him," Plaxico says.

"You two are real tolerant."

"I guess."

"I doubt it. But what you wouldn't get anyway is that people like him are bad for us."

"I thought you were all Muslim," Dorian says.

"Yeah," says Khaleela.

"You mean, like, Sunni and Shia," Plaxico says.

"No, I don't mean Sunni and Shia."

"Then what."

"Look, dude, they never should of let them out—it'll just make it harder for the rest of us."

"Shut up," Khaleela says. "He's coming back."

"You shut up."

"Don't say that to her," Dorian says.

"What if I do."

"He might do a slide tackle," Tarriq says.

Dorian (attempting to keep his voice steady): "I just told you—"

"Yeah, yeah," Omar says. "We know. It wasn't you. It was some other Aryan. Sorry, you all look the same to us."

Karim walks into the kitchen where, set out on an arabesque table-cloth acquired by the old guy in the days of the third war, is the kind of thing he would've wished for back in the camp had he ever found a magic lamp occupied by a solicitous djinn. There are two giant serving dishes piled high with shaved lamb and chicken; a stockpile of pita bread; a bowl of hummus the size of a wash basin; and a pitcher of tea crammed full of ice cubes. But he can't eat. He picks at the food while the others stuff their faces and chug the sweet minty tea. The old guy is looking at him, as he looked at him earlier when he walked in the door and found him sitting at the table crying. *Don't cry now. God, please don't let me cry.* The reason for tearfulness is: in his mind, he is still talking to the sheikh. Saying: *No, don't leave me here.* Which are the very words his mind spoke and re-spoke to his mother and father in the days and months after the drone strike; not the first or second day and night, when he had wandered the streets of the camp in a state comparable to that of a computer after the crashing of its systems, but in the days and weeks beyond, when, having been identified as "displaced" (as if this hadn't been his condition already), he was appended to a new household unit with a woman and a man whose presence only confirmed more fully the unbelievable absence of his real family, until at last—putting some food and a blanket in a backpack, and carrying his mother's cracked eyeglasses in the pocket of his filthy blue jeans—he left like a runaway. He went to where the street grid of the old city ended. There was a last gasp of forsaken warehouses and factories; and alongside a sewer of a creek, a shantytown, like the settlement of some sad band of pioneers. Then farmland. Sterile and flat. Karim walked across it for hours. By midday, he could see the reservation fence. By sunset, he had reached it. Ten-foot electrified barrier of interwoven wire stretching like time in two directions and bending (as perhaps time bends) to form a closed loop all around him. He wrapped himself in the blanket—and while he slept, a surveillance drone must have heat-sensed him because he came shocked out of a dream in which his parents were not dead into a whirl of rotor dust and a darkness slashed by lines of green light that seemed to impale and hold him fast to the cold ground until a vehicle braked a few yards away: in all, four soldiers (not counting the helicopter pilot) armed with laser-sighted assault rifles to apprehend an eleven-year-old boy carrying a pair of broken eyeglasses. When one of the soldiers patted him down and found the glasses, Karim was afraid they'd be tossed away or ground into the dirt with a boot heel. But the man just handed them back. On the return trip, Karim held them in his trembling fingers, his mind saying, *No, don't leave me here*, as if he had expected mother and father to appear on the other side of the fence and they had not come—as if beyond the fence is where they were: another world, but how do you get there from here?

In approximately half an hour, when the sun is paused directly overhead as if balancing on a pinnacle of sky, the party will fail like a ceasefire. Only one of them can feel it coming. That one is not Will Banfelder, in whose opinion the whole affair is going off without a hitch. After noon prayer, he'll break out the croquet mallets; he set the wickets up last night on the other side of the pool. It's not Tarriq Malick, who hasn't had such a wicked good shwarma since

95

that restaurant in the capital closed after someone threw a concrete block through the front window and torched it. Not Zebedee (born Plaxico) Hightower, who is wondering what that phone call was all about and why Karim Hassan-Banfelder all of a sudden has the nervous shrinking look of a dog just kicked by its master. Not Dorian Wakefield, in whose head the voice of Khaleela Kingsley won't stop echoing: *I need mouth to mouth!* And not Khaleela Kingsley, who is catching Dorian Wakefield stealing a glance at her over his shwarma. And finally not Omar Mahfouz. Who never did think that Dorian Wakefield was the slide-tackler from last summer but does intend after lunch to see how the little shit will react to further provocation. None of these know. Only Karim. He alone. Knows though not what. Perhaps when our hearts emit a pulse of commitment, then an echo of an action not yet taken and yet to be devised by the imagination can return to us. As Karim is feeling the echo, the phones of the faithful are awakened from sleep mode by their salat reminder applications. *"Come to prayer,"* the muezzins chant, one, then another, then another. *"The time is here for the best of deeds."*

Dorian knows about this from the Islam chapter in Social Studies. Five times a day. And that's not counting weekly services at the mosque. Doesn't know how they do it. His own family, when they first moved from California, had tried religion. They couldn't even manage once on Sunday. Dorian can't really remember, but the experiment and its failure has stayed with him—and the sight of the church sometimes gives him a guilty feeling, as when passing the home of a friend made and then forsaken. He can hear them now. By standing in the doorway of the bathroom. Their voices rising up the short staircase from the basement. Her voice in prayer. Sweet and serious. Check your breath. It smells like shwarma. On the sink lies

96

a tube of Mentafresh. Squeeze some onto your finger. Suck it off, mix with saliva, swish, and spit.

One o'clock or so.

That hour of a summer day when anyone can start to feel a little crazy. Even in long lost times, before the planet's dangerous warming, it was so; but with this dizzying heat and the noise of cicadas like schizophrenic voices in the head and a feeling in the heart that you are betraying your family and your god . . .

The partygoers are in the yard. Karim holding in his hands something usable as a weapon. The game is called croquet. The other day, the old guy had taken him to play mini-golf and Karim used a metal stick to tap a little ball over fake grass in the direction of a tin cup. Now he is using a wooden hammer to hit a bigger ball over real grass through metal hoops. Games for spoiled and lazy apostates. *How could I have imagined, even for a few short days, that maybe I could live like this?* As he holds the mallet and watches the kid from across the street (the one set apart from the rest by white skin and light hair) clubbing his red-striped ball, Karim feels a correction in course. You can do it. You can do the thing you have been called to do. Though you must admit: What the sheikh said is not unwarranted. There have been moments when you've doubted your resolve— (Like the other evening, waiting your turn at the ninth hole of the mini-golf course at that place called Oasis Family Funplex, where the sails of a miniature windmill were turning and turning, and there was a baby secured in a sort of vest to its father's chest as if the infant were a type of explosive, which made you ask: *what if I was wearing the belt now, what if this was the appointed time and place*)—

"Nice shot, what's your name again?"

"Dorian."

"Oh, yeah. Aryan. Aryan, how come you're not in soccer camp this summer?"

"Don't call me that."

"Because they suspended you is what I heard."

"I'm not that kid."

You would, Karim answers himself now, *pull the cord. You will. Wherever, whenever. So prove it. Prove it to the sheikh.*

"Omar," the girl is saying. "Just cut it out."

"Khaleela. Just shut your mouth."

"Hey—"

"Forget it," she says to the white kid; and she's holding his arm, touching him—which, for some reason, makes Karim even angrier and more certain that the time has come, the sun at a tipping point, time for an action that will prove his willingness and his readiness for the greatest of actions. If only the sheikh could see. And then he realizes: *The camera, the camera in your phone.*

"I told you before, don't be rude to her."

"You told me."

"Now if you do it one more time, one more time, okay, and I'll knock the towel off your fucking head."

"*What?*"

"You heard me."

And while the other kid, the black one, is saying, "Okay, bro," Karim is dropping his croquet mallet, not simply dropping it but throwing it sidewise over the grass. It's a gesture everyone sees. So sudden and dramatic that all speech and thought comes to a momentary stop.

What came next: I just stood there, not getting what he was walking at me for. To tell me something, was all I could guess—like he'd chosen me as the keeper for some secret. Even after he drew his arm back to hit me, it seemed I was still waiting to see what would happen. So he got me full in the stomach. While I suffocated, no one moved or spoke. Then my breath came back. Omar grabbed my shirt from behind. I swung a fist over my shoulder and caught him in the jaw before the other two got me by the arms and neck. Everyone shouting in Arabic and English. This time it came even more out of nowhere. Flash of blindness, then the pain across my face, like a baseball had taken a bad hop. Then blood. On my upper lip and into my mouth. I heard Karim saying: "Hold him down." Which they did. They wrestled me to the ground and the next thing I saw was the kid standing over me with his phone, positioning the camera eye above my face, snapping a picture.

7

Mitch had found the photo. There were about five hundred in the folder. So it had taken him nearly an hour of looking. Then, there it was. The three of them, in the days before Dorian, on a beach. His son was right: a low angle. Unlikely, maybe impossible, that the camera had been been set down in the sand and programmed to work its own shutter. The people were too precisely framed and the horizon of ocean too true. Now that he could study it, Mitch noticed other things. First of all, on the left side of the image (to the left of Kathryn, in the distance, in the water) stood a rock arch. Instantly he knew it. Goat Rock. About a half hour's drive from their old house, where the Russian River ends its southward course and fresh water commixes with salt, and where, in the springtime, on the plateaus of sand to either side of the estuary, harbor seals birth and nurse their pups.

As he stared at the image on the computer screen (he was in his office, in the summer-deserted halls of the department, the building quiet as a church between services), Mitch tried to call to mind the friends who would join them in those days on such outings, and which member of that disbanded league would've conceived such a photo and lain prone in the sand to realize it. Fourteen, fifteen years ago. Perhaps the photographer had also pressed upon Kathryn the sunglasses with the tea-saucer-size lenses, an accessory she would never wear for any effect but comedy . . .

He sent her the picture.

Five minutes later, she replied: GUESS I REPRESSED THAT TRAUMATIC MEMORY OF FASHION—AND YOUR SON AND HEIR WAS A FAT LITTLE S.O.B.

And Mitch wrote back: BUT DO YOU REMEMBER THAT DAY AT ALL? SEE GOAT ROCK IN THE BACKGROUND.

And she replied: VISUAL EVIDENCE NOTWITHSTANDING, I'M PREPARED TO SWEAR UNDER OATH THAT I NEVER PUT ON ANY SUCH PAIR OF SUNGLASSES.

He closed e-mail, closed the jpeg, thinking there was nothing to it—what could there be to it? And yet he didn't send the file to his son. And the next day, when Dorian wrote Mitch wanting to know if he had found the photo, Mitchell lied and said he'd forgotten to look. As if he knew of a reason to keep it from him.

•

On Saturday, while his son is bleeding from his nose and possibly his mouth, Mitch—who all morning has been writing (which is to say: typing sentences, whole paragraphs, only to have them miscarry before completion and then he starts anew, like someone punished with an eternally futile labor)—opens the photo again. It has gotten into his head. Last night, he dreamed a kind of explanation for it. In the dream, Dorian was his eleven-year-old self, but his older brother was still two. They were all on the beach at Goat Rock and Dorian said: We have to take a picture before the radiation gets here . . . Now, looking at it again. Kathryn on the left with the sunglasses, Cliff in the middle, himself on the right. The ocean in the background and a rock sculpted by a thousand years of surf into the shape of a portal. Suddenly, his mind cognizes a detail that the nerve cells of his retina had sensed from the start: The sunglasses, a reflection in the lenses.

He copies the photo to the college server and goes into the department office and starts up the PC with the twenty-three-inch monitor.

Clicks on the file: The picture twice as large now.

There.

In the lens on the left. The one adumbrating his wife's right eye—and most of her right cheek and a fraction of her forehead, too. Something there. An image. Though hard to tell what. He clicks on the magnification slider and moves it up halfway. His older son's face fills the window. Then he moves the pointer onto the image and drags right—to his wife's lips—and then down, until the sunglasses come into view. First the curving frame front. Then the lens. The reflection in it. Close up like this, all you see is a grid of black and white squares, not dissimilar to an unsolved crossword puzzle. But zoom out a few degrees: and the pixels will come smashing together into a shape. A person. Isn't that what it is? A child, isn't it? Blurred by low resolution and warped by the bend of the mirroring surface. But yes. Prone in a brightness that can only be sand, holding something that must be a camera. Long hair lifting like smoke. On the shoulder, the dark line of a swimsuit strap. A girl.

They have him pinned to the ground. Tarriq is kneeling on his right arm; Omar's got the left one and also a fistful of Dorian's hair. Pulling on the hair to tilt the face up so Karim can take another picture and thus the blood is running throatward and causing in Dorian a sensation of drowning. In his eyes the sun is a blinding bulb of unfathomable wattage—and though everyone is talking at once, he can't seem to hear anything but the cicadas like a sound blasted without mercy through an array of loudspeakers. Through it all some part of him asking: *Dude, where the fuck are you?* Well, where else would Plaxico Hightower be—a boy with the reflexes of an emergency responder and the heart (even if he himself does not fully know it yet) of a pacifist—but sprinting over the lawn to enlist the aid of a peacekeeper?

Sliding the door open while slamming his open hand on the glass. He can see through the kitchen to the living room and the baseball game on the flatscreen.

"Mr. B!"

Will is already on his feet, mind daymared with the vision of a kid floating face down in the water of the pool. Across the patio and almost to the steps when Zebedee calls: "No, back here!" He rounds the pool. Sees the children in the grass. Standing among the arches of the wickets and a litter of balls and mallets. One on the ground: not his son; his neighbor's son. Blood on his face, but Will can see right away that this is nothing. An accident. Careless swing of a croquet mallet. Although when he gets closer, he is surprised by how much blood there is, on Dorian's shirt as well as his face, and how black the substance is in the sunglare—and the poor kid also seems to have gotten it in the mouth.

"Jesus H."

"We didn't start it."

"Start what," he says, kneeling down. "Dorian, you all right?"

"I dunno."

"Bonk in the nose. Jesus, though. I hope it's not a posterior bleed."

"Sir . . ."

It's the girl speaking: she looks terrified.

"He hit him."

"Hit?"

She points to Karim. A few feet away. For some reason, phone in hand.

Zebedee says: "It's true, Mr. B."

"We didn't start it."

"Start what, goddamn it."

Dorian sits up, touching the teeth in his mouth; all are firmly rooted. He spits into the grass. Blood still draining from his nostrils. He stands and starts walking. Behind him, he can hear them arguing:

103

"He used a racial slur . . . They used one first." On the front lawn he is safely out of sight. A sob and then the tears come. Swallows. Clot of blood down the throat and a nauseated shudder. He leans over. A few feet ahead, The Negro hunched and proffering his open palm. Approaching from behind, his best friend. Saying: "Bro, lemme help." But Dorian doesn't want help. Needs help, but doesn't want it. And won't accept it. So walks off at a rate of speed and with a bearing of body that says *don't fuck with me*—and, to punctuate the message, gives the lawn jockey statue a vicious karate kick to the head.

You never hit anyone before this. Not in the face. One time in the camp, you punched Hazem in the stomach; and when your friend crumpled to his knees, you kicked him, kicked him hard in the arm and the ribcage in a furious panic because he had used up—all by himself, in violation of the pact made by the three of you—the last of the opium. But you have never hit anyone in the face. Until now. And you wouldn't have thought, had you ever given thought to the idea, that hurting someone else could cause so much pain to your own self: your right hand feels cracked and sprained. You never made another person bleed until today—and because you hit him (at least once, maybe more) after the blood had started, some of the boy's blood is on your hand, smeared and starting to dry.

"Go to your room."

The man who wants to be your father says this in Arabic. In a tone of anger being used for the first time. Go. Do as he says and don't waste time. Because soon he will come and demand an explanation for your behavior, at which time he may take away the phone. So what you must do quickly is send the pictures to the sheikh. Run. Across the lawn. You didn't think this far ahead. You have never sent a photo. But you will find that you, like all children of your time, are instinctively inclined toward basic technological operations. When you reach the room, close the door. In the photo album are three pictures. The first is no good. The boy had moved and the camera captured only grass and a clump of yellow dandelions. But the second one is clear. A bloody face fills the frame and the blood looks very dark on the white skin. Tap this image with your fingertip. Symbols will appear at the bottom of the screen. The leftmost one (an arrow in a square) makes a kind of sense. Touch it. Yes: a menu of commands. Choose the one on top. The picture is now a message. But a message with no destination. You don't know what to type—and for a moment you think there is no way to know. But notice. Another symbol: red circle with a plus sign. Touch it and the number of the phone he called from will be revealed to you. Touching that number will cause it to be pasted into the address line. Just one last thing to do now. But before you tap the green button, touch the subject line. You will see the letters of the alphabet in random order. Search through and press one at a time until you have spelled out: I DID THIS.

As soon as I kicked the statue over, I felt guilty about it. I actually stopped and looked back. Plaxico was fixing it. For some reason that made me feel worse. But I kept walking. Where Poospatuck intersected with Onondaga, there was a culvert, a big concrete pipe underlying the road. When we were little, we'd pretend we were caving or traveling through a wormhole to another universe. I had outgrown those games, but it was still a good place to disappear into. I crawled in a ways. Dipped my hands into the trickle of water and dabbed at my face. Fat lip, one eye swollen nearly shut. The kid had gone completely ape shit on me—and I had done *nothing*, said *nothing* to him. I sat there listening to the water falling from the culvert into a little stream that went through the woods and I started thinking of my grandma's house in the Oregon Territory. Because I guess that's where I wished I could be. In that house that wasn't much more than a cabin on the shore of a lake, so far away from everything and so alone in the mountains. I was always the first one awake there. Before the sunrise, I would go down to the dock and look into the fog and sometimes a loon would call out from the heart of the lake, and something about that haunted sound made the world I had come from—the real one with all of its problems—seem like a dream . . .

When I opened the sliding glass door of Keenan's in-law apartment, I found him on the carpet with his girlfriend, Amber Kakizaki, both of them fully clothed but attached to each other like mating insects.

"Got any ice," I said.

Amber saw me and started going, "Oh, Oh." Keenan said nothing. Just walked calmly into the kitchen while I sat on the couch. The apartment, even after several months, still had the smell of his grandmother: baby powder and prune juice.

"You talk to Plaxico?" I said.

"Yep."

He handed me the freezer pack and I held it to my face. Again, he walked off. Returned with a tin of breath mints and said: "Have a synthetic opiate."

I shook my head.

"Look. Don't be such a pussy. Your goddamn nose is broken, you're blind in one eye, and have you looked at your shirt?"

"You could be nicer," Amber said.

"I agree," I said.

"Nicer. That'll work. Let's everybody be a little bit nicer. The real point is, what are we going to do about this."

Do, I thought.

"There's four of them, right? Jig-Abdul from across the street and the other three go to Crescent."

"What are you talking about?"

"I'm talking about what are we going to *do*, Dorian. I mean, Arabs come into your neighborhood and beat the crap out of you. Now what do you do."

Silence.

Then the grandfather clock played Westminster Chimes.

Then I said: "I gotta pee."

In my friend's grandmother's bathroom mirror, I finally saw my face. Pocked purple, smeared with blood. I ran the water and cupped my hands. Once I'd cleaned up, I could see the damage wasn't so bad. Four times he'd hit me, maybe only three. And he was not a strong kid, not a big kid. Now, what do you do?

Around three o'clock, Mitch gets a text from his younger son. Wants to know if he can spend the night at Keenan's house. Mitch does not like the kid. Likes his parents less. And Kathryn likes all of them even less than Mitch. The kid, as he understands it, has been allowed to move from his bedroom into the in-law apartment recently vacated by his grandmother. The scenario would be funny if it wasn't so poorly supervised. He imagines . . . what ? *Chill out, man. They're only eleven years old. And even if eleven is the new thirteen. So they're playing video games and smoking some greens maybe. And maybe some girls arrive at some point and they pair up and turn off the lights and make out. Like you did at their age if you correct for inflation.* He tells him all right.

As he sets the phone down, Mitch sees the time. He has been at this computer, manipulating the picture in PhotoWizard, for nearly three hours. At one point, he had heard footsteps in the hall outside (and felt, as they faded, a needless relief, as if he were about some business both secret and forbidden). Now, without warning, a key is being inserted into the lock and the door is opening.

"Oh, Professor Wakefield!"

"It's okay."

Of the three books in her hand, library books the size of stone tablets, one has fallen to the floor. Mitch moves to pick up the book, then takes the others from her and sets them down on the faux-wood countertop. He recognizes her. A student assistant. The reason he didn't hear her coming: bare feet (toenails painted black).

"I just came to do some copying," she says.

"All yours."

He bends over the computer and closes the file. Logs off. There are eight printouts of the photo spread over the desk.

"You're a photographer, too?"

"Me? No."

"Looks like a photo. Or is it a painting?"

(Glancing at her while completing the shut down.) "What's your name again?"

"Chloe Bennett."

He nods, then holds out one of the printouts: "Chloe, what does this look like to you?"

"Hmm . . . Man Ray?"

"What? No," Mitch says. "I mean, does it look like something. Can you tell what it is?"

After quite a long time, she says: "A quasar."

"A quasar."

"I took Astronomy last semester."

"Can you see a girl? See. This is the head, the body . . ."

She squints and tilts the paper. Finally says: "Oh. Oh, yeah."

"Do you?"

"No, I do. It's like she's floating in a fog. That's very trippy, Professor."

"Yeah, it is."

"Is it your daughter?"

He looks at her. First in the eyes. Then, when she looks away, not of his own free will, at her chest. Then away, at her hands holding the photo; and sees on one wrist, a pale pink scar. Says: "No. No, it's not. I don't have a daughter."

The party's over. Guests gone home. The girl, Khaleela, had been the last. Will had sat with her on the front steps in silence, in the hot shade with glasses of iced tea, water condensing on the glasses and gathering into beads that tracked down the outsides and clung to the round bases, then let go, falling to the concrete step. When her father came, Will explained to him (as he had to each parent in turn) what had happened. That he had been wrong. Had rushed the boy into something he wasn't ready for. "It's my fault. I should've known better." And this parent—a tall man, arms crossed at a strong chest—did not regard Will Banfelder (as the others had) with accusatory agreement, but said in a voice whose low pitch seemed augmented by a subwoofer in the throat:

"Don't be so hard on yourself, it was just a fistfight."

As the car backed away, the girl waved from the rear window, a gesture of regret and sympathy beyond her years.

Now here he stands. All around him, the goddamn bugs. Whose chorusing is like a kind of laughter. Inside the house, the boy, his son (think *son*, keep using the word) is waiting. To be questioned, lectured, punished. Just a fistfight. Will wonders if maybe the man is right. *Don't be too hard on yourself. Or him. No one's dead, after all. Just a bloody nose.* But it somehow seems unlikely that the Wakefields are going to be interested in anyone else's idea of what constitutes actual violence. *Don't fool yourself. A harm has been done here, a harm. This behavior cannot be in any way sanctioned. And yet it's your fault, not his. You rushed him. You should've known.*

So goes the thinking of Will Banfelder—not in circles so much as by random turns, as if his mind is blindly navigating a maze—as he returns to the house, opens the glass door to the kitchen and confronts not only the remains of lunch (the dirty plates and utensils, the leftover meat and hummus, a housefly crawling on the waste), but also the specter of dessert: the seven bowls he had set out on the counter. The old man stands there, trying to decide what to do first. Finally goes to the freezer. Scoops ice cream, pours on some fudge sauce, and tops it off with Kool Wip. At the table, with a plastic spoon, he eats it all. Then climbs the stairs, approaches his son's door, and knocks.

•

Clifford Wakefield has never been close with his younger brother. He can still remember when his parents announced the news of a coming baby. (He was six years old and just starting first grade.) First a shock of undoing, as if the fabric of space was tearing along a seam; and then, for months afterward, a sense that the established circumstances of life were not so much changing as being confused with a set of circumstances that were alien and invasive. It wasn't that he couldn't imagine a brother or sister. His mind was not denying the possibility of a mother having a baby. But *this* mother. This mother who was *his* mother. He tried to understand the situation in terms of something his grandfather had used as a soldier in Vietnam, a keepsake he had allowed Cliff to play with at his house in the Oregon Territory—a circular object with a glass cover and a silver needle under the glass, a magnetized needle that, in obedience to physical laws, only ever pointed in one direction: true north. Now, if the needle were to point east and only east. Well, that was impossible. But what if it did . . . They were right, of course, his parents, when they told him he'd get used to the baby. But the next summer when they visited that house on the lake, Cliff, now seven, saw the compass laid out in the same place as always, on a shelf beside an old aneroid barometer (the hand of which seemed never to be pointing left or right, not to the forecast of **RAIN** or **FAIR** scripted on the face, but always straight up, to the word **CHANGE**)—and he picked up the compass and, turning his body in different directions, watched the needle being realigned by the powers of the planet, thinking that, just as the needle of this compass cannot point east, there cannot be a baby, cannot be a brother.

He has been thinking about all of this lately, thinking of it in the light of what his schizo brother has been saying about a sister, and sensing a creepy parallel—and just last night, he had a dream that really scared him, which both answered the question of Dorian's strange behavior in recent months and explained the equally strange conviction from his own sixth and seventh years, as follows:

He was walking in a forest and encountered a man sitting under a tree clothed in a T-shirt and ripped blue jeans (feet bare). The man had long hair and a bandanna wrapped around his head. Also, the man was smoking an old-fashioned blunt. He didn't look especially intellectual. But not only was he wicked smart, he was telepathic, because before Cliff had said a single word, the man said something along the lines of: Let ∞ be a set of universes, U's, of distinct but parallel paths ($A_1 - Z^{100}$), each of which is a set of events, E's, on ordered pairs <rc, fw> (<random chance, free will>), such that any variation in any E will have already resulted in the formation of a new U. With these presuppositions before us, we can now turn to your situation. *My situation?* The one you came here to discuss. Euforia? *No, thanks.* Consider the path you are on ($B_{39} - R^{61}$): You

111

have a brother. On other paths (such as K_8 - E^{76}), you don't. One path is central: M_{50} - M^{50}. If a significant event from that path is sensed on any other path, RS may begin to break down. *RS?* Reality-structure. Awareness of central path events may lead to new orderings of <rc, fw> that undermine RS. *How?* Your current situation is a textbook example. Your brother has become aware of an event that occurred on M_{50} - M^{50}. He is taking actions influenced by that event. *So, we really do have a sister.* Did. *She died.* Correct. Your brother has become aware of that. His actions in B_{39} - R^{61} are being influenced by that awareness and are creating consequents. *You mean consequences.* No, I mean consequents. A consequent is the second term of a mathematical ratio. The first term is called an antecedent. When consequents in one universe have antecedents in a different one . . . *What. What then. What happens then?*

But the dream was about to break up.

The man was not talking anymore. In fact, he wasn't a man anymore, although he still looked like one. He was a cicada. He opened his mouth and out it came, emotionless and unrequiring of breath: the scream of an insect.

•

In the light of day, Cliff has been unable to remember exactly what the man said. The ideas, so logical during sleep, now have a quality of total nonsense. What is staying with him very clearly is the scream at the end. Before that, there'd been a lot of weird mathematical jargon. Something about alternate dimensions and his little brother being not crazy. Well, you never said crazy in the first place; all you said was, there's a need here for medication and the kid better start taking some before he does something more egregious than defacing a bathroom— (Phone ringing.) Speak of the devil. It's four o'clock.

First sign of him since he left for the party. Is it possible he's still hanging with the mozlem?

"Lemme guess."

"Cliff—"

"You're getting a tattoo that says: 72 VIRGINS."

"Something happened," he says—and judging from the tone of his voice, not something good. Better lay off and be supportive.

"All right, calm the fuck down. What'd you do this time?"

"I didn't."

"Okay, okay."

"First of all, there were three of them there."

"Three of who where."

"At the party. Kids from Crescent."

"You mean Muslims."

He doesn't answer; and when Cliff tells him to turn on his video feed and there's still no reply, the silence strikes him as eerie. In these days, the mind is poised always on a kind of ledge above fearful assumptions. You see a backpack on a bench or you hear a siren in the offing and your mind curls around an inner trigger. Perhaps he is unable to turn on the video. Because someone is forbidding it. Allowing a voice call, but no more. But, of all people to call, why *me*—

Then suddenly there he is: Black eye and a fat lip, one cheek streaked with a line of blood, as if painted for war.

Cliff (trying not to laugh now): "So what'd you like crash your bike?"

"No."

"Well what."

He touches his lip and winces. Then says again that there were three. While they held him down, the other just whaled on him.

"You got in a fight," Cliff says. "With Muslims."

"They started it."

"Jesus Christ, Dorian. Mom is going to execute your ass."

113

"Is she home?"

"No," he says. Then goes downstairs. Because someone is ringing the doorbell. He walks with the phone in his hand and his brother's face on the screen; and when he gets to the door and peers through the fish-eye peephole (while Dorian is going on about how he never said anything to the kid, not a word the whole time, and the kid just went ape shit on him), whom should Cliff see standing there on the front step but the very same assailant. Son of suspected terrorists. The new kid on the block.

I could hear the doorbell through my phone and I could tell that Cliff was opening the door. What wasn't clear were the first words spoken. Then my brother said: "Dorian, it's for you." And then, on my screen, I saw them. Mr. B was squinting, shading his eyes, leaning closer to the camera. "Dorian?" he said. Beside him: Karim. Wearing khakis and a polo shirt. "Dorian, we— I mean, listen, son. Well, here." (Glancing at Karim.) "Karim has something—" Which was the last thing I heard. Because I had ended the call . . . Not in anger. Not because I refused to speak to him. At the time, I myself didn't understand the reason. Now I know. That for the first time I was seeing myself in him. Marched to my house as I'd been dragged back to the mosque. We were to admit our wrongs, we children: from whom loved ones, futures, entire worlds had been stolen without apology. Somewhere deep inside, I was thinking: Why should either one of us be sorry.

8

That night, Karim Hassad does not sleep much. But around four in the morning, he has a dream of going back to the camp. Sent back because he attacked the boy next door. It unfolds realistically—like life, only in reverse. The old guy is driving him (not east to the Provinces, but west to the Territories); and instead of a dread of endless deprivation and sickness, Karim feels the promise—stronger with every passing moment (moments perceived by his dream-deceived mind as hours)—of the deep peace and amnesia of opium, which is itself a dream. And then the dream is over. Though dreams do not end so much as fade out of sight of the mind's eye, as conversely they may fade back into sight when the other eyes, the ones made of veins and muscle and vitreous, are open. Which is what happens the next morning. Karim is awake in the bedroom given to him by the old guy out of the kindness of his heart. As he lies on the bed, staring at the ceiling, the lingering pain in his fingers makes him wonder how much pain the other boy is in, and the thought of the other boy acts like a rush of sunlight calling forth a shadow: the sudden memory of a dream of being taken back—a good dream, full of the simple feeling of going home.

In the kitchen, Will Banfelder is making breakfast. He has cracked four eggs into a frying pan and the whites have joined together, creating the impression of one giant egg with four yolks. In a second pan, a dozen turkey sausages sizzle and tremble. He puts a glass lid on the pan and watches as the links of encased meat, of their own accord, start rolling around and bouncing into one another.

"Salam, jaddi."

He turns and sees the boy. Who looks absolutely terrible, like he didn't sleep a wink. Which would make two of them.

"Tired, huh."

Karim cocks a shoulder and goes to the table, sitting in the same place as yesterday and the day before: They have settled naturally into this one small routine. He asks if he may drink the juice, and Will says, Of course. He drains the glass. Then refills it from the pitcher. Then returns it with exactness to the place mat.

"I had a dream," he says.

"Tell me."

"I was going back to the camp. You were taking me back."

"Hey," Will says. "Look at me. Karim, look at me. I would never do that. I told you yesterday . . ."

"I know."

"Okay, then. So cut it with the dreams and make some toast."

The boy gets up and removes two slices of bread from the bag and drops them into the slots. Their shoulders are almost touching. It would be a simple thing for Will to put his hand on that shoulder. But same as yesterday—when, after the children had gone and he was sitting beside the boy, asking him to explain and then listening to his explanation (given in Arabic and broken by the arrhythmic breathing of a child holding back tears), and their bodies were very close—same as then, Will is scared to touch him now. Too soon for that. Do it too abruptly and you will startle him. Do it too freely and you cheapen the action. For now, on the subject of breakfast, the adoptive father simply says:

"Over easy, or sunny side up?"

———

The plan was to spend the night on Keenan's grandmother's couch—but every sixty minutes, the grandfather clock played Westminster Chimes and then tolled the hour; and finally at four o'clock Dorian had enough of it and slipped out the back door and walked in the darkness up the road to his own home. The cicadas were silent, not sleeping, he imagined; waiting wide-eyed for the sunrise. The door off the den (referred to by his brother as The Door of Stealth) was the one he entered through. He hoped to see, in the bathroom mirror, that the evidence of the fight had miraculously disappeared. Overall, however, he looked worse than yesterday. Though the swelling in his lip had gone down, the right eye was no less bloated, and the bruise was bigger and darker and ringed with a sickly yellow. He padded upstairs in bare feet, past his parents' half-open door (through which he heard one of them turning and releasing a breath), then safely into his own room, where he lay on his bed and everything went black until a rude shaking and a shining of light—

"Yo, nitwit."

"Stop."

"Time to face your doom," his brother says. Then informs him that the rents are waiting in the kitchen.

"So you explained it," Dorian says.

"I told them the party didn't go so well."

"That's it?"

"I told them that, in my expert opinion, you are not to blame, and Mom said, Blame for what exactly."

"And then what."

"Then I came in here," Cliff says. "And BTW. She's got some serious post–date night stress disorder going on."

———

117

She is waiting in the kitchen, with a terrible hangover and a cup of coffee—for what, she is not sure. For some kind of bad news. In my expert opinion, her older son had said, he isn't to blame. Blame for what, she said; and he said, He really is the victim here; and she said, Victim of what; and he, gesturing with a forefinger, said, I'll go get him . . . So Kathryn is waiting, with a feeling like her brain is trapped under rubble, for the next wave of domestic drama. While she stands by the sink, her husband sits at the table. He looks worse than she feels. He removes his eyeglasses; they dangle from one hand as he stares into the astigmatic distance. Finally saying: "They're not coming."

"Mm."

"They're tying the sheets together and escaping through the window."

"Good luck to them."

He puts the glasses back on and gives her a little smile: "But last night, you did have a good time, right."

"Heck of a time."

"It's just we're not thirty anymore."

"We're not forty either."

"Well, we aren't fifty," he says.

It's the kind of exchange that can turn, suddenly, stupidly, into an argument. She shrugs assent. Can't say that, in the literal sense, he isn't correct. And the truth is, she *was* having a good time last night. All through the first set (stretched out on the blanket, on the grassy hill above the amphitheatre), Kathryn had felt happy. Happier with every song and every drink of wine and every hit from the old-school joints that Deven had brought: five of them expertly rolled and neatly lined up in an antique cigarette case. "Where's it from?" she asked; and he answered, "Humboldt. But don't worry, this farm took readings and tested the soil for years. It's way north of the zone." He started one and handed it to her. A while since she'd smoked anything other than a factory green: just one small hit brought everything around her into a sharper softer focus. The music started; the joint circled back. She felt like something adrift brought to shore on a breaking wave of applause. She lay back on the blanket. Saw one white star: like a faraway idea in the almost-dark sky. Not until intermission, when the music ended, did her mood begin to change . . . She was lying supine with her eyes closed, people conversing all around her, but their voices were a sound without signification, like wind in a forest. She was thinking of the pot farm in Humboldt—not far (a hundred-something miles north) of the old house in the river valley—and of what their friend had said about its distance from the radiation zone. Which made her think of the city. San Francisco. Most beautiful city in the New World. Place where she and Mitch had started loving each other, and where, also, she had come to know the other. (Don't think his name; try to snuff it out as you would a flame.) Place also of unplanned pregnancy and of no baby. Whose beauty might have been for all time, but had instead been ruined in an instant, blasted and burned up and poisoned . . . On the hill above the amphitheatre, she was crying. Hearing the past speaking to her from a great distance. Despite the sounds all around her (the people talking to each other and the crickets calling to one another in the nearby woods), Kathryn Wakefield could hear very clearly a message of confusion, anxiety, and fear: Her own past coming to her across the reaches of space and time. And as she lay there under the stars of the future, a next wave of applause heralding the return of the musicians, she felt she was feeling an impossible sense of interconnection and dependence: as if not just her son's fantasy of a sister, but even the death of that city where the fantasy had lost her life, had followed somehow from her.

———

119

It's like a movie he saw once, where a prisoner was going to get shot at dawn: His brother escorting him down the carpeted hallway which, through some trick of mental editing, seems longer than it can possibly be. Up ahead, on the right, is the kitchen. Inside, Mitch and Kathryn hear them coming—and they can tell when Dorian stops just shy of the doorway. "Can we get on with it," Mitch says. Cliff takes his brother by the elbow and steers him across the threshold. At the same moment, they see him; and though each parent is viewing the same damage, only the father makes the correct inference. The mother is thinking: *Stupid choice; skateboard; on a dare, maybe.*

"Oh, god," Kathryn says. "Clifford, did you take him to the hospital?"

"Me?" (The thought hadn't crossed his mind.)

"It's just a black eye," Dorian says.

Kathryn (kneeling now): "Something could be broken or fractured."

"It's not, Mom."

"Who did it?" Mitch says.

For a few seconds, Kathryn's mind, suffering the backlash of last night's intoxicants, can't catch up with the question. Then suddenly—

"You got in a fight?"

He looks away.

"You got in a fight at that party."

"Kate," Mitch says.

Cliff (raising his hand, but not waiting to be called upon): "Mom, it wasn't his fault."

"Did I ask you?"

"Dorian," Mitch says, "sit down, okay? Kate, please sit down and listen to him. Cliff, just don't open your mouth."

"Do I have to be silent in a standing position?"

"Sit."

120

He sits. Dorian is already in a chair. Kathryn looks at the three of them, all seated at the table now: a confederacy of males. Standing alone against the sink, she says: "I can listen from here."

She listened. She listened quietly to my whole story. Standing the whole time on the other side of the room. As if she didn't want to be near me. I told the truth. That four other kids had been invited. All of them Muslim, though one not Arab. I said that everything had been fine for a while. We were swimming and the girl even wanted a picture with me and Plaxico. But there was this one kid, Omar. Who kept antagonizing me. Which didn't bother me so much, and I didn't say a thing back. But when he told the girl to shut up— ("And what was her name?" my father asked. "Who." "The girl." "Oh. Khaleela." "Khaleela," my brother said. "A lovely name.") And I continued with the story, explaining how I told Omar to not be rude to her. And how he called me an Aryan. To which I didn't say a thing. Just walked away. And then there was lunch. ("What'd you have?" my brother asked. "Shwarmas." "Mm.") And then after lunch, we all went out to play croquet. And I wasn't saying anything. I was just playing the game and he started it again. Used that word like it was my name. And the girl ("Khaleela," my brother interjected) told him to cut it out. And Omar told her to shut up again . . . My heart was beating fast now, you could hear it in my voice. I'd thought the emotions had died down, but they were still hot. Like with embers; if you blow on them, the fire starts again. ("Go ahead," my father said.) And I told them that I told Omar that if he spoke to her like that one more time—(I took a breath and let it go)—I would knock the towel off of his head. ("And then," my mother said, "he hit you." "No." "You hit him first?" she said, and my father said, "Will you let him talk, Kate?") And then I told them that I never did hit him and he never

121

hit me. Omar and his two friends held my arms. The one who threw the punches was Karim.

As he finishes speaking, it seems to Dorian that his parents are separated by a vast distance. He is right—and also wrong. Because even as Kathryn and Mitchell Wakefield foresee the coming schism (we are not going to view this the same way; we will not agree on what to do about this), they are also bonded, as atoms are bonded by the sharing of electrons, by the unstoppable empathy of mothers and fathers: they both feel the same pain and shame—and, also, the same exact hostility. Mitch's imagination is under siege by a vision of himself chokeholding an eleven-year-old orphan so Dorian can bust up his face without interference. And Kathryn wants a phone number. She wants a number to dial and someone to tell off. A voice in her head already rehearsing the diatribe: Who the fuck do you people think you are? *But that's not my voice*, she thinks back. *That's not me.*

She says: "So you used a racial slur."

"Yes, but—"

"In front of all those kids you said that."

"Mom," Cliff said.

"Did I ask you," she said fiercely. "If I want your opinion, I'll ask for it. Goddammit, Dorian. What is wrong with you—"

"Look," Mitch says, "they ganged up on him."

"Three against one," Cliff specifies.

"Actually, four."

Their father (taking a deep breath): "We should probably report this."

"Report," Kathryn says.

"To the police."

"No way."

"Kate, they assaulted him."

"We are not calling the police. We are not going to get a kid from the camps mixed up with the police."

"What would happen," Dorian says.

But no one answers. None of them moves or says anything more for a long minute. Finally, Mitch gets up. To make some food. He lays a hand on Dorian's shoulder. Then opens the refrigerator. At the sink, Kathryn has turned her back on them. She is looking out the window—and from the table, Dorian is looking at her. Both listening to the fragile shells of eggs being broken, one after another, against the rim of a bowl.

What would happen.

The question is on Will Banfelder's mind, too. He has always been friendly with the Wakefields. When he crosses paths with one of them while driving on the cul-de-sac, he waves hello. In the autumn, when the lawns of the subdivision are overspread with red and orange leaves, should he see Mitchell with a rake and a bucket, he will walk across the road and start a conversation about the weather or the foliage further north. But maybe "neighborly" is the more accurate word for this kind of relationship. Truth is, he is not close with them. In a way, it could be said he doesn't know them very well at all. So how can he blame them (any more than he can blame Dorian for ending that call yesterday) if they report this incident to the police. Put yourself in their shoes:

What if Karim came home bloodied and bruised—and you found out that three white boys had held him still while a fourth . . .

But that's different. How? *The two situations are not the same.* Yes, they are: four kids versus one; you can't argue with numbers. *I'm not talking about numbers.* What then. *Power.* Power. As in, who has it

123

and who doesn't. *Right. The two situations are different because of the power dynamics.* You learned nothing over there, did you. *There wasn't anything to learn.* The war couldn't teach you anything? *It was senseless.* You and your platitudes. Thirty years later and you're no smarter now than you were then. That's why you're still fighting, and there's still no end in sight. *I'm not fighting.* Yes, you are. You're all fighting, every one of you, every single day. On desert sand and in corporate boardrooms, in the blogosphere and in the sphere of memory and even in the sphere of dreams. You are fighting this war in your sleep . . . While, upstairs, Karim Hassad stands at the bedroom window. Holding a smartphone as if it's a kind of buoy keeping him afloat. Twenty-four hours have passed—a whole afternoon, night, and morning—since his touching of the command: SEND. There has been no response from Abdul-Aziz. He must have done something wrong. Or perhaps the picture was lost and the sheikh received only the words:

I DID THIS.

This.

A word referring to nothing: You did nothing.

But I *did.*

He is looking through the window at the place where he did it. Beyond the swimming pool. In the grass. Where the elements of the unfinished game—the little silver arches, the wooden balls and the mallets—are as motionless as objects in a painting. One mallet (mine, which I threw before hitting him) lies far away from the others. That is where. But maybe the sheikh received the pictures and the message made perfect sense. Maybe he understood what I did and why. But saw no worth in the action. *You struck an infidel in the face. So what. What is this supposed to prove, Karim?* (He can hear the voice, deep as the skies of Dakota.) *It doesn't change anything. You are no martyr. You are nothing but a boy with nothing . . .* And yet isn't this exactly what the sheikh had told them—Karim, Hazem, and

124

Yassim—over and over again in the camp. That they were nothing, but there was no shame in this. For in their nothingness was a great power. It is hidden in each of you, he had said, this power—and he touched each of them in turn, touched a finger to the breastbone of each boy. You know about the atom and its energies. No? How particles of matter too small to even be seen, when properly influenced, can produce a power as strong as the sun. This is what God did on 8-11. It is said by the infidels that *we* used the power of the atom against them. My sons, do not believe that lie. There was no plane. There was no bomb. In a great explosion generated from nothingness by the will of the Almighty was that city of sin destroyed. As an example to us of the power of our own nothingness. Each of you is likewise an atom. And when you become a martyr, the power hidden within you will be released and you will become pure energy, the energy of God, and you will travel at the speed of the angels (which is fifty-thousand years to a day) along the celestial ladders, which the Qu'ran calls the *maarej*, feeling no pain, only a sensation like being carried on a wave, which will be a wave of pure and heavenly light, and the energy you have become will pass through the doorway held open for you and in this way, in a fraction of a second, you will find yourselves in another universe called Paradise.

•

He hardly slept last night. Between the grandfather clock and the pain in his face every time he rolled over. Now it's early afternoon. Since the conversation in the kitchen, Dorian has been in his bedroom, in a sort of self-exile. At some point, he pulled down the translucent solar window shades; and now, lying on the bed—not in darkness, but in the kind of shadow that can only form when light is obscured but not extinguished by an occluding object—he is unable to keep his eyes open. He is asleep for two minutes and thirteen seconds when the landline rings: a mechanical trill. The waves of sound cause his eardrum to vibrate, but his brain is not processing the resultant electrical impulses. Which is to say: He doesn't hear . . . In the living room, Kathryn takes the receiver from the base. *F. MAHFOUZ*. She doesn't recognize the name, but the number is local.

"Hello."

"Yes, hello. Is this Ms. Wakefield?"

"It is."

"My name is Fawzia Mahfouz. I am calling to apologize for what happened yesterday. To your son."

After a calculated pause, Kathryn says: "You're one of the mothers."

"Of Omar."

"Omar."

"His behavior," the woman says, "is inexcusable." And as she goes on to explain that she is the leader of the youth group at Masjid al-Islam in the capital, and that what her son and the other boys did is completely contrary to the mission of the group, which is to promote not fisticuffs between children of different backgrounds, but rather understanding, Kathryn is experiencing a feverish flush of humiliation. In this woman's place of worship is where Dorian wrote those words.

"Ms. Mahfouz."

"Yes."

"My son is Dorian Wakefield. Is that a familiar name?"

"It is, yes."

(Silence) . . . While in the house above the bay, overlooking the water and the bridge, Noah is saying: Mesopotamia with a hotel, five hundred. Dorian turns away from the window to the boy, whose facial features are enough like his own to give the sense, as he speaks, that he is speaking to himself. I'll pay the rent, he says, if you promise to not look out the window. With two fingers, Noah makes a peace

126

sign. Then Dorian feels a realization: The money is in the other room. The one where his sister writes. Wait here, he says. Then he goes into the other room. From there, the scene outside is more frightening because the window is much larger. Skyler is at the table. Watching the spaceship: a silver disc of unbelievable diameter and circumference that appears to be spinning on a central axis as it hovers above the two towers of the bridge. In the last dream, he made a mistake. He waited too long and then it happened. Now he can feel a vibration in his mind meaning: Say her name. To say it is to slow the spinning of everything, from the planets in their solar orbits to the thoughts in the vortex of your mind.

Skyler . . .

She turns to him, and looks at him, her eyes saying: I know you, even in worlds where we never met.

Now he notices the computer on the table; and on the screen, the photo of his parents and his brother on the beach, which he understands to be composed not of pixels but of all the words she has been writing. The picture is the story. In the sky above the bridge, the spaceship is turning again, faster and faster. Before it happens . . . His thought only complete when she completes it. By laying her fingers on the laptop. Pressing a key. Holding it down while pressing a second. Operation invoked. As a new window appears, she says: I'm saving it to the cloud.

9

While that digital photograph from Path M_{50} – M^{50} was becoming a consequent in pathways including, but not limited to, B_{39} – R^{61}, Kathryn Wakefield and Fawzia Mahfouz were speaking of forgiveness and reconciliation, teachable moments, and a lesson their children would carry into the future. After the conversation, Kathryn opens her Lifebook page. To find the friend request—and an image of the woman to whom she has just spoken: a smile showing white teeth; eyes like black pearls. Later that same afternoon, Dorian gets an e-mail that reads (in part): YOURE NOT A ARYAN OR YOU WOULDNT HAVE EVEN COME . . . I WAS A MAJOR DICK . . . SINCERELY OMAR MAHFOUZ.

With these words echoing in his mind, he goes to the garage and takes out the lawn mower. Inserts the battery, turns the key, starts pushing. The drone of the engine cannot drown out the chorusing of the insects, which are not only in the trees, but in the grass. Nothing to do but go over them. The dream seems so fresh, almost like a wet painting. He thinks of it and something—not color, but a kind of pigment—is left on his mind. The spaceship, for instance; the blur of its spinning hull. He had read, just a few days ago, on some web portal, that theories of alien responsibility, which have always occupied a middle ground between the explicable and the supernatural, are becoming more prevalent—that nearly one in five Americans now believes that 8-11 was an act of "extraterrestrial terrorism." Pushing the mower forward, stopping at the property line, reversing direction, Dorian thinks: *What if. If that's what really happened, then what about the internment camps and the drone strikes (if there ever were any)?* Suddenly, the mower stalls out. The battery is dead. Has he really been turning these thoughts over in his brain for a whole hour? He carries the bag of clippings into the woods by the gazebo. Mixed in with the grass: the body parts of cicadas, some cleanly severed, others mucked with what belongs inside. Then he sees one moving. Alive and whole. Drawn like the others into the updraft of the whirling blade, but miraculously spared the violence of it.

So the sheikh was correct. Of course correct. As everything he has ever said to you and your friends was true. How could it be otherwise? How could a messenger of the Almighty speak anything *but* the truth? And yet you. You listened to another voice. Chose to listen to a voice that said: Why call the number today? What's the rush? What is one more day in the scheme of eternity? Heaven isn't going anywhere, is it? How clever that voice was. To not issue commands. Only to pose questions. And not even in words, but in the form of hot food, a soft bed, a cool pool of water . . . Well, what is so wrong with food and a bed and water? Wouldn't your mother and father want you to have these things? Didn't they speak, often, of how the internment would end some day, some day soon—and you would all return together to a life in the real world? (He is holding the eyeglasses.) *And it did end, and here you are. Without us, I know* (the voice his mother's now), *without me, I know, but yesterday you had friends—friends, habibi—and even that boy so unlike you, with skin unlike yours and a history so different. Even he. I understand why you hurt him. And, of course, of course, I want to be with you, also. But think. Think, Karim—*

"Allahu Akbar . . ."

"Allahu Akbar . . ."

It's the muezzin calling him to sunset prayer. He turns the sound off, sets the eyeglasses on the desk.

Downstairs, the TV is tuned to a baseball game. The old guy on the couch. Asleep. The sportscaster saying: *"After one inning in Houston, Yankees 8, Colt .45s nothing."* Karim can see, through the bay window that looks over the front lawn and the road, that the boy is in his yard again, pushing the mower. He watches him steer the machine, moving it across the grass in straight parallel lines. The job almost finished. Perhaps a dozen more crossings from one end to the other. Karim watches him cross once, twice. Then, very suddenly, thinks to himself: *I am going to whisper now. If the old guy wakes up, I go down and pray maghrib; if he stays asleep, I go across the road.*

"Jaddi."

Not a muscle in the sun-browned face so much as twitches. As Karim steps onto the patio and eases shut the sliding glass door, he can just hear the words: *"Top of the second, heart of the Yankee order coming up . . ."*

Time of a summer evening when the world is being downsampled toward grayscale. The air cooling, a change that seems to be caused less by the setting of the sun than by the fading of color; and the legions of cicadas falling silent, as if color was the thing driving them mad and making them scream. His mother told him to think: words not from beyond the grave, but from a current of mother-talk that moves like constant water through the mind, carving out ideas and shaping beliefs. Unsure at first what she meant, beyond a caution to think twice, think carefully before taking actions that can't be taken back. But now, turning the corner of the house, Karim Hassad is

130

thinking (insofar as acting is a form of thought), that perhaps one must know not only what to do, but also when to undo actions that *can* be undone. He walks down the slight grade of the driveway, the nerves in the soles of his feet sensing that the asphalt is still warm . . . Dorian doesn't see him coming. His eyes are fixed on the last line drawn in the grass by the lawnmower, which is getting harder to discern as the light slips away. Then all of a sudden the kid is standing there, like something pasted from another window into a destination image. He startles and lets go of the bail bar. The engine dies, the wheels stop turning; and there they are, facing one another in the gloaming.

"Sorry," Karim says. "I mean, for scaring you."

"You didn't scare me."

"Oh."

"Anyway, it's too dark now," Dorian says. "I was gonna stop anyway."

"You're almost done."

"I know that."

"So you should just finish," Karim says.

"Did you ever cut a lawn?"

"No."

"Well, it's too dark now to see the line."

"What line."

"That's the point," Dorian says. "If you can't see it, it's too dark."

Karim looks up at the sky.

"Anyway—"

"No, wait," Karim says, pulling something out of his pocket. "You want a green?"

"*Here?*"

"Yeah, why not."

"What," Dorian says, "does he just let you smoke?"

"Sort of."

131

"Whenever you want."

"Two a day," Karim says. "Until the agonies stop."

"The what?"

Returning the box to his pocket, he says: "I used to smoke Dream."

"Dream," Dorian says. "Like, opium."

The kid nods.

Dorian has heard the rumors. Not only that opium was used in the camps, but that government agencies—in league with traffickers allied with anti-Islamist rebels in the Caliphate—actually helped to introduce the drug and to keep it coming through the fences, thereby reducing the people within to a state of perpetual semiconsciousness. A conspiracy theory. Same as the drones. Same as the allegation (so outlandish, it made the notion of aliens from another galaxy seem credible) that 8-11 had been planned in Washington and carried out by a secret command of the Defense Department. Dorian has never believed such things. But speaking of things hard to believe: Here he is, standing on his front lawn in the gathering dark of a midsummer night, having a reasonable conversation with a Muslim who jacked him the day before during a game of croquet.

"I guess you're pissed," Karim says.

"I dunno."

"I hit this friend of mine one time. I thought he was the thing I was mad at, but I realized later . . ." (Silence.) "Have you ever?"

"Hit a friend?"

"Hit anyone."

"Not really. No."

Again, Karim looks up, as if waiting for something to appear in the sky, a star maybe, and says: "I have some issues that require professional help. That's what the old guy says. I call him jaddi, which means grandfather, but . . . I don't know what I should call him. Anyway, if it wasn't for the issues— I mean, what he thinks is, if I talk to someone, I won't do anything like that again."

"You mean therapy," Dorian says.

He nods.

As each waits for the other to say the next thing, both realize that the cicadas, too, are silent.

Karim says: "They finally shut the fuck up."

"I know."

And as if to underscore the cessation of the din: here and there, the mute flash of a firefly.

"Well, I better . . ."

"Yeah," Karim says. "But one more thing. You know that girl from yesterday? She wants to friend you but she doesn't know your last name."

"Oh."

"She's one of my friends, so if I friended you . . ." (Voice trailing off.) "Or I could just tell her."

Now, in the space between them, the pale green strobe of a firefly. Each flash like a dot in a line of demarcation disappearing even as it's drawn. Dorian says: "Whatever, sure . . ." A few moments later, Karim is walking slowly (almost thinking, *home*) over the freshly cut grass, making the walk slow because he knows the boy is watching. Then he hears the mower being maneuvered, the turning of the wheels on the axles. As the garage door goes down, Karim stops. Waits. Watching the space around himself—standing at the heart of a neighborhood dark and somnolent—until a firefly appears, like a mote of magic dust. He reaches out with both hands cupped, and misses.

•

Work. As methodical as the cutting of stones, laborious as the plowing of a field. This is what writing is—or at least, what it always has been for you. But that night, for the first time in almost twenty years,

133

something mystical happens. You wake up in the smallest of hours—and a character is speaking to you. It's the girl from the photo. Not addressing you (not calling you by name), nor pronouncing words in a literal sense (that would be impossible, wouldn't it, since the voice—if it can rightly be called a voice—is located in the abstract space of the mind). No, not a voice speaking words. More accurately, a flow of encoded data. Dimensionless. In fact, in this received form, *meaningless*. Without you, the voice cannot make sense. Get out of bed. Notice, without in any way factoring the information, that the time is 1:57. For all you care, the time might be $\Delta t = 2T_c + 4T_a$. In the bathroom, fill cupped hands with cool water and raise to your face. Be as quiet as possible. Don't wake up your wife. If you do, her voice, a real one, will speak over the wordless one speaking to you, then you also will have to speak. Downstairs, do not power up the computer. What you want is paper—a notebook, wirebound and ruled at intervals of seven millimeters—and a pen, black pigment ink, with a very fine tip. And don't stay in the room. Where you want to be is out in the night. Exit through the door your sons use when they don't want to be heard coming in after curfew. On your way across the lawn (still scented from the recent cutting), look up into the sky; and before you reach the small outbuilding under the trees, you will see a planet, set like a precious stone in the zodiac. In the gazebo, switch on the lamp. Place yourself in the rounded spot of light. Open the notebook. Uncap the pen. So this is inspiration. So there really are goddesses to help us and holy spirits to speak through us and divine winds to bring us visions . . . Of a ghostly shape. Could be a quasar, but could just as plausibly be a girl. Now observe the bigger picture. The girl is a reflection in a tinted lens. The lens is attached to a pair of sunglasses being worn by a woman. This woman is the mother of the girl in the reflection. Beside her, two other people lie prone on the sand. A very young boy and a man. The boy is her son; the man her husband. Now watch as the picture is set in motion. Seven years will pass. And another child, a second boy, will join them unexpectedly—at the very edge of the woman's potential for such a thing. The daughter (a teenager, beautiful and brooding) has been slipping away from the family, growing distant, moving towards nothing, just moving away. The baby will bring her back. When he is in the womb, the girl puts her fingertips against the mother's transforming belly, and, with her lips close to the smooth taut membrane of skin, speaks to him about things they will do together; at the birth, not only does she want to be present, she wishes to cut the cord—and after the boy is out, covered in blood and fluid and vernix, does so with the shaking hands of someone performing the first of countless important acts of responsibility; and in the early days, in the night when he can't sleep, she spells her parents, holds him and walks throughout the house whispering to him with gentle patience—or, better, if the night air isn't too cold, carries him outside, where a pale green moonglow or the sparkle of the galaxy works a quieting magic. The parents think of it as devotion. Their new-age friends call it astroharmony, a clear-cut case of Pisces and Pisces. But to the girl, turning fifteen, then sixteen (as her brother learns to crawl, speak, walk), the emotional reality is more complicated. At the beginning, she fears he'll die in his crib—and she checks obsessively to be sure he's sleeping on his back. Later, it's the stairs: what if her other brother, a careless seven-year-old, forgets to secure the safety gate. Yet these kinds of worries, about accidents preventable through vigilance, are nothing compared to the darker visions of dangers we can't control. She can see now (the baby has shown her) that to be in the world is to be in danger; and to move through the world is to be in a constantly shifting relationship with tragedy: we avoid it by a wide margin, or we narrowly escape it, or we feel it suddenly upon us, a thing too big and fast-moving to be outrun. The boy is two. They give the crib away and he starts sleeping in a single bed; and gets into the habit of waking in the middle of the night and migrating into his sister's room. According to the parents: not a good idea. *What happens in a few months when you leave? Granted, you're not going far, just into the city—but the point is, you won't be here anymore, and he's becoming more and more dependent on you.* The conversation brings tears to her eyes. A couple of years ago, she was wishing away the rest of high school, dreaming of a faraway college in the New England Colonies. Now the idea of moving just two hours away is more than she can bear. In this fragile state of mind, she says foolishly: *You should've had him sooner.* (They try not to laugh.) *You think it's funny. No, but— I'm going to miss everything. Honey, we didn't intend to have him at all. Well, you should've messed up sooner* . . . And so on, until Mitchell Wakefield has filled ten, twenty, almost thirty notebook pages with words that are neither memory nor fiction, nor a writer's elementary commixing of the two, but something *other and more* (though he can't imagine *what*), until around four o'clock the pen slows down, and he can't think of what should come next. Because the voice is gone, like a spirit that has ceased, suddenly and without explanation, to participate any further in a séance; and the moment he realizes he is no longer writing is like the moment when you wake up and realize you're no longer dreaming.

•

First there had been the phone call from Omar's mother. Then the e-mail from Omar. Then out of nowhere, Karim. Not apologizing, thank God. Not making me accept an apology. But the way he came over and all the stuff he said: it was like, if he could, he'd go back in time and do things differently. After he left, I wheeled the mower into the garage, took a cold shower, and found a message in my inbox: KHALEELA KINGSLEY WANTS TO BE FRIENDS ON LIFEBOOK. I confirmed the request instantly. Scrolled through her feed. Found the photo of me and her at the party, and became the twelfth person to like it. One of the other likes was from him. Which made me think. The kid came to you. Then he gave her your name so she could find you. The least you can do is add him. Five minutes later, there he was. Number 526. A little after that, my father appeared at my door to ask if my face still felt as bad as it looked, and also to say:

"This is your call."

"What is."

"What to do now. You remember what I said before. You want to go to the police, I'll take you there."

The next morning, I was looking in the mirror. The bruises weren't gone, but they were starting to disappear; a few more days and no evidence would remain. I couldn't figure out how I really felt about it. The police. That idea was way behind the curve. But was the incident really going to just fade out of sight and mind, like a post that no one cared about, that wasn't even worth a comment?

No. Because even if, on that same morning, Keenan Cartwright hadn't told a counselor at Invention Camp (an engineering major from the Rhode Island Colony, who had suggested to Keenan the week prior, that you had to watch Muslims very carefully in a camp that teaches electronics skills potentially usable in the construction of remote triggering devices)—even if Keenan had not told this young man about what had happened in his neighborhood over the weekend, the incident would not have been forgotten. In fact, over time, it would have been spoken of often, as all concerned parties, children and adults alike, came to see that something good can come of violence: that the prejudices that lead to violence can be overcome—not *through* acts of violence, but by *passing through* such acts . . . Although an outcome of this type is purely theoretical.

Because Keenan Cartwright is a constant across all pathways. When given the option, he will always tell his counselor at lunch on that Monday what occurred at the pool party on Saturday—and by Tuesday will be in receipt of an e-mail from a representative of the local chapter of a nonprofit organization called the American Resistance Alliance. *I'm sure you've heard of us.* Keenan has not. But he needs no information beyond the profile picture on the group's Lifebook page—the flag of the Islamic Caliphate going up in flames—to know that he (along with 3,582 other people) likes them, and that they should talk to Dorian.

Which brings us to Wednesday.

Same old drill. The four boys return home from their separate summer camps and convene at the in-law apartment. Today, Zebedee is first and claims prime real estate under an ancient window air conditioner as large, loud, and energy-efficient as a jet propulsion engine. Second is Dorian. Whose face, having taken a hit during a morning game of Bombardment, is in a fresh state of pain. Last comes Dean. Totally chonged, wearing a shirt with an iron-on marijuana leaf.

"Yo, Rastafari-mon," Keenan says.

"Hello, mons."

"In your honor," Keenan says, "we play some Old Testament." He scrolls on his handheld and switches to a song from the days before digital downloads: *I shot the sher-riff, but I did not shoot the dep-yoo-tee.*

"I bet your grandma listened to this," Dorian says.

"So?"

"So play something that doesn't suck."

"Sure. As soon as you *do* something that doesn't suck. Deal?"

"Do?" Plaxico says.

"Yeah, *do*, my Obama. About Saturday."

"You have any sodas?" Dean asks.

"There's juice boxes."

The grandfather clock plays Westminster Chimes. Strikes the hour of five. There comes a knock on the sliding glass door. They can all see him: a guy much older than they. Probably a friend of the family, Dorian thinks; expecting, when Keenan lets him in, that he will shortcut without ceremony through the apartment. Instead, in a strangely official manner, he says: "Hello, gentlemen." Older than their brothers though younger than their fathers. Blond hair so perfectly barbered it might be chipped from stone. In one hand, a tablet computer in a leather case.

"Let me guess," he continues. "You're Dorian."

Dorian nods.

Then, in a tone somewhere between reassurance and disappointment: "You don't look that se*verely* fucked up."

"You shoulda seen him on Saturday," Keenan says.

The guy ignores this, and holds his hand out. "I'm Jon-David," he says. And though some voice inside is saying *Don't take it*, Dorian can't see another choice. They shake. Awkwardly. Hands not quite locking together. Then he's requesting some bottled water, sitting down on the couch, and saying: "Is there a smell in here?"

"Prune juice," Dean says.

Keenan, returning with the water: "Used to be my grandma's apartment."

"You use this water exclusively?"

"Yes."

"He bathes in it," Dean says.

From the look on his face, it's clear that Jon-David doesn't find the comment very amusing. To Dean, he says: "You drink tap water?"

Dean shrugs.

"In this county alone, there are thousands of miles of unprotected pipeline. Any raghead with a bicycle pump and a grade-school understanding of hydraulics could introduce botulism, plague, you name it, into the distribution system. See, there's this thing going on called World War III. Or have you not heard of it?"

"Sorry," Dean says.

As Jon-David uncaps the water and takes a long drink, Dorian is thinking: *I know who he is. I've seen people like him downtown, standing on corners, handing out flyers. One time, I accepted one, and my mother immediately took it out of my hands and crumpled it into a ball* . . .

"But I shouldn't have to tell you guys. A battle was fought here." (Gesturing at the battered face.) "Guess who lost."

"I wasn't there," Keenan says.

Dean: "Me neither."

Jon-David nods, as if these qualifiers are perfectly understandable. Then, closing one eye, he says: "Well, where the fuck *were* you?"

Dorian waits for his friends to explain about the Calypso Fest and the fractured femur.

"Some people think the war is in the Middle East. But the real war is right here. In America. You have to remember that. In the schools and in the backyards. There are four of you. There were four of *them*, correct? If you'd all been there, it would've been a fair fight." He takes the pad from the case. "Would could should. Let's talk names."

"Ab-Del-Karim," Keenan says.

Jon-David, fingers darting around the keyboard: "Last name?"

"Hoo-sane," Dean replies.

Keenan shakes his head. "No, Hassad."

"This is the kid across the street," Jon-David surmises. "Father's name?"

"Banfelder."

"House number."

"Thirteen."

"Okay," says Jon-David. "The other three."

Keenan gives Dorian a look.

"What?"

"He needs the names."

"Can I ask a question," Plaxico says.

"Shoot."

"You take these names and then what?"

"Kidnap the suspect, tie him down on his back, and you get to pour water over his face and into the breathing passages."

"Are you fuggin serious," Keenan says.

"No." Then, looking directly at Plaxico: "I'm with a watch group. We investigate incidents on a local level. I gather information, like names, and type it into a database. While we're on the subject, what's yours?"

"Zebedee."

"Very unusual."

Dean says: "One of his ancestors got lynched."

"About a millennium ago," adds Keenan.

When Jon-David asks Plaxico if this is true, Plaxico says not a thousand years ago, more like eighty. Then Jon-David, laying his tablet aside, asks in a very serious voice to hear the story. Which all the boys know. Mississippi Territory, 1959. Time of relatives they would never see except in the shifted hues of chromogenic photographs. Great-grandparents, great-uncles and great-aunts. Great-Uncle Zebedee, whose own great-grandfather (this was a whole other story) had sailed in chains from Africa to New Orleans. One afternoon, Zebedee runs out of gas on a dusty road and a group of white men in a pickup truck offer to drive him into town. But what they actually do is take him away from town. They tie one end of a rope to the hitch of the truck and the other around his two hands—and they drive. They drive to a meadow and with the same rope hang him from a tree until dead . . .

Thunder.

Far off, but louder than the drone of the air-conditioner. Dorian glances at the window. The sun is gone. Finally, it's going to storm.

"That," Jon-David said, "must have sucked . . . at least as much, possibly more, than getting abducted by Islamo-fascists and locked in a closet for several days, waiting to find out whether the United States government will agree to unconditionally surrender. And when it decides to *not* unconditionally surrender, you get your head cut off on videotape and your body gets chopped into ten pieces."

Another rumble, closer this time.

"Let me ask you something. You're at the mall. You're gonna throw a penny in the fountain and make a wish, and when you step up to the railing there's a pink backpack there, just sitting there, unattended. What do you do?"

"Blue phone," Keenan says.

Jon-David (nodding): "It could be some girl's schoolbooks. Or it could be a remote-control bomb laced with radioactive medical waste. No responsible citizen turns away. Same thing here. Muslims being violent. You don't just turn away from that. The other day, it was a bloody nose and a black eye. Tomorrow, a knife, a gun, or worse. The other day, Dorian. Tomorrow, maybe you, Zebedee. Because this isn't about white or black. We're equal now. We're truly equal. Because there's an evil out there and it wants every single one of us."

He reaches for his tablet.

"Now how about we get down to business and you give me the rest of the goddamn names."

10

When Jaddi had spoken of therapy and serious issues requiring professional help, Karim hadn't been sure what he meant. Therapy, the
old guy explained, was merely talking. Talking about what, Karim
had asked. And the old guy took a deep breath and started to respond, but then seemed to forget; and then said, in a voice that was
gentle in a strange way: "Anything, bud. Anything that's on your
mind." Karim nodded. Then said: "Did you ever do it?" "Do what?"
"Therapy." "*Me*," Jaddi said. "Yeah, I did—a long time ago." "So you
had serious issues, too?" And then the old guy breathed another
breath. He seemed to be going deep inside himself for an answer,
which turned out to be: "I'd say everyone does, at one time or another." Again, Karim could not quite find the meaning. Yet there was
something clear about the vagueness, a comforting blur of sense.

So, on Monday morning, he did not resist getting into the Argo
Electric for the drive across town to the appointment with the psychologist. In fact, as he sat in the passenger seat, securely strapped
(thinking about the night before, of going outside and speaking
to the boy next door, whom he could now, in a way, call a friend),
Karim's heart was seeping a feeling so long unfelt that, if asked to
name it, he would have hesitated, unsure, before saying:

Hope.

They arrived ten minutes early at a small white building on a residential street. A sign by the door read: THE PLACE

143

WITHIN—PEDIATRIC WELLNESS. Jaddi opened the door. They spoke to someone at a desk. Then paged through magazines until a door opened and a woman (not old, not young; in a dress not bright but colorful) introduced herself as Dr. Khaled, and guided Karim, hand on shoulder, into a room that was windowless and dimly lit, and furnished with a couch, two chairs, a low table, and a small machine emitting a constant shushing sound, like an urging of secrecy. At first, it was just as the old guy said it would be. A simple conversation (in a weave of English and Arabic) about what was on his mind. Her told her, for instance, that he now had five friends on Lifebook. The fifth he had made just last night. And he told her willingly about the party—what he had done to the boy who was now his friend, and why he thought he'd done it: because of the drugs he used to take, which led him to the subject of his other friends, his old friends from the camp, their names were Hazem and Yassim . . . All of this spoken of his own free will—and as the words came out of him, that long unfelt emotion flowed more freely from his heart. More than confident, he felt certain, as if life were a math problem with only one possible answer, that everything was only going to get better from here on. Then Dr. Khaled said she wanted him to try something.

"I want you to think," she said, "of a favorite place."

"Where," he said.

"Anywhere."

"I haven't been any place."

"That's all right," she said. "It doesn't have to be somewhere you've really been. It can be a place you imagine."

He sat on the couch, listening to the meaningless whir of the noise machine.

"Have you thought of a place?"

He shook his head.

"Karim." The doctor leaned forward. "I want you to think of somewhere you wish you could be. The best place you can think of."

The next instant, it came to him. The answer was obvious now that he understood the question. Karim thought the doctor would want to know what place he'd chosen. But she only asked him to hold a coin, an old silver dollar with the head of a president he didn't recognize, between his thumb and first finger—and to look at it, just keep looking at it. "That's good. After a while, your fingers will begin to get a little tired of holding it, that's all right, and the coin can fall down to the floor. It will be safe there. You can get it later. When it falls, that is your signal to yourself to let those eyes close by themselves. That's right. Now I would like you to see yourself, feel yourself in that favorite place. Look around and see the shapes and colors, hear the sounds . . ."

Strange.

How a moment ago, he was in the room holding the coin, but he doesn't seem to be holding the coin anymore—and he doesn't seem to be in the room either. He knows he is, but it's like the room has crawled out of itself like one of those crazy insects, left itself behind like an old skin, and now he's in a completely different place, though one that was *in* the room all along and in a way still *is* the room . . . **What do you see, Karim?** *Green. Green hills.* **What else?** *A lake, a really big one, with mountains on the other side, and down at the end of the lake, there's a fountain.* **A lake with a fountain.** *Yeah.* **Tell me about the fountain.** *It goes high up, really high, so high that it's making a rain.* **So a wind is blowing?** *Yeah.* **Strong or gentle?** *Gentle.* **That's nice. Warm or cool?** *Both.* **Can you feel the rain?** *Yeah.* **How is it, touching your skin?** *Really soft.* **Good. Are you comfortable?** *Yeah.* **You feel good?** *Mm-hm.* **When you feel comfortable, let me know by lifting a finger.** *(Lifting a finger.)* **Good. Now I want you to really be there, on one of those green hills feeling that gentle rain, because you really are there in your daydreaming.** *(Being there, really being there.)* **Now, while you're feeling very comfortable, very good, with the gentle rain falling softly on your skin, I**

145

want you to look all around and tell me if you see anyone else. Is anyone else there, in the place where you are? (Looking, through the mist, the myriad droplets of which are reflecting and refracting light and causing a rainbow to appear before his eyes, through the colors of which he sees them: his mother first, then his father, then his sister; and he walking now in his daydreaming toward them and they seeing him, too, and smiling, and now opening their arms.) Those are pretty, sparkling tears, Karim. Can you cry some more of them?

•

Finally, it's going to storm. They have all been waiting, desperately: for a wave of northern air as big as a nation to clash with the heat and drive it away, if only for a time. When Dorian and Plaxico exit Keenan's place, just before five o'clock, after a half hour of talking with Jon-David Sullivan III of the Saratoga Chapter of the American Resistance Alliance, the sky is dark and wind is thrashing the leaves on the trees. "C'mon," Dorian says. They run across the Cartwright property. To the Wakefield house is a sprint of no more than a hundred yards. But the two boys can't beat the rain: an instantaneous downpour that soaks their clothes through in a matter of seconds.

They duck into the open garage.

Flash of lightning.

Both of them nervous after having given the names; winded from the run; and now a crack of thunder—like a shot from some impossible gun—jolts their hearts. Almost gasping, they watch the rain beat violently upon the driveway.

"Who was that guy," Dorian says.

"I dunno."

"Some kind of Aryan?"

"Well, he's not from Greenpeace, is he . . ."

A car comes up the road, which is a sluiceway now. Tires fighting the current and churning water. After it's gone, Plaxico says abruptly:

"Didn't you see me looking at you?"

"What . . ."

Plaxico shakes his head and Dorian wants to know what he was supposed to do, just get up and leave? His best friend wanders around the cavernous space of the garage, saying nothing, finally taking an umbrella from a peg on the wall.

"What are you doing?" Dorian says.

Though it's obvious what his friend is doing. He's taking an umbrella from a peg on the wall. At the threshold of the garage, he pushes it open. "We shouldn't have done that," Plaxico says—and then he runs into the storm.

As you well know, Kathryn Wakefield: A drug is moving constantly through your bloodstream and circulating through your brain. You ingest it, in pill form, every morning, without fail. What the drug does, from a pharmocological standpoint, is: it boosts levels of seratonin (which you don't have enough of in your synapses), allowing for successful transmission of important messages about emotion and behavior between neurons. In more human terms, its purpose is to keep you from experiencing sadness and fatigue to such a degree that your sense of reality starts to slip and you find it difficult to load a dishwasher much less shower and dress, drive twenty miles, and perform for eight hours the duties of a general counsel. In the winters—the gray cold days of the Northeastern winter—the disorder gains strength (or the drug loses power), so you have learned to increase the dosage for a five-month period. But this is not December or February. This is June.

Why is it happening now?

You go to your doctor of eight years—who, after stating the obvious (*you usually feel pretty good in the summer*), asks you rote questions (*is there a problem at work, how is everything at home*) before writing a new prescription. On the way to the pharmacy, think about the answer you gave her and the one you might have given. You told her: "There have been troubles with my son, the younger one. Going back to last fall." But the truth about Dorian is: He has scared you and worried you and made you angry, but he has not plunged you into a darkness. Depression came last winter, the punctual visitor it has always been; and left, as always, with the melting snow and the appearance in your garden of the delicate shoots of the first perennials. Now, two months later, here it is again, out of time. The reason you might have given is: *The other night I got to thinking. About her . . .* I say *her*. Of course, I can't know what the sex would have been. Yet I do seem to remember having a feeling back then, a sort of theoretical inkling, of two X chromosomes, not an X and a Y. In the generic terms of science is how I tried to think. All my life, I had been moody. But in those days after, I felt as though much more than the embryo and the placenta had been removed from me. (I could call it an emptiness. But that's not really what depression is. Depression isn't having nothing in you: it's the absence of things without which you feel like nothing.) Afterward, I was using up sick days and spending them in bed, curtains drawn against the sun, wanting darkness, wanting always to be asleep, which is a way of wanting to be dead. But if you wait long enough, if you can stand the wait, the missing things do get returned and you want to live in the light again. And I have been trying, ever since, to stay in the light—or at least not allow the darkness to get a good grip on me. But the other night, at the amphitheatre: I got to thinking about it, and I started feeling about it the way I had back then, and now I can't seem to stop. Thinking: She would be twenty-six now; and eight years ago, when something happened above the Golden Gate Bridge—a thing that, even now, no one can really explain—she would have been eighteen; and she could have been there, in the city, on that day. And so I start crying, and I want to be covered by darkness at the thought. Just the chance. That had she been born, it would have been possible for her to die that way.

●

Late at night, three days after therapy, he is sitting on his bed, hypnotizing himself. Holding the coin that Dr. Khaled gave him—and pretty soon the coin is falling out of his fingers and he is in that place which she has told him he should go to in his imagination one or two or three times a day, a place which is always there and to which he can go anytime because he is in charge of his imagination: where he can always talk to his mother, because (as Dr. Khaled said) he knows her so well and they love each other so much that he is able to hear her voice and feel her love in his inner mind. What they are doing tonight is this: Sitting on the green grass alongside the shore of the lake, looking at the word of God. Not the new Qu'ran given him by his adoptive father. The one Abdul-Aziz gave him in Dakota. The front cover is torn. Some pages are water-stained, others speckled with mold. Here and there, a winged insect has been crushed into the shape of a letter from some unknown abjad; and on one page in particular (the one open before him and his mother now) there is a smear of blood where, months ago in the camp, Karim killed a mosquito that must have been feeding on him or one of his friends while he read. On this page, just above the blood, are the verses about a place of gardens and fountains, of eternal peace and safety, where hearts will be freed of hatred . . .

He falls asleep.

(Or perhaps he has been asleep for some time.)

When he wakes up very suddenly, he thinks he must be having

a dream about waking up, because the old guy has thrown open the bedroom door and is standing at the threshold, holding a gun.

"Stay here," he says.

"Jaddi, what."

"Don't go out of the house. Don't go out of any door. Got me?"

From the phone in his other hand comes the voice of a woman: "*Nine-one-one. What's your emergency?*"

"There's a fire on my property," he says. Then he's moving into the hallway, towards the stairs, and Karim hears him say the street address but can't make out anything else. He gets up from the bed. Opens the window. The floodlights are on, shining on the swimming pool and the patio, but nothing is burning behind the house. So he goes to the room across from his own—and opening the door, sees it framed in the window: what appears at first to be a small tree on fire. Though it can't be a tree, because there are two straight lines of flame, one vertical and one horizontal, connected, crossing at their midpoints. Not a tree. So, what is it? The boy can't begin to guess. Having never seen such a thing, nor heard of one . . .

Whereas, I, across the street, knew exactly what was burning over there. Two pieces of wood nailed together, a cross, which must have been splashed with a fossil fuel before someone put a match to it. I could smell the fumes through my open window, just barely. Gasoline or kerosene. That deadly sweet odor handed down from the past, like a heritage. As I watched the thing, I was thinking of a dream from the night before. I was back at the party, but it was pouring rain. A muezzin was chanting somewhere. I knew that the song was my sister's name in Arabic. Karim was there, but he looked like Omar. Suddenly, Keenan appeared. To help me hold him. The same way the Arab boys had held me. I could feel the rain soaking

150

through my clothes, warm like blood; and I understood that Karim was the muezzin and if we just kept him here in this storm, he would begin to experience a sensation of drowning. Keenan was saying: *Speak English, nigger. Tell us the name.* Those words. Some part of my mind couldn't stop repeating them while I watched the thing burn, brightly enough to give a pulse to everything nearby. The face of the house. The trunk and lower boughs of a maple tree. And at the foot of the driveway, The Negro. The way its shadow kept shifting in the light of the fire, it seemed to be coming to life.

The next morning, a Saturday, at eight-forty, scared murderously shitless, Dorian Wakefield and Zebedee Hightower march across the cul-de-sac to kill Keenan Cartwright. The if-onlies in the situation are starting to pile up: if only you didn't call him towelhead, if only we didn't go to the stupid party, if only they never closed the camps in the first place. But the revisionary wish that seems most crucial at this point is: If only we didn't give him the names. Which follows directly from: If only Keenan had kept the fuck out of it. They find the sliding glass door of the in-law apartment locked, the vertical blinds drawn across. Also the shade down on the bedroom window. After rapping on it to no effect, they go up the steps to the deck and see, in the kitchen, Mr. Cartwright, one hand holding a cup of coffee, the other down the front of his boxers, scratching.

Knock knock.

He turns, looking at them in sleepy confusion, blinking as if to blink away the hallucination of a couple of leprechauns, then finally comes to the door.

"What do *you* want."

"Keenan."

"Don't be a smartass, Wakefield."

Zebedee says: "We're sorry to bother you, but his door is locked."

"That's cause he hasn't unlocked it."

"Oh."

"Oh, what. You late for a pancake breakfast?" Then, looking at Dorian more closely, his face in particular: "Bastard got you pretty good."

"I guess."

(Drinking some coffee.) "I don't suppose that could've been *your* idea last night."

"What."

"That little light show."

While thinking of the burnt ground down the street, Dorian's heart expands like a balloon, full to bursting, until this man in underwear, with enough hair on his chest and back to qualify as a member of an earlier hominoid species, finally grants them entrance to the house. Through the kitchen they go, down the stairs, into the apartment with its swamp-gas smell of prunes, and into the bedroom.

"Wake up, you idiot."

"What . . ."

Zebedee says: "You have to call that friend of yours."

"What friend."

"The Nazi," Dorian specifies.

Keenan, fumbling for his phone: "What the hell are you guys talking about?"

"Don't you know," Zeb says.

"Know what."

Incredibly, he slept through the whole episode, including a 120-decibel fire engine siren. As they fill him in now, Keenan Cartwright's eyes get clear and his nostrils sort of flare—and when a smile dawns on his face, a feeling moves through Dorian, a kind of emotional address to the self, that goes: *You never liked him. You were in third grade together and last year in fifth. But you were never friends until the thing at the mosque. After that, while half the world was harshing on you, he was on your side. But even as the bond formed, you knew it wasn't strong and it wouldn't last . . .*

"You have to call the guy," Zeb says.

"Sure."

"Now," Dorian says.

Keenan raises a hand in an appeal for patience. Then, walking into the bathroom, drops his briefs and pushes down his boner. As the piss streams: "What about the other three? I wonder if they all got torched. Prob'ly not. It'd be too obvious. But that woulda been epic. You took some pictures, right?"

Dorian doesn't answer. He watches him shake off some pale yellow drops and pull up his underwear. Watches him reenter the bedroom. Mostly naked. Still talking about pictures, when Dorian, using both hands, shoves him so hard and unexpectedly on the chest that all the boy can manage is one awkward backward skip before head and ass hit wall and floor—after which he lies there, clenching his teeth, fighting back tears, and finally looking up with the abashment of a dog that can't understand what it did to warrant such cruelty. And Dorian does not feel a tinge of remorse as he says: "Now call the guy, you shithead, and tell him to stay away before we all wind up in fucking juvenile court." When Zeb offers his hand to the injured, Keenan just slaps it away. Then Zebedee follows Dorian out the back door, hearing a voice telling him: *You should've done that. But all you ever do is turn away or run away while other people fight and hate rises up from its own ashes. By what right do you take my name? I who died for you in a past of burning crosses . . .*

•

On his front lawn, a circle of scorched earth like an impression left by a science-fictional laser beam. Could've been anyone. (Well, not anyone. What he means is: anyone with enough malice in him to set fire to a cross.) Happens all the time. (Well, not all the time, but pretty often, and a lot more frequently since the closing of the camps.) He just read a story the other day about a nationwide spike. Most of them supposedly the work of organized reactionary groups. Not lone wolves, not neighbors. *I feel like a shit for even letting the thought occur to me. I've known Dorian since he was four; the kid isn't capable of something like that.* Well, not on his own, anyway. *Meaning what.* The Cartwright kid, or the older brother. *The brother.* Makes sense, doesn't it. *Maybe, but not Dorian.* So Dorian is immune to anger, is he? *I didn't say that.* A real dove of a kid. *They worked it out, and now they're Lifebook friends.* Lifebook. *The gesture means something.* It means nothing. A click you can take back with a click. *It wasn't him.* Sure, whatever you say. Everyone is exactly who they appear to be. Except you, right? You're the only one with secrets . . . All of this to himself, within himself, while sitting on the porch, looking out at that scar on the lawn, while the sun goes down, while the sound from the trees gradually dies away, that sound which every day elicits in his mind another comparison: the din of a madhouse, he thought today, the incomprehensible ranting of the insane. Nine o'clock. Ten. The boy is upstairs. Reading calmly at his desk as if nothing of concern has occurred. Unfazed is the word. Well, why be surprised? Why would something like this frighten him? After years inside that fence. He who has sensed many a time in darkness a presence, something stalking him, almost silently, and has turned to behold it, behind and above, inhuman and unmanned, hovering and watching, seeing him with the perfect clarity of the blind, beaming at his body coded pulses of invisible light from an electro-optical infrared system, acquiring him as a target, then thinking and deciding, in the way a robot thinks and decides, if he shall live or die. A boy with such experience is supposed to be intimidated by a couple of burning two-by-fours.

By eleven o'clock, Will Banfelder is keeping watch from a room on the second floor. He sits in an armchair by a window affording a view of road, driveway, front yard; and streams on his tablet a replay of the baseball game, with the sound muted, so he can hear, through the screen of the open window, any noise from outside. Around one in the morning, the next thing will happen.

A car appears.

He doesn't notice it at first. Because it is being driven slowly, with only the parking lights on. Then there it is. Slowing—as it comes even with the driveway and mailbox—to a crawl. He sets down the tablet. Picks up the handgun. The car is stopping now. Brake lights casting a red glow. He slides the safety pin to the left. It is an action the driver seems to sense: soon as the weapon is ready to be fired, the car moves again. Forward. Disappears around the downhill curve of the cul-de-sac. It might be exiting the circle, turning right on Onondaga, and leaving the subdivision. But as Will watches, the headlights reemerge from the trees at the foot of the hill. The vehicle is coming back. He goes downstairs. Eight steps, short hallway, front door. He enters the unlock code. Then transfers the gun to his dominant hand. Opens the door a crack. *What if it's him, or the brother.* Slowing, same as before. But also turning. The front wheels roll onto the driveway. Stopping. Passenger door opens and someone gets out and removes something from the backseat, though it's hard to tell what. The trespasser comes onto the lawn and into the weak light. A few yards, a few more. Then Will unlatches the screen door and pushes on it, and says: "Put that down. Put it down and don't run. If you run, I will shoot you in the back." And the man puts it down. A large pot with a handle on the top, a pressure cooker. He sets it on the ground and then he runs. Thinking perhaps that you won't shoot. That you'll still be standing near the bomb when he reaches the car and the driver sets it off with an electrical charge from a wireless device. But he is not going to reach the car. Drop him. A single shot between the shoulder blades. Before he hits the ground, fire again at the windshield. Fragments of glass ring over the hood. The car freezes. Then all of a sudden moves. Lurches forward, halts, leaps backward. Empty the clip—and though the driver by now is more or less dead, a reflexive depression of the accelerator will carry the vehicle in reverse across the road and onto the neighboring lawn, at which point even involuntary movement will end, the foot slipping off the pedal and the car slowing, coasting like a thing falling asleep, drifting into a peaceful rear-end collision with a birch tree, directly under the bedroom window of Dorian Wakefield.

11

The life of the Great Eastern Brood is once again coming to an end—as it has every seventeenth summer since the ice went from the land and a habitat of deciduous forest, a hundred million acres strong, grew up for them to sing in. In school, back in May, the three fifth grades had done a joint project: AMERICAN HISTORY THROUGH THE EYES OF MAGICICADA SEPTENDECIM. 2021. 2004. 1987. And so on through the centuries. Back to 1630, a decade after the arrival of the Mayflower. The question of the assignment was: How much does a world change in seventeen years? What Dorian and his friends discovered is that a world can change an awful lot. For example, the cicadas had completely missed the Second World War. The pupae had been underground, blindly feeding on tree roots, when Pearl Harbor was attacked, and were still five years from emerging when America, in 1948, after a long and bloody invasion of the Japanese mainland, finally dropped the atomic bomb on Tokyo. The insects had missed the Civil War, too. When the Brood of 1851 died out, Plaxico's great-uncle's grandfather had been the property of a white plantation owner in the Mississippi Territory; by the time the next generation came to light, he was a freedman.

And yet. It is possible, too, for a world to change very little, to be stuck in one place, or caught in a kind of loop, so that even the magicicada, a creature which disappears from the face of the Earth for so long a time, may reappear to find conditions not much different from those left behind. To find the same war still being fought. Even after so long a wait . . . For this world has become stuck. Caught in a loop. As it was in the time of our progenitors, so it still is. So it may continue to be, even in the time of our progeny. Unless the cycle is somehow broken. *Unless the course of a given pathway can be altered by a person gifted with an awareness of other pathways.* Listen now. When we tell you that among the countless thousands of reality-structures comprising the parallel planes of ∞, there is one in which orderings of random chance and free will are such that this war without end never began. Can you sense that reality? Where the ones you've lost are still with you and the ones you stand to lose will always be safe. Listen. To the sound we make. If you listen now, if you let the sound in—don't fight it off, don't shut it out—you will hear what we have been saying all along. You will hear her name. Skyler, Skyler, Skyler.

•

Into his dream comes the gunshot. Even as his sister is turning, moving to cover his body with her own, Dorian is awake and alone, in his real bed—and there are five more shots in rapid succession, glass breaking, the sound of a car engine revving, and when he gets to the window that faces the road and the Banfelder house, headlights are swerving weirdly through the dark, coming towards him though not casting light in his direction, tricking his brain into thinking that time can move both forward and backward. But no. Only the car is going backward. Driving in reverse onto his lawn, heading right for the tree under the window, and as the rear end strikes the trunk, the alarm goes off, three deafening horn blasts followed by a whooping siren. And someone else is coming. Across the road. On foot. Visible in the glow of the headlights. Dorian ducks out of sight. As if in fear of a mad assassin who will shoot anything that moves. Then a voice:

"Mitch! Kathryn!"

His father, from somewhere below: "Will?"

"Hold on!"

One more cycle of horn and siren, in the course of which Dorian's bedroom door swings open. Cliff. In mid-howl, the siren is squelched.

From the lawn: "It's me, Will Banfelder. Goddammit, Mitch."

"Was that you?"

"Just me. They did have something. A pressure cooker, I think. The police are coming. Are the boys awake?"

"Dorian?" Mitch says.

"Yeah."

"Cliff?"

"Present," Cliff says.

Will (with a tremor in his voice): "Boys, don't come down here."

"Is he dead," Kathryn asks.

"Yeah." A pause. "Yeah, he is."

"Who is he."

"Not Arab. A DT, for sure . . ."

And then their neighbor, who has just deposited a dead body and a car on their lawn, runs back across the road. To make sure his adopted son is safe. Saying he'll be right back, as if to promise that the mess will be cleaned up. Cliff says he's going down there. Dorian does not move. Doesn't even look. He just sits on the floor under the window, feeling: I am in trouble. I am in deep and troubled waters. Okay, someone else threw the first punch, and someone else set the wheels of revenge in motion. But why me at the center? This can't be a coincidence. Some dark desire has drawn death in my direction. I must want these things to happen. Deep inside, I want the trouble to get deeper still.

———

Residents of Poospatuck Circle, and Members of the Community Lifebook Page: You know from Kathryn Wakefield's post (2 minutes ago via mobile) that the Wakefield family is safe. It is a post that does nothing to mitigate your collective fears and curiosities about what is happening where you live. The time is two in the morning. Are people supposed to go back to bed under these conditions? Step out onto your porches, your decks. Depending on your view, you may be able to see that a car has crashed backward into a tree, or that the ambulance which came screaming into the subdivision is now just parked in the road, no longer in any kind of a hurry. Most of you, however, can't see anything but the colored flashes from a police cruiser. What are you supposed to do? Make coffee and sit around until sunup, wondering and worrying? Get dressed. Go out into the darkness. At the foot of every driveway is a light. A lantern on a pole or a simple cylinder jutting not far out of the ground. Everyone, go to this place. Stand in the light and see a neighbor standing nearby in another oasis of light. Call out: *What's going on?* **You saw the post?** *Yeah, but.* **There were four shots.** *I think I heard six.* **You think it's related?** *To what.* **Last night.** *The cross, you mean. I think it must be.* **Two nights in a row.** (Move closer to each other. Drift into the road.) *It's all related. The fight was the first thing, then the cross, now this.* **I wouldn't call it a fight exactly.** *What do you mean.* **I'd call it assault with a specific intent to commit battery.** *Banfelder has really opened a can of worms here.* **I know.** *I mean, this isn't just his problem now, there's a dead guy on someone else's lawn.* **Look, another post.** *From who?* **Moses Nkondo. Says there's two dead, DTs, and they had a pressure cooker bomb** . . . So there you have it. Two right-wing haters trying to first-degree-murder your neighbor with an IED ran into a little more resistance than they bargained for. Or maybe the way you see it is: Two self-appointed guardians of the American way, making a statement about what will and will not be tolerated, have been gunned down in cold blood by a man whose loyalties are none too clear. The interpretations are irrelevant. The fact of the matter is: A conflict is under way—and escalating. Right and wrong. Don't waste time on that debate. Just everyone pull together and do something before violence gains the foothold of an invasive species and spreads faster than you can fight it off.

At the time of the six gunshots, he had been in the study on the ground floor. Writing with pen and paper. As he has been doing every night for five nights now. Mitchell Wakefield is becoming something he never was before: nocturnal. Around nine o'clock, when the cicadas stop chorusing, is when the voice starts speaking. A sentence comes into his head; and once he has written it down, the space after the period or the question mark is immediately filled by another sentence, and the next space by another sentence, the pen moving as constantly as the needle of a polygraph. Tonight, the pen had done something different. Stopped mid-sentence. Frozen in the white space between two horizontal lines. Confused, Mitch removed the canalphones from his ears. He had been listening to ocean waves and the interrupting noise seemed to have come from somewhere on the shoreline. Maybe he hadn't really heard it. Then—again—another explosion, followed an instant later by a sound like a micrometeoroid smashing through a roof window . . . Now Mitch is standing on his lawn, in the strobing lights of two police cruisers, a few yards away from a dead person. Man in a car, windshield scattered in pieces on the hood and on the dashboard and also (even this next detail he can see from beyond the yellow tape marking the borders of the crime scene) on the shirt and in the hair of the dead man, who is still upright in the driver's seat, one forearm draped over the steering wheel as if cruising the main drag of some bygone town, shirt sopped with

161

blood and a gash across one cheek, a furrow so deep you can see bone shining through the skin.

"Mr. Wakefield."

Beside him: one of the neighbors. Whose first name Mitch can never remember. Deepak or Deepesh. Doesn't know the wife's name either. But both of them are surgeons. One operates on brains, the other hearts.

"Doctor, this is . . ."

"Very disturbing, I agree. But not surprising. Where Muslims go, violence follows."

Mitch looks at him, a face flicking in and out of sight with the rotation of the lightbar beacons, skin shaded now red, now blue.

"I don't say this in a prejudicial way."

"No, I know."

Looking at the car, the doctor says: "It's obvious who this man is. So, what is he doing here? Have any such people ever come to our street before? No. They're only here because that boy is here."

"That boy."

"Mr. Wakefield, let us face the facts. The boy was brought here. And then his Arab friends came and they assaulted your son . . ."

Dorian catches some of this. He has been standing a ways off, near the thicket of trees surrounding the gazebo, as if guiltlessness is a function of distance. He takes a step closer now, as his father says:

"Doctor, we've put that incident behind us."

"Obviously not."

"I'm not sure what you mean," Mitch says. "This? I don't see the connection."

"Mr. Wakefield. You don't know us well, me and my wife. But you know what we are. You know I'm a brain surgeon. You may not know that my wife's patrilineage is Brahmin, but you know she is Indian-American. You know we're Hindu. But the man in that car, he does not know and he doesn't care. Indian, Persian, Pakistani, Iraqi.

162

It's all the same to him. Now, this man is dead. One less ethnocidal maniac. So, one might think our neighbor has improved the state of things. But in fact he has made things much worse. Because this man has confederates who will soon be very angry. Let us not delude ourselves. The question is not if they will come back. The question is when. And when they do, we will all be in danger. My wife and I for obvious reasons. But all of us by simple association, by reason of our inaction. We cannot sit by and do nothing."

"What can we do?"

"Press charges. Press charges against the boy for assaulting your son."

"We can't do that," Mitch says.

"Why not."

(Dorian doesn't want them to notice him, but he takes another step: closer to his father and the yellow tape, the car and the dead man, because some words of the conversation are still unclear.)

"What if we did."

"If you did," the doctor says, "then maybe we could stop this violence before it gets worse. Before more of us get drawn into it."

"And what about the boy. He ends up where."

"Where he belongs."

"He's just a boy," Mitch says. "Same age as Dorian."

"Mr. Wakefield, I've operated on children younger than your son. I've saved the lives of children. But a doctor also knows about hard choices. Think of 8-11. Should every victim have been helped and saved? Of course. But in certain eventualities—"

Ringtone.

At which sound the doctor will turn and see you. Stand your ground for a moment. Look your father in the eye. Then remove the phone from your pocket. *UNKNOWN CALLER.* Take a few steps toward the trees. As you answer, a voice will say:

"Dorian."

Ask: "Who is this?"

"Who am I. Who the fuck do you think I am? What did I tell you. Tomorrow a gun. Well, it's tomorrow, my friend."

End the call.

Turn around. Your father in conversation now with a police officer. But your neighbor still looking at you while the lights of the cruisers flash like nerve impulses carrying messages between neurons . . .

•

The next day is Friday. The old guy can't take him to jummah because he has to be at the police station with a lawyer present answering questions about the night's bloodshed. So Karim gets to "hang out" for the day and go to prayers with Omar Mahfouz. At nine on the dot: the doorbell. Mrs. Mahfouz. Who appears none too pleased with the situation. The old guy asks her to come in for some sweet tea. She declines. Karim gets in the car and they drive for a good five minutes in total silence before she says: "I'm glad you're safe, Karim. But what was done last night is not God's way." And so on. Karim sits in the passenger seat, pretending to listen, nodding from time to time. Knowing perfectly well that God has more ways than one. The house they arrive at is larger than the one he is living in. With an in-ground swimming pool and an in-ground basketball hoop with a glass backboard. Inside, downstairs, there is a room dedicated exclusively to a giant wall-mounted television: which is where Karim finds Omar, controller in hand, on a couch that seems to be digesting him slowly and alive.

"Hey," Karim says.

The other boy, over and over again, is pulling a sort of trigger. On the screen, not people, but vaguely human beings with gray skin and unseeing eyes, are being shot repeatedly; and though their flesh is tearing off in clods on impact and blood is spraying everywhere, they don't appear to be dying.

"What are you doing?" Karim asks.

"Dumb question."

"What are those things?"

"What things."

(Pointing to the television.) "That you're fighting."

"Are you kidding?" Omar says.

Only when the action freezes and GAME OVER appears on the screen does the other boy look at him.

"You want to play?"

"No."

"Suit yourself," he says, and starts it again, while Karim stands there and finally sits on the couch. Speechless for the duration of another massacre. When it's done, Omar, like a follower of timeless rules of hospitality, again offers his guest the controller. Karim ignores him. Gets up and leaves the room. Mounts the stairs of the strange house and enters the kitchen, which is wide-open and silver, and still. He opens the refrigerator. What he wants is a soda; and like a wish granted, there it is. He sits by the pool and drinks it and thinks about taking out his coin and practicing his meditation, but he doesn't want Omar to come out here and find him in a trance state. So he takes out his phone instead and checks Lifebook. There's a post from the girl, Khaleela (two hours ago, in Washington, D.C.: standing beside a giant statue of a guy in a chair, a president whose name Karim can't remember). Forty-three people like it and he adds himself to the list though he doesn't actually like the picture. He links to her page. She has more than a thousand friends. He goes to his own page. Nine. One of whom is the boy downstairs. What kind of friend is he? It doesn't matter, because with the coin Karim can go there any time; and even when the time is over, he can go there in his mind again tomorrow and be with her in his mind. Which is good.

It is. And yet. *I don't want to pretend. I want to go to Paradise for real. And for always.*

"Hey."

Turning. And Omar, from the door of the kitchen, saying: "Dude, time to hasten to the remembrance of Allah." As if prayers and God are a joke.

When they get there, a recording of the azan is playing over the parking lot. Karim and Omar go through the men's entrance. Mrs. Mahfouz falls in behind a couple of grandmothers in long shapeless robes. The hall is on the second floor. They climb the stairs together and remove their shoes together. But as soon as Omar puts his loafers on the shelf, he leaves Karim there, on one knee, untying his laces. When he finally walks in, the musalla is half-full: maybe a hundred men and boys doing their rak'ahs. Karim takes a rug from the pile. Omar off to the left. Beside him: one of the other boys who was at the pool party. Don't. Don't make a fool of yourself. Go to the middle of the room. By yourself. Say your prayers. (To one side of you, a guy in a Yankees jersey; to the other, an older man in a dishdasha.) Bow, kneel, touch your forehead to the rug—and after the second cycle of prayer, waiting now for the arrival of the imam and the start of the service, survey the hall: Omar and the other one whispering and joking; the mothers and girls and the littlest children roped off in the back. Maybe two hundred people now. Not just Arabs, but lighter-skinned Middle Easterners and dark-skinned Blacks. Even a white man. Whom you can't help but stare at and be suspicious of.

Watch him lower his head to the floor. As he does so, the person just in front of him and to his right will come into view:

A boy.

The resemblance in profile so strong you would swear . . . Then he turns, to his left and back, where you are—and you squinting in disbelief. But it *is*. It's Yassim, making a face that seems to say: Oh, there you are.

•

Dorian down arrows until he is back at 2:09 a.m. *UNKNOWN CALLER*. And there is the number. An area code unrecognized. Why talk to him? Not because he wants to. Only because he has to. Because what if his neighbor, the doctor, is right? Last night, a couple of strangers killed: men enlisted in a kind of army, soldiers fighting a war, ready and willing (or so one might assume) to die for what they understand to be their country. *But what if someone innocent were to die tonight, and I never even tried to stop it?* He walks outside, out the sliding door and onto the deck, where there are some Adirondack chairs and a gas grill and a bug zapper, non-functional, hanging from the eave of the roof like a memorial to generations of executed insects. And over the cul-de-sac: a crescent moon, a waning crescent. Horns pointing to the right. An Islamic moon.

"Who is this," he says.

"Um. It's Dorian Wakefield."

"I can see that."

"Is this—" (Don't call him by name: address him personally and you only make borders less secure.) "Is this the man from that organization?"

He laughs.

"You called me," Dorian says.

"I called *you*?"

"This morning."

"I don't recall the conversation. I probably made a hundred calls this morning. I'm very busy. Some haji-lover killed a friend of mine last night—"

"Wait."

After a period of silence—a time long enough for the siren of an ambulance to reach Dorian's ears and fade away—the man says: "I'm waiting."

167

"I guess you were right," Dorian says.

"Was I."

"Look. I have to talk to you . . ."

"Really. Well, you didn't want to talk to me this morning. It's coming back to me now. You're the kid with the black eye. I called you and you hung up on me. This isn't a good time. Your neighborhood has gone flashpoint. There are more than a hundred comments now."

"About what?"

"The post. I sent you the link, Dorian. I come out there, I blog about you. Last night, a guy loses his life and you can't be bothered to open your mail."

"It's not that."

Silence again. Then the man says, in a changed tone: "No, it's not, is it. It's not that you don't care. It's the exact opposite. Let me guess. You want me to exercise the better part of valor."

"I don't know."

"Do you know what the better part of valor is?"

"No."

"Discretion," he says. "That's what a famous coward once said. Is that what you'd like me to do?"

The boy looks at the moon. Not far from the lower horn: a planet. A pearl of light. And hears himself delivering an address about his neighborhood. The Nkondos' son, Ryder. Fighting in Persia. The Ganeshwarans. Hindu, not Muslim. And William Banfelder. Had served in Gulf War III . . .

"And what about you," the man says.

"Me."

"Yeah, what are you?"

Not sure what he means. Last year's genealogy project had revealed a backstory of embarrassing blandness. Anglo-Saxon. Last name derived from a place in England. (Meaning, literally: Watch over an open pasture.) But maybe the actual question is not *what were you born as*, but *what will you be*.

"Are you there," the man asks.

"Yeah."

"Tell you what. No action in your neighborhood tonight."

"Really."

"Mm. If you come to a meeting tomorrow. Of the local chapter. I'd like to expose you to a few ideas . . ."

And under the crescent moon with its subscript of star, Dorian types the information onto his notepad, not even thinking to *not* agree to the man's terms—a meeting, just a meeting, yes, all right, agreed—full not only of relief, but a sense of accomplishment as well; not to mention of optimism that this process of negotiation can be continued, and the whole situation defused gradually, and no one else hurt, and no one ever to know with whom he had to consort to make things right.

12

Time is a constant across all pathways. Though there may, and al-most certainly will, at corresponding geographies, be differing weather patterns (violent thunderstorms on one path, a placid blue sky on another), all dates and hours will be synchronized to the mil-lisecond. So, when Dorian Wakefield, at 2:33 a.m. EST on 2 July 2038 in B_{39} – R^{61}, is asleep in the Province of New York, he is also asleep at 11:33 p.m. PST on 1 July 2038 in R_5 – B^{94} in the State of California. In R_5 – B^{94}, his family never left California. On that path, his sister is alive, because on that path nothing ever came hurtling out of the skies over San Francisco. On R_5 – B^{94}, the city is undestroyed and Skyler Wakefield is alive; and at 11:33 p.m. PST on 1 July 2038, she is on a beach on the northwest edge of the city, at the strait that links ocean and bay—not far from the bridge whose main cables plunge and rise to the pinnacles of twin towers and whose suspension ropes uphold a roadway that has joined the city to the headlands for more than a hundred years—and she is worrying about her brother . . .

She is with friends on the beach. Fellow students from the art in-stitute. They have been drinking wine around a bonfire and pass-ing around a ceramic pipe packed with some very exquisite sativa from an indie farm up north. The flames are so bright that, from her vantage on the landward side of the fire, there seems to be, to the west (where the ocean should be), nothing but a blackness, as if everything, all the real world, might have winked out of existence, or never existed at all, and maybe they, Skyler and her friends and the man she is in love with, are floating in some allegorical space, like characters in a parable, whose situation is meant to instruct us and show us a way.

They are all in their mid to late twenties and studying to be artists. Skyler is twenty-six and learning to be a fictionist, a path her father had tried to stop her from going down, avouching that a future of cooking and ironing would be preferable to the humiliations of the writing life. But she hadn't listened, and she knows that her father is secretly glad of it. She gets up and walks away from the fire, the sand cold on her bare feet. Her brother is eleven. Not a little boy anymore, but still, when he answers, she uses the nickname they have called him by ever since she can remember . . .

"Dodo?"

"Skyler. What. What time is it?"

"I woke you."

"What are you doing," he asks. "Where are you?"

"Baker Beach."

She turns the eye of her phone (and the image of his face) toward the bridge, though she supposes the video won't show much more than the vapor lamps of the roadway like a trail of stars in the dark.

"What's wrong," he asks.

"Nothing."

"It's after midnight . . ."

"Is it?"

She sits on the sand with the image of him, grainy and monochromatic. Watches him wipe the last of the sleep from his eyes.

"Weird," he says.

"What."

"This dream I was just having. All these people in our yard. But it wasn't our house. Some other house."

"Yeah?"

"There was a car and . . . a guy dead in a car. I can't remember now."

"Just a dream," she says.

"Yeah."

"Anyways, I was going to ask you the same thing."

"What."

"If anything's wrong. I just, I got this—" (*sort of sensation*, some part of her is thinking, *as of standing with you at a precipice, a dizzy anxiety that some force will pull you over regardless of how firm my hold on you might be*)— "This sort of, I don't know," she continues. "That you're in some kind of trouble."

He shuts his eyes.

"Are you?"

"Sky," he says. "You know what I said to Mom the other day?"

"No, what."

I said, "'You know what, Mom? You're worse than Skyler.'"

"Mm."

"I'm serious. It's like . . ."

"What's it like."

"I don't know," he says. "But I'm not in trouble. It's summer vacation. I'm playing soccer, I'm doing my summer reading list. I'm trying to get a good night's sleep cause I've got a game tomorrow."

(and some part of her thinking: *Something not right, though I can't say what it is. A feeling I keep getting. {{examples}} That nightmare I have in which the bridge is gone. I'm babysitting a boy who is Dorian but also isn't. {{where}} I'm in a house I was in once, up on the hill in Presidio Heights, and I can see everything from up there: the bridge, the headlands, the bay, the ocean. Something happens. {{clarify}} I don't know. An act of war, an act of God. The bridge is gone*

172

{{dead link}} and the Marina District is burning. It wasn't a bomb, but then it is and I know I should be sheltering in but I'm not, because my brother is in very bad shape because he was looking when it happened and he was watching through a window: his face is bloody and his eyes are sightless. So I carry him on my back until we find a hospital—and that's where I lose him. No choice but to leave him there, but how can I leave him? {{disambiguation needed}} Leaving him. In other words: leaving home, going to college, moving to the city—when he was so attached to me, dependent on me. {{retracted}} That was nine years ago, nine years. The dream is not about that. It's not an expression of guilt or fear or maternal instinct. It's not telling me how I feel deep down; it isn't telling me that I'm ready to have children or that I'm not. What it's telling me is that something is wrong—something bigger than myself, of which I am (we are) only a small part. {{elucidate}} I can't. Except to tell you that the feeling seems to come from over there. {{specify}} The bridge. Whenever I'm near the bridge—like now—and much more so when I'm crossing it . . .)

"Dodo," she says. Are you there?

His image is frozen.

"Dorian, can you hear me?"

Low bandwidth. The call has dropped. He looks less alive than archived. Grainy, grayscaled, and motionless. As you must look to him. Why does that scare you? He is in his bed at home, breathing, as you are on this beach, breathing. And the bridge is there. It was never not there.

•

In the morning, Dorian wakes with a start and checks the community Lifebook page. A night without violence. As promised. Peace for a night. Now—how to keep it? Go to the meeting and then what. What will they ask of you next? Slippery slope. One step down and

you'll start sliding. Don't even go near the edge. *But if I don't* . . .
He gets on his bike and goes to a place he thinks of as his alone:
a wetland area on the east side of town, where a creek flows over
rocks and into an expanse of reeds and cattails. The multi-use trail
ends, suddenly, at the interstate: the creek disappears into a dark culvert ablast with the thunder of traffic headed toward Albany or New
France. Before that, you can enter the water and wade to where the
tall plants protect you like ramparts. He shouldn't go. He should go
to the police instead and tell them what he knows. But as he sits
there in that place of contemplation—atop a rock amidst the blades
of the reeds and the strange brown spikes of the cattails—it seems
to Dorian that to tell what he knows will not solve a problem so
much as create a new one, a worse one. He can set this right on his
own. Without anyone else getting hurt. And with no one ever knowing he had a connection to any of it. As he stares over the marsh
into the heights of the deciduous trees, he will come to feel sure of
this—and he will suddenly see, perched on a branch like a speci-
men from the state museum, an American eagle, which all at once,
with a shrug of wings, will come to life and fly away, silent as a
drone.

At first he couldn't believe it. But in the days since encountering Yassim at the mosque, Karim has come to feel that what is actually hard
to believe is that there is nothing unbelievable about the appearance of his friend. Hadn't the imam said in his sermon, two weeks
ago, that some of us become lost on false paths, but if we pray well
and honestly, Allah will guide us onto the path of our true and best
destiny—which will lead us finally and unerringly to the gardens of
Paradise? *I became lost*, Karim thinks to himself. *I became lost and I
didn't even know I was, but God has sent Yassim* . . .

174

After the service last Friday, the two had slipped out of the prayer hall together. On the playground, surrounded by squealing children and beyond the hearing of the mothers standing in the shade of the main building, Karim smiled and fought the impulse to embrace his old friend, for if he did, he was sure to cry.

"Yassim," he said. "I thought—"

"What."

"Nothing."

"You mean you thought I was . . ." He pantomimed an explosion by a sudden unfurling of his fists . . .

"I guess."

"I am, dude. I'm a ghost come to haunt your ass from Paradise. Shit, man. Can you believe this?"

"What."

"All of it. These fuckin mozlems."

Karim looked around and saw: little boys with neat haircuts, little girls wearing shiny shoes, mothers in fancy hijabs texting on smartphones. Nice families, each with a car in the parking lot and a home to return to.

"The sheikh wasn't kidding," Yassim said. "They're all infidels."

"But Yassim . . ."

"Mm."

"What are you doing here?"

Yassim smiled and put a hand on Karim's shoulder. There was nothing sarcastic about this action; no joke. His old friend guided him a few feet away from the play-structures, away from the mothers and the children. Under a line of trees, a few boulders were left over from when the land had been excavated. On one of these rocks, in the shade, Yassim produced a smartphone, touched the screen, and handed it to Karim. A video started up. A boy, robed like a little scholar in a short-sleeved dishdasha, a kufi on his head, looking directly at the recording device, said: "Peace be upon you, my

175

brothers." The voice. That's what made Karim realize that the boy on the screen was someone he knew. Realization in the form of a denial (*not him, ears too big*), even as he understood that the ears had been hidden before under hair that had since been cut, and that the boy on the screen really was Hazem—the very boy with whom Karim and Yassim, for half a year, had slept on a twin-size mattress under a lean-to made of scrounged sheet metal and particle board; the same boy who had been joined with them in dependency upon a drug that bore the three to a place far away from where they truly were; the one among them who had always been a true believer, never doubting what the sheikh told them (that, for example, if you lay your life down in the path of God, you will feel nothing when your body explodes). And yet, now—on a playground in the Colonies, a world away from Dakota—Karim still felt a weird doubt. Peace be upon you, my brothers. A thing Hazem would never say. And yet it *was* him. *Was* him wearing a suicide vest and standing in front of the flag of the Caliphate, saying: "Every one of you who feels you have no future now but the future of a dog. I thought that was my future. But I have found a new one." *It's him*, Karim thought. *Him and not him*. And what a strange notion came to Karim next. That this was Hazem's very self trapped within the screen of the phone, like a djinn in a lamp . . .

"So, he's dead," Karim said. "He's a shahid."

Yassim nodded.

In a tone falling somewhere between reverence and incredulity, Karim said: "He really did it."

"Just like we will."

"We?"

"It's a joint operation now," Yassim said, as a child skinned her knee and broke into tears. "That's why I'm here."

———

176

The Algonquin: A very big and very old building on Broadway. A four-storied castle of red brick with arches and columns and balconies, made during that gilded age when the town had lured people with its healing waters and horses. Once a hotel, now rental apartments. As he locks his bike to an iron rack near the entrance, Dorian realizes that he never has looked at the building closely. There seems to be something false about its grandeur. He walks up to the door. No video intercom, just a silver frame with black buttons and a speaker. No name next to 30½. He presses the button. No answer. But an interval during which he thinks: *You've come to them, you're asking them to let you in . . .*

Through the speaker: "*Yeah.*"

Dorian's voice sticks in his throat.

"*Hello?*"

"Yes, he says. I don't know if this is the place, but—"

The buzzer cuts him off. He hears the lock of the inner door click. Then he is in. He goes down the dimly lit hallway, past an elevator, and enters a space his mind links to an illustration from his fifth-grade history book: The theater where Abraham Lincoln was shot. What was once a lobby looks now like an empty stage. Two wide staircases sweep up to a second-floor balcony, then a third-floor balcony . . . Up the stairs. Every door is red with gold numbers. On the third floor, different hallways lead to the ends and corners of the building. He goes down one of them and, not finding 30½, returns to the center and tries the next one, and like a mouse in a maze turns around again. Smell of snuffed-out greens and cleaning agents, and sounds from behind closed doors of videogame warfare and doom metal. Finally, he finds it. Knocks. Door opened by a girl with stretched earlobes. He has seen her before: one of the baristas at Café Pravda. She says, "Dorian, right? God, look what they did to you." Touching him. Laying her hands on his face, one palm against each cheek. (For a second, he thinks she might kiss him

177

on the mouth.) "C'mon," she says, and leads him into a room with big arched windows, uncurtained. Not a place where anyone lives. It's set up like an office. Several desks. A printer on one of them; a scanner on another. Bare white walls. He sees a kitchen and smells coffee. Then he sees the second room, where a voice is coming from. Something about the minutes from the last meeting. Corrections, additions. Eight men at a table, each with a palmtop or a tablet, including Jon-David, from whom he gets a look of acknowledgement, at which a kind of relief moves through Dorian, the kind he feels whenever he starts anything new (a team, a camp, a club) and sees among the new faces someone with whom he shares a background of friendship.

"Who's this?"

"Poospatuck Incident," Jon-David says. "It's on the agenda." (Turning to Dorian.) "Here, I saved you a seat."

"What's your name?"

"Dorian."

As the man types it, Jon-David lays a hand on Dorian's back and whispers: "Congratulations. You're officially present."

•

She wakes up on the couch and recalls having woken up several times already. Each time glimpsing the television, but seeing only vaguely what it was showing her, and not really hearing what was being said. On the table between herself and the television: an ashtray and the small ceramic pipe she bought in a head shop in Haight-Ashbury long ago (before the bridge fell, before Dorian) and a small plastic zip bag with a few buds of the stuff they'd had the other night in the park; all this beside a wine glass and a bottle of red, half empty. One of the times she'd awakened, she had become cognizant first of the television and then of Dorian, who was sitting on the couch beside her, looking into her eyes and touching her shoulder, prodding her gently, saying:

"Mom, Mom."

And Kathryn had responded with something like: "Hm? What. Dorian. Are we all right?"

"Here," he had said.

What he wanted to do was help her up. But she was alert enough to not want him to think she couldn't do it on her own . . .

And so finally he had left her there, with the TV still on, thinking that's how you end up when you don't carefully consider every choice in life, one thing leads to another and you find yourself middle-aged and stoned and asleep in front of a neoliberal news program at nine o'clock at night. *Why is she the one I want to talk to?* Because, if she were sober, she'd drag it out of you. What's the matter, she would say. Where were you tonight? She would take you by the shirt sleeve, grip your arm and make it hurt, making you believe there are things a mother is powerful enough to disallow. *And my father.* Won't pressure you at all. Because deep down, he doesn't want to know. If he stays ignorant, he won't have to act. He can stay in his own world of stories.

Still, go looking.

You won't find him in the room downstairs, or in the bedroom. But through a window onto the back yard, you will notice a light in the trees. Go out there, cross the lawn, and stand by the door of the gazebo. He is inside. Writing in the light of a camping lantern, by hand in a notebook. Address him through the screen.

"Dad."

The pen will stop moving. Perhaps only coincidentally. He didn't hear you. Just a pause in composition. But then he closes the notebook and caps the pen and turns to you and says: "Hey."

"Hey." (Open the door.) "What is this, like, your new office?"

"Sort of."

179

The little screened-in outbuilding is furnished with a rattan couch; a small glass table, on which the lantern is set; and a lawn chair, in which you now seat yourself. Notice, on the couch, in addition to the notebook and the pen, a couple of old-fashioned books, a pod and a pair of earphones. And something else. A print-out, a picture. Grainy and ghostly, like a diagnostic medical image.

"Where were you tonight?" he asks.

"Nowhere."

He sees what you're looking at. His eyes go from you to the picture and back to you again. A moth is outside, trying to get in. Wings beating against the wire mesh of the window screen in a kind of code.

I knew what it was even as he gave it to me and said: "It's the photo you wanted. I zoomed into the sunglasses. That's the reflection." The strange thing is, I couldn't see it at first. Couldn't see the thing I was consciously looking for: a girl of eight or nine, holding a camera or a phone in front of her eyes. I couldn't see that. Still, I thought: I have not been wrong. I haven't. He altered the image . . . Then suddenly the truth was obvious and clear. I saw through the illusion of the white and black pattern. The flowing lines that seemed to be the lightplay of an aurora were actually strands of long hair (there must have been a wind coming off the ocean). A sloping shape, almost whited out by a brightness that could only be the sky, became the outline of an arm and shoulder. The darker vertical line was the strap of a swimsuit top; and the dark blur making it hard to discern a face was the device that had taken the picture in which she herself had been captured.

"It's her," I said.

"I know it seems that way," my father said.

"It *is*."

"Dorian—"

"How did you do it? Erase everything. I search her name and there's nothing—not even deep-archived."

"Dodo, listen to me."

"Don't call me that. *She* made up that name."

"You're seeing something that isn't there. So am I. It's happening to me now."

"What is," I said.

"It's hard to explain. It's what I'm writing. I don't know where the words are coming from. Something's going on. Maybe in the water supply or in something like milk that we consume on a regular basis. I don't think it could be airborne, but— A kind of hallucinogen. A drug that affects memory . . ."

Soon as he says it, he wishes he hadn't. Because he does not himself believe it. A drug in the water? If they were under the influence of some kind of chemical, so would countless others be. There'd be widespread reports of people remembering family, friends, lovers who never existed. No, this isn't pandemic. *It's specific. To us.* Us. *Yes, us. It's happening to me now.* Nothing's happening. You're simply seeing what you want to see. She's nothing but a dream. *The pregnancy was real.* And it might've been a girl—is that what you're thinking? And it might've been yours. *All of it is possible.* Okay, fine. Let's say it was yours (which there's an even chance it wasn't), and it was a girl and you kept it and had it. So one day, eight years later, you could've been on a beach in California and she could've taken a picture of you and her mother and her brother (and herself), and let's say ten years after that she was in the city when the thing happened, just like Dorian says she was, and let's say she died there. How did you—all

181

of you—forget all that? *Maybe that's it.* Maybe what's it. *The drug. It doesn't create false memories, it erases real ones.* Christ, would you listen to yourself . . . Listening, insofar as words not spoken aloud can be heard again in memory; and as Mitch listens, he speaks further still, saying it can't be that kind of drug either, because a life cannot be made to vanish totally: not from the cloud, nor from the mind. Yes, certain links can rot, or be deliberately broken. But Dorian said it himself. There are archives. It's the same with memory. We can take a pill for grief or trauma. Mitigate the pain of a loss. Even forget the day it happened, the specifics of the event. But we can't erase a life. The life will always be a part of us, and always *will have been* a life. And if some force came hurtling out of the sky over San Francisco, not a hijacked plane or a meteor but something infinitely more powerful, enough to crash entire systems of reality . . . if that's what happened that day over the bridge and she was there, then all this—the words I am writing, the dreams my son is dreaming, the photo his hands are holding now—these things would be recovered fragments of the life we lost . . .

Stand up now.

Don't let him go away thinking: *I am still alone, my father won't listen or believe, no one ever will.* Say: "Dorian." Stop him. Hold him still. Hold him. Over his head, notice a moth clinging to the window screen. Pale green. Eyespots on the tapered hind wings. Not an uncommon type but rarely seen, for its existence is so brief. Because of your light, perhaps it will not die in darkness.

13

This is the season when thunderstorms form as if summoned by a wizard, over one town or city but not another, golf-ball-size hail falling in one area while somewhere else the wind twists itself into a whirling funnel. In Kathryn Wakefield's office in the provincial appeals bureau on the twelfth floor of Agency Building 3, the text of a severe weather warning streams along the bottom of the computer screen—

... THE FOLLOWING COUNTIES UNTIL 5:30 P.M.: ALBANY, DELAWARE, GREENE ...

—while she looks through a plate glass window down at Empire Plaza, at the flux of human bodies, dozens of people walking on differing paths, each on his or her own small and private journey, and yet all of them (she is thinking) somehow united, part of a choreography of motion around the giant quadrilateral of the reflecting pool, which now, at this hour of the middle afternoon, is showing an image of a bruising sky so color-saturated and sharply focused it might be made not of light and water but of megapixels. She is looking down at the plaza when it happens.

The tone.

A high-pitched, nails-on-a-blackboard screak. But she does not reach for her mobile device. Doesn't stop the signal, though the signal will keep sounding until she touches the screen and opens

183

the message. Instead, she keeps watching the plaza, all the people whose personal paths through the collective transit had appeared to her, a few moments ago, at once volitional and predetermined. She watches them come to a stop. All of them—all of a sudden—motionless. Holding their phones, touching the screens, stopping the signal, reading the message. Well, not *all*. Here and there, Kathryn notices, a pedestrian hasn't even paused, hasn't broken his stride, as if terrorism does not pertain to him . . .

Five minutes later, she is in the garage under the plaza. In her little plug-in, in a jam of vehicles inching toward the exits. It will take upwards of thirty minutes to simply get out onto the street. Then she still has to get down the hill to the on-ramp. Could be an hour before she's even *on* the highway. Think about alternate routes. Problem is: this is a specific threat against capital cities, based on intelligence credible enough for the threat level to be raised to severe, meaning attacks are almost certainly going to happen. Every artery out of the city will be clogged, not only with commuters, but every resident with enough brains to get beyond a potential hot zone of radiation. She tries her husband again. No good. The networks are overwhelmed. Nothing to do but sit still and inch forward. A driver further ahead leans on his horn for seconds on end—and the sound, as it echoes through the subterranean chamber, brings tears to her eyes. And then she sees. Someone, in an attempt to back out of a space and join the line, is refusing to give up his claim on the queue, while the person he is trying to precede, won't back up to let him in, or perhaps can't because the next car is up against his rear bumper. The ultimate effect, after a revving of engines and a yelping of tires is of the interjected vehicle being rammed, at a forty-five degree angle, into the rear of another parked car, setting off its alarm. Someone else, two cars ahead, attempts an end-run around all of this, causing a new collision. Cover your ears with your hands. Open your mouth. Maybe if you scream, all these goddamn fucking people will prove to be nothing but ingredients of a nightmare.

Twenty or so miles north, in the town where she should be, the sky appears to Dorian Wakefield exactly as it had appeared to his mother in the surface of the calm water twelve stories below her office window . . . While she was staring out of that window, Dorian was walking through the ruins of the old race track, thinking back on what his father had said the night before, feeling that there was something to be done now, something they had to do, he and his father, both of them together, in order to . . . (This is where he lost his sense of direction.) To do what? Dorian doesn't know. All he knows is that his father believes him. But is belief in the claim of another an admission of dishonesty? The question is: Do you believe *him*, when he's been lying to you for so long, when all of them . . . This was the argument he was feeling inside himself when it happened.

The tone.

For a few moments, Dorian didn't really hear it; or, rather, the temporal lobe of his brain failed to interpret it correctly. Because of the cicadas. Because the tone of the advisory system (a combination of sine waves in the 800–1000Hz range) bears a striking resemblance to the song cycle of a periodical insect. The delay lasted a few moments only. Then the neurons in his auditory cortex responded, and Dorian Wakefield felt his heart catch fire. Like millions of others from the Original Thirteen to the Acquired Territories, he reached for his mobile device. Touched the screen. Stopped the signal. Read the text of the alert. Saw the time and thought: *She is still at work.* He stood there long enough to try a call—"*due to a surge in wireless*

185

traffic"—and then started running. Across the thicketed infield, past the dead tote boards and toward the ruins of the main building, making for the pavilion where he'd locked his bike, while overhead the sky took on colorations suggestive of the bruise that had faded at last from his face, so that, despite the clear and present fear that his mother might not get out of the capital before something went down, the image on his mindscreen was Karim coming towards him across a green lawn and drawing his arm back and the sensation in his gut seemed to be the convulsive pain of a fist striking him there. By the time he reached the pavilion and the fountain, he was gasping for breath, as if all the air had been forced out of him once again. He went down on his knees beside the bike and grabbed at the locking mechanism. Four numbered disks that he had turned probably a thousand times to a combination that he had chosen—and that he now cannot remember. He closes his eyes. Thunder. Like giant pieces of sky smashing into each other and subducting. Then the numbers come to him and the lock is open; and as he stands up on the pedals and starts pumping, a drop of rain hits his face, another his arm. A moment of silence all across the environment (magicicada does not chorus in the rain)—and then a noise like innumerable bullets being shot down from the sky onto rooftops, foliage, concrete. Suddenly, the air is half water. Sensation as reference (`var rain : Rain = dream of Rain`), so that, despite absorption in clear and present fears, he is also seeing-as-accessing a dream authored and saved on 07.02.2038 in which it was pouring rain and a muezzin was chanting. Karim was there, though he looked like Omar . . . I could feel the rain soaking through my clothes, warm like blood; and I understood that Karim was the muezzin and if I just kept him there in that storm, he would begin to experience a sensation like the one I was experiencing now, one of drowning caused by moving through a downpour of water while taking the deep and rapid breaths of someone in a state of terror. Gag and spit. Is there a taste to it? One there shouldn't be?

186

And I feel something, too. On my skin. That's called water. *No, like a burning.* Are you sure? *No, I mean, I don't know.* You're imagining that. *But it's possible, isn't it. To fly a plane carrying a nerve, blood, or blister agent into a line of storm clouds.* Yeah. Calm down, stop breathing so hard. *I can't, I think there's a taste in my mouth.* And watch where you're going. *It'll take her hours to get home.* Red light. *She's probably not even on the highway yet.* (Car coming from the left; braking, hydroplaning, barely missing him.) Hello, what did I just say, are you trying to get us killed? (Eyes burning, too. But don't your eyes always burn a little when you're crying?)

We live, day to day, with the chance of something violent, something tragic happening at any moment. Yet wondering *when* suggests the possibility (however faint) of *if*, allowing for the hope that the thing you fear may not happen after all. But when you know when, you can't hope against the coming. All you can do is wait . . . And that is what Karim Hassad had been doing ever since that day at the mosque, when his old friend had told him: Within the week. Some time in the next seven days. I don't know what, I just know soon. Now, listen. Give me your number. After which the two had parted company. Karim was brought home by Mrs. Mahfouz, and he found Jaddi at the kitchen table, cleaning his gun: inserting a small brush into one of the parts.

"How was masjid?" the old guy asked.

"Good."

He nodded, but didn't look up until Karim said he'd met someone there. "A boy like me, from a camp." And that was when Karim started lying. Saying first that the boy had been interned in the Wyoming Territory; and second, that the boy and his parents were now living with extended family in a town twenty minutes away. "He invited me over tomorrow," Karim said. "Can I go?" The reaction on the old guy's face was not one Karim had seen so far. An expression that reminded Karim of the way the nuns had looked at him back in Dakota when he would nod in the affirmative after being asked: Are you staying away from Dream? But then the tension, like a thin layer of ice quickly melting, was gone, and the old guy said, "Sure, bud."

The next day, Karim was with Yassim in the backseat of a car being driven by a man who had introduced himself to Jaddi as Yassim's uncle, Faraj. The man (maybe his real name was Faraj, maybe it wasn't) had been polite and amiable at the house; in the car, he shook off that personality, and adjusting the rearview mirror so he could see Karim and Karim could see him, explained in Arabic that there was not much time now. "If you had made contact three weeks ago, when you were told to. But because you failed in that simple task, we must move you quickly toward your goal, which will now be a shared one. A new era is about to begin. Within the week, the first lines of a new chapter are going to be written. We will give you a role in this heroic epic, and the action you perform will be added to the like actions of a thousand other shahids, each one of you like unto a wave which when joined together will form an ocean, and all of you will live as heroes in Paradise. But we will not tolerate any further problems from you. Am I understood so far?" Karim nodded, and Yassim said, "You'll have no problems from us, Uncle. You just tell us where to go and we'll be there." The drive ended in a rural area, on what seemed to be an abandoned farm. Yassim got out, Karim got out. The first thing Karim noticed was the barking of a dog. As usual, the buzzing of the insects was all around him. But he had become, in a sense, deaf to that noise, so all he seemed to hear was the dog, which judging by the hoarseness of its voice, had been barking for a long time without cease. "I already did this," Yassim said. "Did what?" Karim said. The man, motioning to the boys, walked toward a building painted the color of dry blood. Inside there, Karim realized after a few steps, was where the dog was. And as he perceived also that the building (the word came to him: *barn*) was falling apart—walls buckling, roof crumbling—Karim was blindsided by the thought of his mother telling him about a time, the summer before they were interned (he was three), when they had been at the beach, making a sandcastle, and a wave came and it fell apart, "and you started crying, habibi, and scolding the ocean." Door opening. Sunlit inside because of a hole in the roof; and leashed to a post, the dog. Whose barking, at the sight of them, changed from a distress signal beyond hope to a wild expression of thanksgiving directed at the beings who had finally responded. When he saw the gun in the man's hand, Karim thought: *Where did that come from?* The man walked up to the dog, pushed the gun into the short coat shrink-wrapped around the ribcage, and then shot. The animal yelped and leaped sideways: the leash stopped it short, and so it sat humbled in the dust. Blood dripped from fur matted with blood. It opened its mouth and hacked. The man said: "Now, take this—" (a different weapon in hand, a knife with a long curved blade) "—and cut the throat." In the three days since cutting that throat, Karim has come to see that it is true: He had not so much killed a living thing as ended the suffering of a pointless life. *For what kind of life is it to be chained up, alone and starving. And how are we—me and Yassim (and don't forget Hazem)—any different from such a dog? They fenced us in and made us orphans and the hunger we feel can never go away. Not in this world. So what will it be to take up a knife and cut our own throats?* And amid or laid over (or perhaps running simultaneously with) this voice-as-feeling was the image-made-from-story of a beach and a wave and a castle made of sand, and his mother; and all of this thought-as-seen when suddenly—from his phone and scaring the shit out of him—came the tone. Which he had known was coming. But foreknowledge of the coming was no protection. To the contrary, foreknowledge only pushed his fear into a dimension without boundaries.

189

•

In B_{39} – R^{61}, Karim Hassad has cut the throat of a dog. This action is repeated on many other pathways, though the cutting of the dog's throat is by no means a constant, any more than is the issuing of a terrorism advisory alert three days later. On many pathways, random chance has *precluded the cutting of* a dog's throat—for example, through antecedent events that lead Karim to a point other than the barn on the afternoon of 07.06.2038 and from that point to other points, none of which ever coincide in spacetime with the barn (not to mention the fact that on certain pathways the dog was never captured and imprisoned in the barn, and on one notoriously malfunctional path, which has been under review for some time by the appropriate RS subcommittees, the barn was never built in the first place). While on many other pathways, free will as exercised by Karim has *deselected the option of* the cutting of the dog's throat, a choice that will lead, on some pathways (though by no means all), to future events and fates radically different from those in B_{39} – R^{61}.

But.

The possibilities are infinite; and we could easily lose our way at this point (and could have long before now) by considering endless variations: which is to say, we could incapacitate ourselves with thoughts of what we might have done, what might or might not have been and what might be, if only we had done this or not done that. Such differences can concern us only insofar as they inform (and potentially impact) events on B_{39} – R^{61}: a path on which Karim Hassad *does* cut the throat of a dog and on which a terror alert *is* issued on 07.09.2038; where Dorian Wakefield is riding his bike through a rain he fears is poisoned, where Kathryn Wakefield is mired in a vehicular exodus from a city specifically targeted, and where the possibility of Skyler Wakefield once existed but where Skyler Wakefield herself does not exist.

190

All that concerns us now—and it is arguably the only thing that ever concerns any of us—is what happens next on the path.

Is a dirty bomb (hidden, let's say, in the falafel truck that parks every day alongside the very plaza that Kathryn Wakefield was gazing down at a few short minutes ago from an upper story) about to be detonated? Or is a blistering rash even now appearing on the skin of Dorian Wakefield? Are we fated to lose forever the ones we love? Or will the long-lost, in the end, be miraculously returned to us?

●

What happens next is not much. By dinnertime, the Wakefields are all together, safe and sound (though the car is scratched and dented on the passenger side and the cheap thermoplastic bumper is cracked, Kathryn isn't hurt), and nowhere in the country has anything happened yet. There was no chemical in the rain (Dorian feels stupid for fearing there could have been, something he saw on a television show probably); and the storms are wheeling off to the northeast, the harmless precipitation welled like tears in the flower petals of gardens and dripping tear-like from the rounded and pointed margins of leaves, while the clouds break apart, light of a setting sun pulsing through the fissures, a phenomenon you could describe as a kind of molting; and with the end of the rain, the cicadas, a few at first but soon all the millions of them, are once again singing their weird requiem.

It's a Tuesday.

Family dinner night. And if there is one cliché Mitchell and Kathryn Wakefield can get behind, it's that terrorism should not disrupt our way of life. Or, in the words (more of less) of their older son: A hundred years ago, people collected scrap metal; today we do our part by sitting down to eat, in a calm and civilized fashion that sends a clear fuck you to the enemy, a bacon-wrapped meatloaf.

"You'd rather have bread and water," his father says.

"Uh-uh."

Dorian (looking down at the apportionment of meat, potato, and vegetable on his plate): "Thanks, Dad."

"You're welcome, Dodo."

It's an exchange that Cliff notices and finds curiously sincere, and that Kathryn is aware of, too, through only obscurely, through a mood darkening by the hour like a day coming to an end. Earlier, when she got broadsided on the highway, pushed over the rumble strip of the shoulder and onto the grass of the median, she had sat there for a half hour. Now she is expected to use a fork; and the idea of a meatloaf made of veggie burger crumble expressly for her is too sad to bear . . .

"Kate," Mitch says.

"Mm."

"Should we serve you? Here—"

"I'm not hungry."

Dorian (picking up the carving knife): "It's veggie, Mom. Just for you."

She gives a kind of smile. "I appreciate that," she says. "But please don't guilt-trip me right now."

"It's not a guilt trip," Mitch says. "It's dinner."

"I said thanks."

Silently, Dorian puts down the knife. Feels his lip trembling. Goddammit, if you cry now. *Well, what do you want out of me.* I want you to cut the baby shit. *She could've died.* But she didn't, did she. *She hates me* . . . Too strong a word, and inaccurate. Hate is that cross that burned the other night. Hate is whatever is coming next, might come at any moment, but probably after we're asleep— after struggling to keep our eyes open and we just can't anymore, then it'll come, because they want us to be dreaming about it when it happens. But this. This not-touching, this not-looking—this is something else: harder to understand, more frightening even than hate.

After dinner, Mitch goes up to the safe room in the attic. Earlier in the day, right after the alert, he had come up here and checked the taping along the sill, frame, seams, and joints of the one window, and then covered the window with fresh sheeting and sealed the sheeting to the wall. Pinned to a corkboard on a different wall is a list of supplies. Check list against items stacked and stored: Ten gallons of clean water, first aid kit, box of safety matches, four N95 particulate respirators . . . For chemical or biological, nothing else to do. The main thing is an upper floor and no cracks. As for nuclear. There are people (some of them friends) who dug up their backyards after 8-11 and had a 7' x 8' x 30' box made of plate metal buried underground. Last semester, a student told him that all through her childhood she'd hosted sleepovers in a five-room underground bunker complete with a digital home theater . . . flashlight, twelve rolls of toilet paper, hand sanitizer gel . . . Of course, he and Kate had discussed it when they moved here, how they'd be living thirty miles from the capital and on the outskirts of a major tech corridor. What if the very worst were to happen? It wasn't a question of money (they could have financed it like anything else, a house or a car), but there was another kind of cost to be weighed against the benefit. Living with that thing in your yard. Your children grow up playing on top of it. You trim the grass around the blast door. A cold form of comfort. If we need it, it will always be there—and always it will be there, reminding us that, at any moment, we might need it. There it will be, hidden but never invisible to the mind's eye, a kind of coffin to step into of our own volition . . . hand-crank radio, pack of playing cards . . . So, if the very worst happens: the fallout shelter at the high school, a five-minute drive, though who knows how long when half the people in the district have the same destination.

Mitchell Wakefield has always said to himself: We can't be that kind of family. The kind that lives in fear. But what are we living in now, if not fear? (Every heartbeat a knifethrust.) We can't live any other way.

•

Has she ever felt this far away? As if all of reality has telescoped out to the edge of a horizon and is going down like a sun into a dark ocean while she, alone on a shore that doesn't exist, watches it disappear.

Kathryn is alone in bed. Her bed is the shore. Even her thoughts are distant, though she knows what she's thinking about: How one night, eight years ago—while to the south the city burned and smoked and sickened—when he was still small enough to be held in her arms, she held him in her arms under the stars and comforted him, and then laid his sleeping body down in the same room where her older son was already asleep; and then—(as she tries to remember, she herself is falling asleep, not quite unconscious but experiencing a déjà vu of the coming dream in which her phone is ringing and a wave of pain crashes against her heart at the sight of the contact photo and the name.

Answer.

And there her daughter is. Crying. Eyes wide and glassy. The night sky behind her like the sky in a medieval painting of hell. Howl of emergency vehicles. Mom, she says. Oh, god, Mom. Please help me.)

14

I had promised him something. I didn't know what exactly. But the next morning, when I woke up and saw the news: **SUICIDE ATTACKS IN BOISE, HELENA, AND CONCORD**— Well, like everyone else, the first thing I felt was relief. It hadn't been much at all. Small planes (light-sport, single-engine aircraft) carrying conventional explosives flown in the middle of the night into three pretty much empty Greek revival and neoclassical structures that had housed the legislatures of the Territories of Idaho and Montana and the Colony of New Hampshire . . . I had been the last to wake up. I came into the family room and found my parents and brother there, with the television split-screened so they could see a live-feed of smoking ruins at the same time that they were watching video footage of the crashes (in Idaho, a direct hit to the dome) while also listening to an argument between two pundits about whether the danger was now over or only just beginning.

I got a bowl of cereal.

Pretty soon, the next wave of news broke. Mosques on fire in the Republic of Texas and the Florida Territory—and as I watched the revenge take shape, I thought of Jon-David, and how I had agreed after that meeting to let him drive me home, because I'd lost track of time and it was nearly curfew . . .

"So," he said. "Are you with us?"

"I dunno."

"Jackson can be kind of corny. All that stuff about dinosaurs and asteroids. But he's right, you know. Our country is going extinct."

The windows were down. Cool night air flowing through the car. On the dashboard, a dead cicada. The way the wings were trembling, it looked like the insect was about to come back to life.

"I'm worried—"

"About what? The future, or your neighbors? I know perfectly well why you came tonight. To buy the old man some time. Well, let me tell you, he doesn't have much. People are upset."

"He'll go to trial," I said.

"There won't be any trial. He hasn't even been arrested. The old man knows his shit. He fired the shots from within a legal radius of his front door. So the hands of the state are tied. Again. And I say 'again' because this isn't the first time he's gotten away with murdering an American. He did it in Gulf War III. I found a guy from the company he worked for. He shot another PMC. Blew his head off. And then skipped out of country with a bank account full of blood money."

Suddenly, we were at the intersection of Cherokee and Poospatuck. He parked and we sat there, the engine idling.

"It's been a pleasure," he said.

"Yeah, but—"

"Yeah but what, Dorian? Let me assure you of something. What the old man did will not stand. Stay out of it. I'm warning you. Don't get involved. As for the Muslim kid. He's a very dangerous type. He's got nothing to live for, but he could have plenty to die for. Common sense dictates: Don't wait and see. But for you I'm willing to wait. If you promise me something in return."

"Promise. What?"

Staring through the windshield into the darkness, he said: "Promise you're with me when the time comes."

———

It is (to the mind of Will Banfelder) not an irony, but more like a trick from up the sleeve of an asshole god, that no sooner does a kid get rescued from the surreal margins of war than he is swept up in the mainstream of its terrors. Ethically speaking (just his opinion, of course), the camps were nothing short of malignant neoplasms on the body politic. But despite the myriad injustices of the institution (to say nothing of its especial dangers and horrors), it did have the one fringe benefit, resultant of bumfuck geographical location, of at least keeping innocent children safe from some of the sicker shit that people plan and perpetrate in the name of their asshole gods. I mean, seriously: *Tell you what, kid. We're going to let you out now (no hard feelings), we're going to make the fence and the psychopathic flying machines disappear (mecca lecca hi, mecca hiney ho), but, be forewarned, it has been determined that freedom can be hazardous to your health and may result in death, permanent disfigurement, emotional trauma (or all of the above) by explosion, poison, and/or pathogen. Rest assured, however, that when intelligence and law enforcement agencies determine that the communication between those sons of bitches who seek such outcomes becomes so active that projected dangers rise to the level of imminent probabilities, we will send you a convenient alert via home screen widget synched directly with the national advisory system that sounds as follows . . .* When Will heard it yesterday, he was drinking a beer and streaming a replay of the game from the night before, a classic pitchers' duel which (to his mind) was worthy of a second viewing, in the same sense that great books should be read more than once. He touched the screen of his phone and skimmed the text, then went directly upstairs, where he found Karim on his bed with his phone in his hands and the signal still sounding.

Will said: "Do you know what this is?"

Karim nodded.

"I don't want you to worry about it. Okay?" (Taking the phone from his hand and silencing the screeching.) "This happens all the time. They're always raising the level and then nothing happens . . ."

Next morning, upon discovering what did happen (not nothing, but for all intents and purposes nothing), Will feels pretty good about his handling of the crisis so far. He told the perfect lie, the type of lie a father tells for the good of his child (*happens all the time, nothing to worry about*), which is not a lie so much as a calculated exaggeration of the unlikelihood that things will be anything but all right in the end, which is what kids, and maybe all of us, need to hear and want to believe as long as circumstances allow for the believing. So, now here they are, father and adopted son, at the breakfast table, watching coverage of the crashes on the little flatscreen mounted on the kitchen wall where once upon a time there hung a clock with hour, minute, and second hands, when the doorbell rings. Get up and check it out. Slide your hand inside your unbuttoned shirt and feel for the gun in the holster. Peer through the window panel. On the porch are two people. Of Arabic descent. The kid Karim met at the mosque and his uncle.

Through the window: "Marhaban, effendi."

He opens the door.

Whereupon the guy takes him by the shoulders and kisses him two times on each cheek, as the kid says: "Marhaban, eboo Karim. Is he ready to go?"

"Go where?"

"Have you forgotten, effendi?"

And the uncle goes on to remind him that it had been arranged last week that the boys would play again today, we were to come here and collect him and they would once again spend the day together—and although, while the man is speaking, there is a thought in Will that something is off about his eyes (like he's blinking without closing them, as if there's a third lid as with certain species of birds and reptiles, a kind of shield that doesn't jibe with the fondness for honorifics and the predilection for cheek kissing), the idea gets lost in the illogicalities of the issue at hand.

"The playdate, right. Slipped my mind, but given the current state of emergency, don't you think . . ."

Touching the boy's shoulder, the uncle says. "Ebnee, why don't you go say hello to your friend. May he, effendi."

"Na'am."

Then, after he's out of earshot: "Best to not discuss this matter in front of the boy. He knows, of course, but why dwell on it."

"You're out in public," Will says. "I'm not so sure that's a good idea."

"No?"

"They're firebombing mosques. A guy got dragged behind a truck in Texas."

The uncle looks away and manages a smile. "You are . . . a good man. But this is not Texas, sadiqi. Even if it were, I would not hide inside my house for fear of what might be done to me. As for my nephew, he has spent enough of his life living like an animal inside a pen. But forgive me . . ."

But the thing is: Will Banfelder doesn't disagree, not in principle, not in his heart. Not that there isn't a counterargument founded on concepts like caution and forbearance, the integrity of which he recognizes. But this current state of affairs could go on for days, even weeks. Are you going to watch over the boy every moment? And doesn't the therapist feel that this relationship (with a friend whose personal history so closely parallels Karim's own) is one to encourage, one that will facilitate both the processing of grief and the adaptation to a new life and world? End result: You let him go. You agree to allow him to get in a car with a man you don't really know the first thing about. Not entirely comfortable with the situation, but accepting of its discomforts, although, as you walk them to the car (which you notice is not electric or even a hybrid, but runs entirely on fossil fuel), you feel oddly troubled by the fact that Karim didn't say anything this morning (such as, *it's almost ten, they'll be here soon*), as if he, too, had forgotten, yet saying a few minutes ago that, no, he had not forgotten, and yes, he still wants to go, though there was something unusual about the way he said so. And now, at the car, something more than unusual. You say: "See you soon, bud." And he, standing by the open back door as if at a threshold, pauses. Then steps suddenly back toward you. The way he does it is awkward and hurried, and the action itself is incomplete. But what he's doing is clear. He is putting his arms around you. Then the door is closing and your son of three weeks is on the other side of the door, the car is backing away, the man glancing at you through his window, and you imagining again, as you make eye contact with him, that strange blink, that drawing-across the eyes of a translucent shroud as in creatures inhuman . . . Despite these portents, you let him go.

And while some people, even now, even as Will Banfelder watches the old Saturn arc out of reach, are sealed in safe rooms or locked in underground shelters bracing for a violence that could recur and escalate at any moment, others, like Khaleela Kingsley (the girl from the pool party who, for nearly three weeks, has been a hope running silently in the background of the mind of Dorian Wakefield), are going on in defiance, or maybe denial, of hard data, so that even as Karim Hassad is being carried past the Wakefield house and is looking out the window of the car he is riding in to try and catch a glimpse of the boy he hit in the face and wishes he hadn't (wishing rather, as he looks and doesn't see him, for an entirely opposite history), Dorian is reading Khaleela's post about a vigil she plans to attend at the park downtown at seven o'clock, and Dorian is clicking on the shared link (The Peace Now Project | Light Up The Darkness) as Karim, obeying the dispatcher's instructions, is fastening his seat-belt and feeling the neighborhood, Poospatuck Circle, which was never his, slip away behind him in the same way that the internment camp, Dakota, a home that was never a home, slipped away beyond the windows of a different car; and he feels stupid for sadness felt about leaving such a place, which is the same stupid sadness about leaving the world, a place also not his and no more real a home.

"Mom . . ."

She is in bed again, already, at ten o'clock. Dorian, in the past, has seen her almost this bad. At the nadir of winter. But in summer, never. This is the mother associated with gray skies and icicles, whom he has agreed, after long negotiations with himself, to accept as an element of that certain term, with the condition that she will get softer and warmer like nature itself.

"Mom. Later today, there's this thing in the park."

"Mm."

He stands there, remembering how last night he had heard her through the wall, not crying exactly, but breathing hard, winded by the shock of waking up from an overwhelming dream, and he had stood at the threshold of the room (same as now), knowing her to be alone—waiting there while she ignored him, enduring it until some force compelled him to move: not away but closer . . . And Kathryn not hearing what her son is saying now as she lies in the bed that he had climbed into and slept in the night before ("a thing in the park, a peace thing, it'll be over by curfew")—not hearing that; not sure at the moment where she is, not sure when, much less who is speaking to her or what is being said. She isn't dreaming. Of that, at least, she feels certain. Earlier, seeing her daughter on the phone: that had been a dream. She couldn't possibly have been *seeing* Skyler because this is a mass call event and not only is the volume of traffic over-loading available channels, video calls have been access-class barred to give emergency responders priority on the network. So that wasn't real. Okay. But what she can't understand is: What is she doing in a bed, dreaming or not, when her daughter needs her? Maybe that's what the voice is saying (*get up, do something, before it all gets lost forever*). She tries to move. Just the intent sets off a bizarre sensation under her skin as she remembers, all at once, that they put fire ants in her circulatory system, the veins and arteries of which are believed by the colony to be a series of tunnels. As long as she stays still, there can be coexistence. But if she moves, they will eat through her from the inside. Wanting to move but unable to, a form of torture no different from wanting to go back and there being no means of travel or locomotion in that direction—and yet she is in a wood now; aspen trees whose leaves in the sunlight and breeze are literally gold coins turning in the air; and the man seated cross-legged at the foot of one of the trees—a Siddhartha clothed in a T-shirt and ripped blue jeans, feet bare, long hair, a bandanna, a spliff the size of a cigar in one hand—is communicating something along the lines of: Let ∞ be represented by a Cartesian grid that extends without borders in all directions. *A what?* (Smiling, smoking): You weren't very good at math, were you? *No.* A giant piece of graph paper. *Oh.* Now you draw a horizontal line: That's the x-axis. Ring a bell? The y-axis is a vertical line intersecting the x-axis. The point of intersection of these two lines is called the origin and has coordinates (0, 0). That's where you are: the present. Behind you on the x-axis is coordinate (0, -1). That's where you were yesterday, last week, last year, depending on your unit of measurement. Ahead of you on the x-axis is coordinate (0, 1). That's where you will be tomorrow, next week, next year. I can see it's coming back to you. *Can I try some of that?* Good idea, because this is about to get tricky. Let me approach the difficulty via a question. If (0, 1) is where you will be tomorrow, what about (1, 1), the coordinate directly above (0, 1)? Kathryn (thinking, smoking): *Where I wish I would be?* A frisky answer, and not necessarily imprecise. It's where you **will also be**, a point parallel to (0, 1) but also distinct from it, because back at, let's say, (–26, 1), using years now as our unit of measurement, you did something different from what you did at (–26, 0). *You mean my daughter.* Correct. *I dreamed about her last night.* (Nodding): In the terms of this discussion, you remembered a coordinate on the grid: $(-8, 12^{13})$ to be exact. Way up in the second quadrant. *She was dying.* (Smiling, gesturing for the joint): Death is nothing but something that happens at one set of coordinates while life is happening at another. You're dead right now, Kate, in more than two hundred thousand present moments. Skyler is alive in four million, give or take ten thousand. *Alive.* Of course, alive. And at several present-time coordinates, you are all alive right now, all five of you, all of you living in California, you and Mitch and the boys still in that same house above the river valley, and Skyler in the city and San Francisco as safe and sound as when you knew it in your twenties (at $x = -26$) when you were faced with a decision containing within itself an energy powerful enough to shape entire systems of reality . . . (But none of this said in so much dialogue, not heard by her as words nor even imagined as speech, but come to be understood through sustained hallucination as new subjects can be learned by study: a mother and wife to all outward appearances sleeping off despair, but really a woman in a wood throughout whose blood ants made of fire are conducting a dark pilgrimage to her heart while her body temperature is climbing as surely as the surface temperature of the planet.)

•

He brakes on the hill above the green and looks down at the war memorial and the carousel and the people gathering.

Seven thirty. The sky bleeding out. The fountain in the pond going hush-hush-hush. Someone strumming a guitar. One of those songs he hates, about a hundred years old and overplayed as a hymn.

Projected mental threat: I swear, if you start singing, I will throw that instrument in the water. Then, sure enough: "*Imagine there's no heaven . . .*" Are you really going down there? You know who these people are, don't you. They're the freaks who stand on Broadway, on the corner by the post office, with their signs. And remember that one time, they were actually out in the middle of the intersection and there was a woman with a megaphone standing on a crate shouting that her son was dead, go look, read his name on the memorial in the park four blocks from here, he was drafted in the last lottery (and pretty soon you couldn't even hear her because everyone was blasting their horns and yelling out their car windows or shouting stupid patriotic shit from the sidewalk). Usually, Dorian would've just pedaled past. But that time he stopped, because there were four boys out there in the street, teenagers a little older than his brother, and each of them was holding up a piece of paper, and one of them got the megaphone and said: "In case you didn't know, they still send actual letters. The draft notice is the one and only form of communication left in America that you can delete by burning." And that's exactly what they did. One by one, each kid lit his on fire. And then the cops came up the street in helmets with the clubs and the handcuffs—and Dorian is thinking now, as he walks his bike down the hill toward the black wall of the memorial, the same thing he was thinking that day: that he will become one of those boys, he will get that letter in the mail and have to make a choice (go or don't go; report as ordered or refuse to report), same one his brother will have to make a year from now and which they have never talked about as a family, as if silence can be a rampart against consequence. *And that surprises you? What have they been doing for eight years now if not trying to make her never exist with silence—* Shake it off: this voice, sectarian and oppugnant to the better angel of your nature, whose accusations (*lying to you, hiding her from you*) you have been repeating aloud for months and believing, as primitive peoples believe in fictitious explanations for phenomena beyond their understanding, when you knew all along (or at least know you should have known): that the truth, be it that of the stars in Heaven or a family on Earth, is infinitely more complicated . . .

"Dorian!"

He turns to see Khaleela running over the green with a glowstick in her hand, the sky above her faintly glowing and the fireflies sparking around her: a picture of her not to be forgotten and to cry over in future times.

"Dorian." (Coming to a panting stop.) "Hi."

"Hi."

"Looking for me?"

He nods; sets his bike against a park bench; and when he turns, she angles the glowstick in his face.

"Bruises all gone."

"Pretty much."

"So it doesn't hurt anymore," she says.

"No."

"Come on, then"—and takes his hand, thinking to herself that life can tear apart at any moment. The Caliphate could nuke the whole eastern seaboard tomorrow. Are you going to leave things up to a boy? As if there's time in this world for the slow confusions of nervous boys, the obviousness of whose attraction to you is rivaled only by the self-evidence of their total cluelessness about how to act on that attraction; while he, heart smacking around in his chest like a bee in a capture jar, knows somehow that the destination of this hurried hand-in-hand transit is the hedge at the foot of the hill—and Dorian knowing what will happen there, what he has to do, which he has never yet done though he has performed the action in imagination and also in dream (remembering suddenly a dream about her: disaster drill at school, basic medical in the fallout shelter, everything like normal except it wasn't a mannequin, it was her; he

205

slid a hand under her neck and pinched the bridge of her nose), and telling himself now, *when you do it for real, you don't breathe into her mouth*—and what in one instant is a yearning-forward shall become in the next the foretelling of a happening willed into existence by the dreaming of it, which is: his hand on the nape of her neck and her palm against his cheek and the two of them kissing at (0, 0) and at myriad other parallel points and sending a spike of love, like an electrical signal neurotransmitted, across the infinity of the grid.

15

As we were trying to figure out how to say goodbye, it happened again. The tone. Khaleela had my phone in her hand because she was putting her number in my book and then the tone was sounding on every phone in the park. And not just the phones. The municipal system was going off, too. Sirens starting up and echoing and multiplying into the sound of a flock of screaming robot birds while a text-to-speech voice, female and ageless, coming from the sky like the voice of a mythological goddess, said: "*Attention. This is the Capital Region Emergency Warning System—*"

"Khaleela!"

It was her father. She waved the glowstick with one hand and grabbed me by the shirt with the other.

"My bike," I said.

"We'll drive you. Come on. What if it's airborne."

She took my hand and we ran across the green, past the carousel, the horses motionless and wide-eyed in the dark, while the voice advised without feeling: "*The following bulletin may affect your area . . .*" Then I was falling into the backseat of her car and there were her parents in the front.

"Who's this," her father said.

"Dorian."

Her mother (pushing the start button): "Seat belts. Where do you live?"

"Poospatuck Circle."

"What?"

I told her it was a tribe. "A tribe of what," Khaleela said. "*Poop*satuck," her mother was saying to the GPS. "*Poop*satuck Circle." Which the GPS of course didn't recognize. "Point me," her mother said to me, and I pointed and said, "*Poo*spatuck," and explained that they were a tribe of Native Americans. Her mother started driving and her father looked back at me with disapproval as he switched on the radio. No one spoke the rest of the way. The only words in the car were the clear commands of the GPS and the vague imperatives of the man on the radio concerning the need to stay informed and follow the instructions of state and federal officials so we could protect ourselves, our families, and our community against an incident of bioterrorism about which no further details were currently known. "*Go point-five miles on Washington . . . There has been a serious incident.*"

Where they are now is not where they were the last time when he cut the dog's throat and he and Yassim, after being measured for the belts, put on make-believe ones filled with twenty-pounds of sand and practiced walking, stopping, and pulling an imaginary cord. That was a farm in the country; this is an apartment on the top floor of a three-story walk-up in the capital, through the window of which (smudged pane of glass, metal screen in the pattern of a Cartesian grid, and small black flies trapped in the interstice) can be seen, down on the street, a smoke shop with a window display of water pipes, and, above and beyond the nearby rooftops, the summits of the pale monoliths of Agency Buildings 1, 2, and 3 . . .

The first thing they did upon arriving in the capital a little before noon was get food from a drive-thru (cheeseburgers, fries, shakes), which they consumed in the backseat of the car on their way to view the target: a hospital named after an infidel saint. They did not go into the hospital, nor even get out of the car; but sat in the car and looked at the entrance to the emergency room, which, sometime between nine and ten o'clock that night, depending, said the dispatcher, upon how soon symptoms present in the general public, you are to walk through. Inside, you will be in a large room filled with people, perhaps several hundred of them. It will be loud and chaotic. Do not look into the faces of any of them. As we practiced, you will walk to the center of the room, cry Subhan'Allah as loud as your voice can go, and pull the cord. That is the hour in which you will meet God . . .

Then: single room with single window, table, television, a few carpet remnants where Karim and Yassim and the man knelt and said the afternoon prayer—in the midst of which the food Karim had eaten not two hours before, apparently not accepted by his stomach for digestion, hit the floodgate of his bowels with a sudden and merciless pressure. As he performed the actions of salat—bending at the waist, bowing, and saying Subhan'Allah—he tried to hold himself closed, clenching the muscles with all his might and eyeing the bathroom: only a few feet away, but also scarcely distinct from the main room itself and with no type of ventilation. You cannot walk away from prayers to take a *shit*. But what if one is physically incapable of prostrating, of kneeling and pressing one's forehead to the carpet, without losing everything one is trying so desperately to keep in? Just a few more minutes, five at the most. But his control slipping with every passing second (that garbage he had eaten, wolfed down as if not having had a meal in days; like a drug while being chewed and swallowed, but afterward, almost immediately upon finishing, how queasy he had felt and full of regret)—every second an eternity and not even at the first prostration and thinking *if you shit your pants right now* and going already for the door, not knowing what in the world he had been thinking waiting so long, unbuckling his belt while angling his backside and going into a squat and begging his body to hang on for just one more fraction of a moment, not caring now about smell or sound, only that he get his pants down, but the body refusing to grant the self even that much latitude, so that what the body refuses to harbor, instead of being contained by clothing, explodes onto clothing *and* hands *and* toilet *and* floor . . .

And now, five hours later: he stands at the window with Yassim, looking down at the smoke shop.

"Wish we could do it one more time," Yassim says.

"What."

"Dream . . ."

And then a knock on the door and the uncle who is no uncle peers through the glassed hole of the door, then unbolts the door and opens it—and a second man comes in, carrying a duffel bag.

Sun going down.

Almost time to pray again. Last time to ever pray in this world. Two, three hours left now (depending on how soon symptoms present). In the duffel: the belts. Not your decision. None of it by your own will. Not willed by you any more than what happened in that bathroom earlier in the day: a thing your body does and cannot be stopped from doing. For it has been written. Written that you would shit your pants from fear seven to eight hours before the achievement of your goal, shit all over your clothes and yourself and the floor of this ugly apartment the way that dog shat on the dusty ground of the barn as you bent over his bleeding body with the knife and held the edge to his neck, he looking into your eyes with his, seeming to know what was coming and seeming to desire it, and yet terribly frightened of it, too. *But you must not think that those slain in the cause of Allah are dead. They are alive and well provided for by their Lord (Sura 3, verse 169).* But what if you, after cutting the dog's throat, instead of relinquishing the knife, had thrust it suddenly into the belly of the man now laying the belts out on the table and had stabbed the point of it into him with all your strength, picked up the

210

gun he would have dropped and, holding it with two hands, pulled the trigger as he had pulled it against the dog whose throat you had already cut. What if you had done that. But more important, Karim: Why didn't you?

And Mitch wishing he had not given in and let Dorian go (which he only did because his son confided in him that there was a girl involved and father-son sympathy won out over vigilance), because now he's not sure where his son is, and, with the stress on the wireless networks, may not be sure of his whereabouts for some time if, as Mitch hopes, Dorian is sheltering in somewhere near the park rather than riding his bike in the open, in air through which something lethal could possibly be drifting right now . . .

As he drives, he tries the call again. Gets another dead beeping signal. On the radio, they are saying bioterror, but unknown whether food, water, or air. He finds the park deserted (though votive candles are lit and flickering all along the wall of the war memorial), then takes the route home his son would most likely take if riding home, which Mitch is confident Dorian is too smart to be doing, but then he remembers yesterday, the panic his son was in after riding through the rain, and he isn't so sure if intelligence or even preparedness has much bearing on human behavior once the energy of an emergency has been released; and who is he, in any event, to be judging the decisions of a boy not even twelve years old when his own decisions yesterday and today have been so unintelligent, ill-considered, and driven by emotions he has no excuse, under the circumstances, for not being able to control . . . *What emotions, what are you talking about?* Don't act dumb. Tell me you didn't leave the house today because of her, to get away from her—after she had gone back into the bedroom and you went in there later and found her in the bed which you had deliberately not slept in the night before because of what she had said to Dorian at dinner ("don't guilt trip me right now"), when all the kid had been trying to do was give her food. You looked at her in the bed: "What are you doing in here, Kate?" She, after a long delay: "I can't keep my eyes open." And you pushed the door closed and asked: "Is this really who you want to be to them?" *Them* meaning: Your children. *This* meaning: An image of weakness, of addiction to your belief in your own weakness, so invested in a sense of weakness that you can't stand with the people who love you, much less stand up to the ones who hate you . . . Words not so much recalled as rephrased in thought as he drives the route his son would most likely be taking. Not seeing him. Which is a good thing (*probably sheltering in, maybe in the old casino building in the center of the park*), yet wishing, too, to converge with him on the road so he can get him into the car and bring him home and keep him close until this thing ends, however it ends. Never should have let him leave the house today, as Mitch himself never should have left it. What is wrong with him? With all of them? A family whose members have not only *not* been together on this defining and exacting day, but have, in fact, one by one, gone missing. She first, to some inner world of despondency. Then he to his office at the college—because when she is like this, she falls into herself like an imploding star that will pull anything in its vicinity over an event horizon of gloom. So he escaped to a place always quiet in these summer months but today nearly soulless, and he sat at the desk in his office and opened the file (listeningvessels.docx) and tried to work on what he's been writing, if one can correctly call it writing, this phenomenon that, all along, has been more like a streaming of content than a composition of words. But how is he supposed to write when the nation is on high alert and he is so angry, not just about this latest episode of depression but also about an ancient history of which the document on his computer is nothing if not some kind of revision—

Well, that's what fiction writers do. What, hold grudges forever? *Fuck off.* No, seriously, tell me. *They write about their lives but they change things.* So that's what this is: a fiction? (Thinking, steering, looking for his son): *I don't know what it is.* Except you do. It's what would have happened if you'd known, when you were twenty-four, that the woman you were in love with was pregnant, and the baby was yours (and not that of the other, whose name we will try not to speak) and had been born instead of not, so you would have had a daughter, and she would have grown up but only to a point, only to die at the age of eighteen trying to save a boy who wouldn't have lived no matter what she did, and in the end her death would've been your fault, because she came to you that year, in the spring, and told you what she wanted to do: live in the city for the summer, in a sublet, and intern at a publishing house and wait tables and babysit, and, of course, write. *Well,* you said, *your mother won't like it.* **I know. That's where you come in.** *Who said I'm coming in anywhere.* **Dad, seriously, c'mon. A little intercession.** With the end result that, six months later, she was present in San Francisco (instead of a hundred miles farther north in Sonoma); in someone else's home (instead of her own, the one shared all her life with you); and instead of watching the disaster unfold on a television screen, she was in it, a moving suffering part of it—and your wife (her mother) able to say to you: She shouldn't be there. She should be *here.* She *would* be here if you hadn't let her . . .

Lost all the same, just in a different and immeasurably more painful way—and the guilt, rightful or not, the father's to bear, but also, at least, the father's to own.

And while Mitchell Wakefield makes one more loop back to the park and along a different series of streets (the keens of ambulances mixing now with the sirens of the municipal warning system), and

Kathryn Wakefield, through the ebbing light of a forest subconscious, is trying to find a place to vomit and void herself of the parasites that are moving faster now, burning up her insides, keyed as they seem to be to the wailing of banshees coming from deep in the wooded distance, the Tesla Electric being driven by Shadea Kinglsey is negotiating with a falsetto squeal the turn onto Poospatuck and Dorian is saying: "A little further. That one, on the left. Right here, this brown one." The car abruptly brakes at the foot of the driveway, bodies jouncing forward and back again, and he about to open his door when the mother says, "Hold on," reversing in order to pull up the driveway while the girl whom he was kissing behind a hedge fifteen minutes ago, first girl ever kissed, is taking his left hand in her right, though not imperatively, not an action suggesting the panic of a separation impending and irreversible; rather, a soft and steady touch that makes him think of the candle they lit together at the park and placed at the base of the memorial. The mother asking: "Do you have an opener?" And he bringing up the app on his phone, garage door lifting, and struck suddenly with a sense of proper comportment in the present situation (driven home, life possibly saved by the parents of a girl suddenly something more than a friend), he says: "Mr. and Mrs. Kingsley, it was really nice to meet you." Both of them looking back at him: the father with an expression like what-planet-are-you-currently-on; but the mother with a well-wishing smile—and then he's getting out, watching the car go away, raising a hand in response to her upraised hand . . . In the garage, only the one car. Opening his contacts and touching the image of his father. Dead beeping signal. Now at the door, keying in the code with the same fingers he had put on Khaleela's neck and in her hair. Bringing the hand to his face now, he can still detect a trace odor of the soap or shampoo he had smelled when, after the very first kiss, he pressed his face against her cheek, as if you can hide behind a cheek, as if there was anything to hide from there, alone with her. "I hope that's not all," she had said; and he breathing then, trying to slow his breathing, breathing in a scent he knew (sweet, verdant) though would not have been able to name; and then putting his hand on her neck and into her hair, eyes closed, not daring to open his eyes but thinking he had to because how else would he relocate her mouth which he never should have strayed from in the first place, but then suddenly there her mouth was, right where he guessed it would be. Calling out now, running into the house and up the stairs, calling to his mother and receiving no answer while thinking *Am I in love, can you be in love from just that much* and *Why isn't she answering*, fearing, becoming suddenly and fully afraid, that upstairs he will find her in the same attitude as when he left her, hours ago. But she can't still be in bed, not now, not anymore, when some kind of biological agent (they don't know what yet, or they just aren't saying) could be floating in the air and coming closer or may already be all around us—taking all at once the easy step over the fine line between fear and anger and imagining that he will find her in the bed, same as he left her, doing nothing and hiding from everything, so he will have to turn on the light and tell her, in a voice steeled by the fortitude it shouldn't be his duty to display, *Get up, goddammit, Mom, get the fuck up*, because it's her, she and all the rest who grew up in the time before, in a peacetime that was nothing but a willful turning away from a war that had already begun: their duty, not his; yet he the one to have to come home and tell his mother that this is serious, that's why sirens are going off and the phone is making that sound, *you pick it up, see, and touch the screen, and then you start trying to stay alive*. But opening the bedroom door will scatter all this acrimony to a kind of wind. Yes, the smartphone, lying on the bedside table, is lit up and the tone is sounding through the speaker. But Dorian can tell, even in the dusk-light, that, although the bed is unmade, his mother is not in it. Not there. He takes a breath. She's probably in the safe room with the radio on. She just couldn't hear him. And he is about to turn away (sorry for the angry thoughts, cognizant that her struggle will someday be his, for depression is in him and waiting for him, an inheritance no parent wants to leave, and none of it her fault, none of it anyone's fault) when a sound comes from the bathroom. A sob, a gasp for breath. Dorian already moving forward and seeing, through the open door, his mother on her knees. That much he can see in the gathering dark. But not until he waves a hand at the motion sensor does the color come clear: the red in the bowl of the toilet and splashed darker on the seat which she neglected to raise; and as the room lights up, she holds up a hand, also blood-stained. Not reaching out to him. Warning him to stay away.

By which time (7:33 p.m. EST), William Banfelder, having driven downtown wearing a half-face particulate mask, had talked his way past the officer on guard at the entrance to the police station, and was sitting in a work cube with a detective who, after listening to everything Will had to say (a computer listening, too, and transforming the spoken words via dictation software into written text), said:

"I'll get him in the national file."

"What file."

"Missing persons. It's premature under the circumstances, but I'll do it."

"Okay."

"Check in tomorrow, if there is a tomorrow."

"But what about this guy," Will said. "I'm telling you, there's something—" But the police detective, heavyset with a long scar on his neck, just shook his head, refusing still to have any truck with the idea that the man who had abducted his son ("you mean," the detective had already said, "the man your son drove away with of his own volition and, I might add, with your permission") was a member of a terror cell with not only no intention of returning Karim, but with the aim of using him, along with the other boy, in some kind of operation, maybe as soon as tonight . . . *Stupid son of a bitch*. Oh, like the feeling isn't mutual. Like he's got time for some stupid old guy who lets an eleven-year-old kid of whom he's been the legal guardian for exactly four weeks and three days get into a car with some haji he hardly knows on the second day of an elevated threat alert and then shows up at the police department five minutes after the shit hits the fan expecting immediate action to be taken in response to groundless theories and accusations— *Not groundless*. Yes, pal. Groundless. I'm not saying wrongful, just groundless, because I couldn't agree more that there is something really wrong with this picture, but face it, you don't have a single solitary fact to back up your gut, which makes you, in the eyes of law enforcement (to take just one example of an objective observer), no different from your run-of-the-mill paranoid islamophobe who sees a conspiracy behind every tree . . . And now almost nine o'clock, and Will Banfelder sitting in his kitchen with a can of beer on the table that he can't bring himself to drink, the handgun on the table just to the side of the beer can, and the television on (more and more people at this hour arriving at hospitals with symptoms, though still no confirmation of what they are sick with, could be Pneumonic Plague, could be Viral Hemorrhagic Fever, "*both of which start the same way,*" an expert now explaining, "*headache, high temperature, chills, then nausea, then worse, both agents Category A, both contagious*"—while on the alert ticker at the bottom of the screen: BIOTERROR ATTACKS IN MADISON, PHOENIX, ALBANY), and he trying the call again, knowing there won't be an answer, only that tone of failed connection like a heart arrhythmia—and knowing that, even if the networks weren't in a state of total disorder, Karim would not answer because the phone had surely been taken from him hours ago and turned off or discarded or more probably smashed to pieces to preclude any possibility of a GPS track.

Lost.

You lost him, Banfelder. Saved him only to lose him. So, total your losses. Because all is lost now—and there is nothing that ever could have not been lost, because the sins were too many, too grievous, the things you (we) did over there, all the evil done and the good deeds left undone of which the not-doing is itself a kind of evil. Listen and you will hear still, even after all this time, the voice of that psychopath from whom you actually took orders, no different from taking orders from a demon, saying: *Chill out, Willem. Ain't no such thing as consequences here.* That any of you could have believed such bullshit. Self-righteously deluded as only those can be whose time of dominance has nearly reached an end, refusing to admit the impermanence of your power though there was no more of it left than the oil in the fields you were so desperate to control (already then: a state of terminal decline), and you really thinking that, just because there was no accountability within any system of human justice, there would be no accounting . . . To the contrary: Your punishment shall be a constant across all pathways—even those in which you never did violence to a single living thing, of which there are many, but nowhere near enough to balance out the genocide committed across the full breadth of the grid, the killings untold of people on infinite parallel planes, men and women insurgent and civilian, whose names and sects you never knew and whose faces are long forgotten, though symbolized in the face of a boy (now lost) through whom you imagined you could redeem yourself—as if his tragedy, created by you, could become, through your mitigation of it, a valid means to personal salvation. For every path you live shall be as a path laid down between two mirrors and leading to the same end, the same loneliness, and the gun the only shade of companionship—and the temptation you feel now (to take one last life and be done with it) as ceaseless and all-important as the taking of breath.

16

Not reaching out. Warning him off. *Get away. Don't come near me.*
For a moment, Dorian can't understand. Then all at once he does.
Five minutes later (having called for an ambulance; having gotten
a mask from the safe room and returned to the hallway outside her
room, where he stands shaking), he hears his brother downstairs,
shouting, "Dad, Mom, Dorian," and can't answer: his voice gone;
dumb as a dreamer in the climactic moments of a nightmare . . .
And Cliff thinking, as he takes the stairs two at a time, that mother
and younger brother must be in the safe room; as for father— Then
he sees Dorian, wearing mask, holding phone, standing outside the
parental bedroom (door shut) and for a second doesn't understand.
Stopping short, looking at the door and then back at the brother; then
the house seeming to shift suddenly on its foundation (like that time
in California, fourth grade year, a magnitude six centered practically
in the front yard, if you could call it a yard, that field of flaxen yellow
grass unmowed and the stand of eucalyptus trees and the smell of
those trees, smell of childhood), and he putting a hand out now to
the wall of a different home and saying: "Oh, man. You called nine-
one-one? Okay. I'm going to get a mask. Where the fuck is Dad?"

Pulling into the subdivision. Onto Mohegan heading for Cherokee
when an ambulance audible for a half minute already and having

219

gotten louder by the moment, shows up in his rear and side view mirrors, and, as he pulls to the shoulder, screams past him, dousing the cabin of the car with tinted light, drowning out the voice on the radio, and then the voice again—*"if you become ill with fever or develop other symptoms"*—and up to speed again, seeing that ahead, the ambulance is making the right he is going to make and proceeding along Cherokee though not turning off on either Cayuga or Oneida, but continuing on, which means it is going to Poospatuck, giving Mitchell Wakefield the sense that he is following the vehicle according to some predetermined arrangement. Accelerate. Keep the lights in sight. If you don't, you'll never find your way. No, that's not it. Get there first. If you're there, even if only at the last moment, the dark angel will be required to pass over your house having been programmed to havoc only the households of fathers past due. But he can't catch up. By the time he reaches the driveway, the thing is off-road and driving up his lawn—and before he is even in park, they (a pair of them, wearing yellow biosafe suits) are getting out of it, one opening the back of the ambulance, the other stepping onto his porch and hammering a fist against the door. Bolting across the lawn now, into the rotations of light:

"Wait, I live here."

Through the respirator of his full-body garment, the one tech says: "When did the vomiting start?"

"What?"

"You said there's blood in the vomit."

"Jesus."

The front door opening and Cliff with a mask on, saying: "She's upstairs. Dad, where the fuck have you been?"

"Looking for Dorian."

"He's here."

(As the other moves past them with a folded stretcher): "We'll mask her, but stay six feet back minimum."

220

"What is it?"

"Don't know yet." (Going in.) "But it's contagious for sure."

Then Dorian. Mitch rushes up to him. Literally picks him up in his arms and carries him several yards over the lawn before putting him down and kneeling in front of him, the lights draining the blood from his face and turning his flesh pale white and cold blue in alternation. Saying, "I got home and went into your room," and Mitch looking into his eyes and telling him it's all right, and she will be all right, "I've been listening on the radio, and it's probably bacterial not viral, so there are antibiotics," half-believing that this is what he heard, saying it as much to calm himself as to calm his son, when what he actually heard on the radio is that they don't know yet, that it could be bacterial *or* viral, and if it is bacterial, it could be a drug-resistant strain of plague, and if it's drug-resistant pneumonic, the mortality rate will be one-hundred percent, and if it's viral there's no cure, and if it's viral hemorrhagic, there will be not only the vomiting of blood, but blood spilled internally, coming in time through every bodily outlet. So what he says he heard is what they must believe, because in any other scenario they are going to lose her *and we can't lose her, we can't*: every cardiac cycle of the father-and-husband now an emotional text-in-code: contraction, dilation, contraction: *and we can't lose her, we can't* . . .

While, in the ugly apartment, the salat reminder application on the uncle's phone is playing the azan, and as the muezzin chants from the phone, the uncle, who is no semblance of a loved one, says to Karim: "Do you think you can pray this time without defiling yourself?" The other man, the bringer of the belts, wants to know the story behind the sarcasm. The uncle tells him. The other: "Well, that explains the odor in here." "So, it is still in the air?" (Nodding): "I thought one of you had stepped in dog feces."

"*Allahu akbar, Allahu akbar.*"

And all through the prayers, the tears in his eyes as hard to hold in as the shit had been, and knowing (as he bows, kneels, prostrates, and a tear slips through a crack in a duct) that soon it will be so with everything, soon impossible to keep anything inside: shit, tears, blood, bone, brain . . . Forehead to the carpet and a baby crying in one of the other apartments, a long drawn-out seemingly eternal keening, like the sound of the homeless and orphaned cats that wandered the internment camp at night trying to find some relief for a feeling that had taken them by the heart and wouldn't let go: a desire not so different in its ruthlessness from the desire in him, and which, like his desire, has one (and only one) means of satisfaction. *To be again with those who have died, you yourself must die.* There is no purpose whatsoever in resisting the logic. And to object, on grounds of unfairness, to the difficulty imposed upon you by the circumstances, only suggests that your desire is not as great as your fear; or worse, that your love for them is less than your love of life (which is ridiculous); and worse still, that your devotion to this world is greater than your devotion to God (which is not only apostatic but impossible, since God would never have put you on a path to martyrdom if He didn't know that you would be thankful for the privilege of dying in His name and surrender completely without being afraid). So, this moment of doubt felt while holding your forehead to the carpet and looking at the stain made there because you aren't strong enough to keep your tears in is nothing but a moment: passing and past; and once gone, something that might never have happened at all. "O, our Lord, grant us in this life and in the hereafter good things." Remembering, even as he speaks the words, that time in Dakota (soon after they had died, before the dream-world of the drug) when he had set out with nothing but a backpack containing some food and a blanket, and his mother's broken eyeglasses in the pocket of the jeans he'd gotten from the nuns, going who-knows-where across the flatness, walking all day, all the way to the fence, until the sun had set, setting same as now, meaning the time had come to take the blanket out of the pack and use it as a thing to kneel and pray on. Except he hadn't done that. Only after the sun had gone completely down and the air had turned suddenly cold did he remove it and wrap it around himself and sit huddled there, making no excuse in either thought or speech (such as being exhausted after having made such a long journey to nowhere), nor promising that at dawn he would make up for the dereliction with a perfect du'a. He simply did not pray. And as the sky and air got darker and colder, he lay back and watched the stars appear one by one and saw one break from the others and fall in a straight white line and thought-as-felt: *up there, beyond all that, that's where Heaven is supposed to be.* An idea that might have been an affirmation if not for the way it progressed into question: *where it's supposed to be; meaning, where they say it is, where I've always believed it to be, never thinking to not believe—but what if there are no rivers or gardens higher than the stars; what if there's nothing but more dark space and stars falling never-witnessed and all of it only getting darker the farther you go?* And if so, then this world is everything and should mean everything to us—and furthermore, if there be no praxis of reward, then what we choose to do (or not do) is far from meaningless; in fact, every action means *more*, not less, because what we do here and now can never be made to seem later—in a heaven bent upon falsifying, like a nation, the truth about actions taken in its name—anything other than what it honestly was . . . All of this the equivalent of a transmission sent by the self over light-years of cognition, sender-self long dead by the time the message goes its distance, yet heard now by the listener, who, staring down into the circular dimension of a prayer rug, is perhaps sensing, at the outer limits of awareness, a way to alter his path.

What she understands is that she is moving—or, rather, being transported at an urgent rate of speed from one place to another. (Could it be between points on the grid, from one set of coordinates to another?) Certainly, she is no longer in the forest. This is some kind of small enclosure: walls, a ceiling, supposition of a floor; and she in the center, equidistant from the six sides of what is evidently a cube moving at high speed, though she herself (meaning: her body) is immobilized, as by some force being applied against her from all directions, as in a case of gravitational collapse . . . Think, Kate. What's happening to you? *I think I'm dying.* Let's not get overdramatic. *I'm serious. This isn't normal.* Maybe it's a dream. (Shaking her head while the tech in the back with her, whom she does not recognize for what he is—seeing nothing more than a yellow blur in partial occupation of the space of the cube—says, "I think she's delusional," to which the driver responds, "Shit, if this is viral.") You could be dreaming. *I'm not dreaming, goddammit, I'm dying.* Okay, you're dying, have it your way. But remember what the guy said: "Death is nothing but something that happens at one set of coordinates while life is happening at another." Think about last night. You dreamed about Skyler. Remember, he told you the dream was actually a point on the grid: $(-8, 12^{13})$. *So?* So think about another one. *Another what.* Another point. Same x, but a different y. *How could I do that?* Simple. Imagine it's eight years ago but you didn't let her move to the city. They tried to convince you, but you put your foot down and didn't let her. Go ahead, close your eyes. *They are closed.* I mean your real eyes. All right. Now. The date is August 11, 2030. You're at the house in California working on a legal brief, right? *Yeah.* Okay. Where is Skyler? *How am I supposed to know? There are a million possibilities.* Actually the possibilities are infinite. Just choose one. She was good with kids, right? *Yeah.* So, c'mon, Kate. *All right. I'll tell you what she did. She got a job as a camp counselor. At the Y in Forestville.* Good. See? You just remembered another point on the grid. *I didn't remember anything, I just imagined it . . .* Which is to say that, while strapped to a gurney in the back of an ambulance—body heat 101.6° F, blood cells escaping by the thousands from veins and arteries whose walls, under direct attack from the pathogen, are becoming increasingly permeable— she is feeling an emotion evocative of how she put her foot down that spring and said: "No, not yet, I didn't have an apartment until I graduated and I'm not saying you have to wait that long but I am saying this is too soon, and if it ruins the rest of your life to not be allowed to live in the city with two other teenage girls after your freshman year of college, then you can hold me personally accountable and never let me forget it." And all through the spring, her daughter giving her the silent treatment, and for a week after coming home, too, and Kate patiently waiting out the repudiation—until, one day, maybe a month into the vacation, she realized that the whole thing had blown over, and her daughter, far from angry about having to live the summer at home, was happy to be there (perhaps relieved to have been disallowed from doing something she could see, even in such limited retrospect, had been more a temptation directed at her than a desire born on the inside). Enjoying her days at the camp, her simple and soft authority over a group of six- to eight-year-olds called the Evergreens; and most days leaving that job (no more classifiable as labor than the story-writing she intended already to be her true and future work), leaving the camp and then—not out of any sense of familial duty, but rather because she wanted to, because doing it gave her personal pleasure—driving to Miss Izzy's to pick up Dorian. It had been her school first, and Miss Izzy her teacher. Fourteen years earlier. And when Skyler walked through the doors of the building now, she experienced (not as memory, but more as a shifting, a gentle subduction of muscles) some sense of the little girl she had been then; and there Miss Izzy would be, different but the same; and there, Dorian (three and a half now), standing at an easel with a paintbrush in his hand, or sitting cross-legged on a rug listening to a storybook, or in the sandbox outside cooking something made of sand on a plastic stovetop, and Skyler watching him, and Miss Izzy coming alongside her to say something like, "He's so much like you," or "He was talking about you today." And then Skyler strapping him into the car seat and the two of them driving up out of the valley, past the firehouse and the wildfire sign, whose dial was set all through that summer of drought to orange or red, and she driving past it and looking at it every day, and her little brother naming the colors each afternoon from the backseat and explaining the significance of each and reporting to her which color the arrow was pointing to: attempting through a repetitive engagement with concrete elements (colors, an arrow: a thing he himself could move if he were allowed to touch it) to apprehend the abstraction that the sign represented, which was not fire itself, but the possibility of fire, the likelihood of danger. And when the day came, the eleventh day of the last month of that summer, the day that some force came hurtling out of the sky over the city, she (at the camp with ninety children, fifteen of whom she was personally responsible for) remembering (again, as a shifting, not a thought) not the sign itself, but the concept and purpose of it, which now seemed to have been to warn them of the possibility, the likelihood of a very different threat: a warning no one had understood and a threat therefore unprepared for, though the building did have a basement, which is where they took the children, out of the summer sunlight into a concrete cave, where she and the other counselors strove to maintain the fiction that there was nothing to be afraid of though half the campers, in the minute of confusion following the first reception of the news, had gone online and read that a meteor had crashed into the bridge and the city was on fire, entire districts burning out of control and further impacts imminent, or that it wasn't a meteor, but rather a jet plane and within the plane had been a weapon, the type everyone had lived in fear of in the last

226

century (her grandparents, her great-grandparents), but had always seemed to Skyler a menace as remote as medieval plague, a thing whose old dark promises—of incinerated cities, megadeaths, and nuclear winter—had become, over time (after decades of never being kept, and decades more of test ban treaties and reduction treaties and the dismantling of arsenals), not just unbelievable, but impossible. And yet now San Francisco was all at once on fire and she sheltering in a basement with little children, the youngest of them taking turns in her lap while she fielded phone calls from parents en route; and letting the campers go, one by one, until finally, her responsibilities fulfilled, she was able to get in her own car, and as she shut the door and turned the keys in the ignition, she realized: *I am here because of my mother. If not for her, I would be there.*

And the father and his sons going into the house, understanding that no one is to enter that bedroom, which Dorian has of course already done, thinking now that his head hurts, thinking he feels both hot and cold, and knowing for a fact that there's a sick feeling in his stomach, though he is aware that it may not be the bacterium or the virus giving him nausea and causing him to shake, but rather the terror they've started in him, infected him with—imagining their satisfaction at how very frightened they've made him, having made him see his mother bent over a toilet, hair viscous with sweat, blood dripping from her mouth, looking twenty years too old as if aged by black magic, and making him fear now that he will be next, looking from father to brother (both touching and scrolling on their phones), reasoning: *in the bed I was less than six feet from her; if the incubation period is twenty-four hours, I'll be vomiting blood in the morning;* and Cliff saying:

"Dad, here's the thing."

"What."

"It's spread through coughing or bodily fluids. So last night . . . Did you and Mom. I'm just saying. If you did—"

"We didn't."

"And you don't have a headache or feel feverish."

"No."

"Or like you're going to throw up . . ." And the voice in Dorian's head going further: *and I kissed someone tonight, and our tongues touched, and if I've got it then I gave it to her*, and moving already, as if being pulled like something roped, across the safe room into the half-bath where he riffles through the medical supplies and finds a thermometer and puts it with trembling hands into his mouth, feeling a rush of heat in his face which he knows may not be due to the bacterium or the virus, but to a terrible sense of responsibility for what he's done and embarrassment at how ill-fated he must be to have done it, imagining some survivor friend of the girl he kissed after all this has run its course and life gone back to normal (though not for him, and not for her, because they're both dead)—hearing the friend saying in a near-whisper, standing by a row of school lockers, in a school decimated and in mourning: *He had it and he kissed her and she died. She died because he kissed her.* And someone else: *Who was he.* And the first: *Who knows. Nobody. Just some boy. His mother was sick all day but he didn't notice. Nobody did. And then he kissed her* . . . By the time his father comes to the door, he's taken the thermometer out of his mouth because he's crying too hard to keep it in place.

"Dorian, we're going to be all right."

(Shaking his head.)

"Dodo, listen—"

"I slept in there, Dad."

Moving away and turning his face away, to protect his father from the spread of the disease . . . And Mitch thinking: *God, that's right.*

228

I went in there around dawn and there he was where I sleep (should have been sleeping) and years since he'd come into the bed and probably wouldn't have if I had been in it . . . While Cliff in the main room is facing (as he has been for the better part of a calendar year) two doors, labeled GO and DON'T GO, and once the envelope comes with the notice inside it—ORDER TO REPORT FOR INDUCTION—he is going to have to open one of those doors and step through it, and thinking now that he needn't be unsure anymore about which: fuck passive resistance and fuck fear of death, like you could sit on your ass now jerking off in some halfway house in New France while she lies buried here and a chance that, over there, you could kill someone who might be said to share some blame, however remote, for what is happening to her . . . As Dorian, having gone to his knees, is crawling into the shower stall and closing the door, telling his father to stay away, "I know I've got it so don't come near me," huddling against the wall and putting the thermometer back in his mouth, knowing he has it and has already passed it on, *so I'll be vomiting blood by tomorrow morning and she by tomorrow night,* a fact his reasoning mind finds hard to accept: an hour ago, behind that hedge in the park, the two of us were just beginning, and already we're over. Thermometer in mouth now, father speaking on the other side of the shower door, though you not listening, phone in your trembling hands, thumbs touching alphabet, backspacing against the errors, then deleting the message before sending or even finishing (hearing that voice again: *And he didn't even call her, he just sent her a text*), closing his eyes, memory-touching his palm to her cheek and memory scripting a link using the scent of her skin as anchor—and in a new window of the mind: *I am coming home from school on a summer afternoon in Northern California, the car (in the back of which I am seated) going up the dirt drive past the eucalyptus trees, through the shadows and the scent of them, closing my eyes and breathing through the open window the infused air (something like the smell of a girl I will kiss eight years in the future: narcotic, pheromonal)* and remembering now, in the corner of the shower stall, how he would be painting at an easel or playing in the sandbox or listening to a story, and would turn or look up and there his big sister would be, come to take him home, and they would drive home together, past the firehouse (he telling her about the wildfire sign, what the colors meant and where the arrow was pointing) and then up the dirt drive through the trees and the smell of the trees. Except for the day she did not come to collect him. The day that something out of the ordinary happened. The school closed early, right before the napping time, so I could hardly keep my eyes open in the story corner while a teacher was reading us a book about a boy and his pet dinosaur, and I remember turning and seeing my mother standing next to Miss Izzy and I took one last look at the book (the dinosaur tangled at the neck in telephone wires) and got up and walked to my mother, feeling like I was walking in my sleep, and almost instantly, as soon as she strapped me into my car seat, I *was* asleep, and when she saw in the rearview mirror that I was, she must have turned on the radio, and I must have been hearing in my sleep what was being said on the radio, because I was having a dream that something had happened in the city: the reason we'd gone home early was that something had crashed into the bridge and set the city on fire: and the reason Skyler hadn't come to get me was that she was in the city: and I (even though I knew I was apart from her) was also in the city: and though I was myself, I was also another boy, an older boy, who lived in a house on a hill overlooking the bridge and we were in the house together: something had happened in the sky above the bridge only it hadn't happened yet: and in the dream, I am looking through a window waiting for it to happen and knowing when it does that everything is going to change and life will never be the same again.

17

In the ugly apartment: a table. On it, the suicide belts, which are more like vests, are laid out. On one wall: the flag of the Caliphate. What they are telling you to do is stand, one at a time, wearing one of the vests, in front of the flag, while holding an automatic rifle, and read something from a piece of paper while one of them points the eye of a smartphone at you and records you holding the gun and wearing the vest and reading what is written on the paper. The problem is, holding the paper leaves only one hand and arm for holding the rifle; and neither one of you is strong enough to hold an AK-47 in one arm. The uncle says, "So, let them sit in a chair." The other (whom you seem to despise even more than the uncle, though he has done nothing special to warrant a greater resentment) says, "One cannot make a declaration while sitting down."

"Uncle," Yassim says. "I know."

"You know."

"I mean, I just have an idea. Like if we were both in the video, I could hold the gun while Karim reads the paper. Then we switch."

For a moment, it seems the uncle is going to spit on him, and Karim thinks of when the uncle handed him the knife, and wonders what if, in a moment of spontaneously channeled violence, he had used the knife on man instead of dog. Why didn't he? Karim was that close to him; close enough that, after taking the weapon in hand and turning to the dog, he could have reversed himself without

231

forethought or warning and buried the long curved blade into the man's belly and sunk it in by pushing with hands and arms while shouldering and running against the weight of his full-grown body, forcing him backward and floorward and falling with him and on top of him, maintaining a firm grip on the handle. And now a situation not dissimilar. The uncle having already put in Karim's hands another (deadlier) weapon, though he had made a point, just before giving it to Karim, of ejecting the magazine and placing it on the table beside the vests, where it is lying even now, as the expression on his face is changing, or maybe staying the same but revealing itself to be something different than what it had seemed to be . . . In any event, he doesn't spit. He says: "Not a bad idea." The other (shrugging): "They will be smaller in the picture." But the uncle is already taking the unloaded rifle off the table and giving it to Yassim, then lifting one of the vests from the table and telling Karim to come, and Karim doing as he says and offering an arm and the man slipping a sleeve over his shoulder. Telling the other: "Think outside the box, sadiq. It will be a message of solidarity, inspiring other young people to join with a friend in martyrdom." And then to Karim: "Don't you think, ebnee?"

Ebnee.

And you thinking: *I am no son of yours.* While thinking also of the man to whom you are in fact a kind of son, who must be sitting in that house now, in the room he made for you, on the chair in a room you will never return to, before the desk upon which you left that old battered book. Open. Open to the page with the blood smear and the words about Paradise. Which you left there deliberately, as if the verses of that sura would explain sufficiently where you have disappeared to. A world of gardens and fountains. And why you did what you are going to do. Because it was the only way to get there. *The only way, jaddi* . . . But how can you? How can you walk into that place called Urgent Care and pull the cord hanging from the front of the vest that you are now wearing (which your body is now registering the full weight of), igniting the explosive liquid in the tubes taped there, and propelling the ten pounds of nails, screws, and ball bearings toward the hearts and heads of a hundred (maybe more) sick and terrified people, some of whom, far from being inimical to you, might be nothing but sympathetic: who, if given a choice of helping or hurting you, would help, just as the old man seated at that desk, looking even now at the open pages of the book, had helped you . . . And while thinking all this, you are also speaking, though not any words that parallel your thoughts. You are reading from the paper while Yassim stands beside you holding the rifle and the second man points his smartphone, you reading though not hearing your own voice though you know a voice is coming out of you and being recorded and the voice which is yours but also not yours, saying: *He ejected the magazine from the gun. But this vest you are wearing. What if you pulled the cord right now. Reached for the cord without apparent forethought and no warning and pulled. The explosive liquid would be ignited here. In this ugly room. And there would be no bombing in that hospital tonight. And the declaration of martyrdom now being recorded will never be uploaded and never viewed, and will never encourage any other boy to do what you are on the verge of doing*—and so it might be said that at the end you did a good thing, Karim, a good thing at the end. To accomplish it you need only move your hand the space of a few inches, feel the cord and pull. Suddenly. Without premeditation. Without reasoning. For all thinking on this subject is nothing but instinct. An omen in the nerves and muscles a moment before the cerebellum sends the requisite command, which it is about to do, about to generate the action potential that will spread through the muscle fiber network and prompt the pulling of the cord when the sound comes through the wall behind you: the baby: crying again: so near, so clear, there might be no barrier at all.

233

What is happening to Dorian Wakefield behind the closed shower door in the bathroom of his family's safe room? Insofar as an "answer" to this question is relevant when so-called physical laws are in the process of being eroded (or perhaps a more accurate phraseology: *when such laws are being, if not revised, than at least superscripted by the human mind*), that answer might best be attempted through a process of historical comparison across the horizontal axis of the grid. At a distant point in the past, in Quadrants I or IV (say, $x = -500$), Dorian's experience in the shower would almost certainly be considered supernatural, a mystical vision or a demonically induced delusion. At $x = 0$ (his present moment), a psychiatrist like the one he saw for two months back in the fall might diagnose a dissociative disorder, possibly an episode of depersonalization brought on by the panic caused by the fear of his mother dying and the fear of his own probable death. At future points on the axis, however (in Quadrants II and III: at, for example, $x = 109$), we know that what is actually happening is this: He is thinking of a point in the far reaches of the first quadrant—and that point, that summer from the past of a different pathway, is the very same one that his mother has been imagining-as-remembering while in the throes of a multisystem syndrome that is soon going to cause cardiovascular collapse. And the configuration of that point, that moment from another past, is so convincing and so longed-for (and we could say *necessary* in the context of a present situation moving rapidly toward total darkness), that Dorian is consumed by a sudden surety that the events transpiring here and now (at 0, 0) are not real at all.

"Dodo," his father says.

"Mm."

"You all right in there."

"Yeah."

"Can I open the door?"

And the door opening and Dorian exiting the little enclosure, unsteady on his feet, a rush of disequilibrium in his head, which might be a symptom of disease, but feels to him more like a kind of physiological adjustment, as if he has been at a great depth of water and is returning now to a surface.

"Dad. I'm going to tell you something. It's important."

"Sure."

"It doesn't really matter what you say back. It's just important I say it, because it's going to help us get out of this."

(Nodding.) "All right."

"She picked me up at school that summer."

(Still nodding.) "Who did, pal."

"Skyler. She was home that summer, not in the city. And you remember the firehouse?"

"Yeah."

"And remember that sign? It told you about the fire danger. Every day, I would explain it to her. Like, it's red, red means high . . . I just remembered that."

"Listen, Dodo. I want you to put this in your mouth and hold it there until it beeps. Okay?"

He does as told. Sitting very calmly and pressing his tongue down, keeping the thermometer steady. His father on his knees beside him, a hand resting nervously on his shoulder. And now beeping. And his father taking it and angling it in front of his eyes. Saying: Normal. 98.6. And then: "All right. Cliff, come here. Listen, guys." And telling them to sit tight. "Stay in this room. Keep the radio on. I'm going to make sure Mom is taken care of and then I'll be back. An hour at the most. Then I'll be home."

And thinking to herself (as she is wheeled unconscious, strapped to a stretcher, out of the back of an ambulance by two EMTs in biosafe suits and through the in-patient entrance of the emergency room, into a scenario of suffering and panic and inadequate epidemiologic response: upwards of a hundred people, the sick mixed with the worried, half of them unmasked and half of those vomiting blood into sickness bags), that the reason she is thinking about all this—about that summer and how Skyler might have been in the city that day but wasn't—is that she drove down into the valley earlier today, surrounded by the hills yellowed by sun and heat and lack of rain, and just as she was passing the firehouse and the fire warning sign (the arrow pointing to orange), she came suddenly, after a curve, upon a car driving slowly and cautiously, with a bumper sticker that said: 8-11 NEVER FORGET . . . Not that I ever do. Every single day, some part of me (if not concretely, then in the abstract) remembers what happened and what might have been and gives thanks (to whom or what I'm not really sure) for my family's deliverance. Still, in the summer, it's different. As we come closer to that date in August, the anniversary of a thing I guess we are just never going to understand, I feel the coming of it, like the fog that builds over the ocean, inevitable and integral, moving closer and massing overhead like memory. So, I was behind that car this morning, which was going far more slowly than the speed limit—and how could I know why. For all I knew, the driver (say, a woman like me: fifty, a mother) was thinking of that day and a child she lost, a daughter or son who *was* in the city on that day, whom she had *not* stopped (and saved) from being there, the way I stopped Skyler—and for all I know, she's weeping right now behind the wheel, the landscape a blur of grief. And my mind starts doing something that it does sometimes, that once it starts I can't bring a halt to, which is: darkly envisioning who I might be—what would be left of me—if she had been taken from me; if, on that day that the city was burned and turned to ash and sickened, my daughter had been *there* and I *here*, a hundred miles away, which might as well have been light-years of spacetime for the impossibility

236

of reaching her and helping. And I see myself in the house with the boys. Waiting and hoping (and praying to a god I don't even know) and trying to keep from Dorian what is happening; and waiting not only to know if Skyler will be all right but waiting for Mitch to get home from Mendocino; and trying not only to convince Cliff that Skyler *will* be all right but myself as well—and *believing* she will be because any credence given to the alternative is an acceptance of an unacceptable fate. (Breathing faster and more shallow now, central venous and arterial pressures falling.) Where was I? Coming into town. Yes. The car with the bumper sticker turning east. And instead of completing the errand I had come to do in avoidance of the brief I didn't want to write, I took 116 west, along the river, all the way to the end, to the beach where the harbor seals birth and nurse their pups, though the seals are long gone by summer. The beach devoid of people, too, and I sat alone against a log, a section of tree which, having been washed long ago into the ocean, had come ashore in a new form, contours rounded by wave action and bark bleached to near whiteness by sun and salt, and I sitting against it now, holding my phone and slideshowing through photos of us stored in the cloud as waves rolled and beat heart-like against the sand, and getting to this one: taken here: of me and Mitch and Cliff (I wearing sunglasses with lenses the size of tea saucers): remembering that Sky, eight or nine then, had lain in the sand in front of us, having actually made a shallow cavity in the sand so she could point the camera *up* at us, though she had managed to bring the ocean into the frame as well as the rock formation in the middle distance: the arch with its archway like a gateway. Which I sent to all of them (the photo, I mean: to Mitch and Skyler and Cliff and Dorian) with a note reading: VISUAL EVIDENCE NOTWITHSTANDING, I SWEAR UNDER OATH I NEVER PUT ON ANY SUCH PAIR OF SUNGLASSES. And I there, losing my connectivity to time, staring out at the ocean and the rock and its archway: no living thing around me, nothing moving on the sand or in the air above, nor the air itself, and at last even the ocean seemed to be still.

•

They sit tight with the radio on. Hearing the same urgent message again and again. "*Officials suspect that a Category A bioterrorism agent has been released in this area.*" Their father gone to the hospital to make sure their mother is being cared for and not lying unconscious on a gurney in the midst of total chaos, forgotten because there aren't enough nurses and doctors and no one to advocate for her and make demands in her interest. They sit tight, awaiting his return, for approximately forty-five minutes, at which time (9:22 p.m. EST) the next thing happens. The power goes out.

Everything dark and quiet.

They switch the radio to battery. Turn on the battery-powered lantern. Wake up their phones and learn that the electrical grid is offline—and not just New York according to some accounts, but everything east of the Proclamation Line and even up into New France, which means the system has been attacked. And now a report of a fire at a substation up north and speculation about a bomb in a tractor trailer or possibly a light aircraft; and an hour gone now and still he isn't back, and he said an hour at most, and no call and no text either, so where is he, and a sense in Dorian that things are coming to an end: an unreal feeling from a dream in which you have glimpsed the fictionality of setting and event but are terrified nonetheless by a seeming realism.

"You okay," Cliff says.

"I dunno."

"Here, take your temperature. It'll still be normal and Dad'll be here any minute."

"You think so?"

"I do."

Dorian puts down the thermometer and walks to the closet, opens it and takes out the air rifle. The only gun in the house. Which is nothing really but a toy. Into the wooden stock of which his grandfather (at ten years of age, almost seventy years ago) had carved: 1962. No sooner is it in his hands than they both hear, through the one sealed window, the car in the driveway below. Through the cloudy plastic sheeting: an aurora of halogen light. "See," Cliff says. "Like clockwork." Leading Dorian out of the room. Cliff with the lantern and Dorian the gun. Into the hall, down the stairs. Intending to open the garage door manually from the inside—and downstream of consciousness, as they enter the garage, a suspicion struggling against the current of presumption (though too weak to stop the actions), so Cliff already pulling the release cord of the machine, then shining the light on the door handle and Dorian ducking first under the lifting door, stepping out into the night to find that the car idling on the driveway is not theirs and the man standing outside it, a shadow in the backlight, not their father, and also another man on the other side of the car, neither of whom is clear to see, and Dorian thinking suddenly of something from a few years back, a kid from a town far, far away who'd disappeared and they'd found the body finally but never the head, as a hand grabs him by the shirt and seizes the rifle as a voice he recognizes but can't quite place (the pitch, timbre, and intensity allaying his extant fears while creating a new order of them) says: "Take it easy. It's just me."

Meaning: the man Dorian met in Keenan Cartwright's in-law apartment eight days ago; who called Dorian six nights ago while another man was dead on his lawn and whom Dorian hung up on and then called a day later in an attempt to stop a flow of violence that seems now so trivial as to be meaningless; whom Dorian told Keenan Cartwright four days ago to call and tell to stay away; and who asked Dorian, two days ago, to be there when the time came. So the time, it would seem, has come.

"Who the fuck're you," Cliff says.

"The cavalry."

"Well, just stay six fucking feet away from him."

"I'm not infected."

"Just move."

"Older brother," Jon-David says. "Chill. We're not here to sneeze on you."

"Give me the gun."

"You planning on shooting some squirrels?"

"Just. Look . . ." (The belligerence vanishing from his voice.)

"Tell me your name."

"Cliff."

"Okay. Cliff. Listen. We're here to help. We're not infected. None of us were anywhere near the zone. And just in case, back at my apartment, I have a thousand 100-milligram doses of Doxycycline. That's the antibiotic for plague and that's probably what those fucks released the other day and I'm going to give you some and I'm going to give your little brother the gun and all I want you to do first is see something."

"See what."

"What I have in the car."

"Look—"

"No, *you* look."

Motioning at the car with the gun. Making it sound like an invitation, a dare, and a command all at the same time. For several seconds, Cliff standing still. Then going to the car. Peering through the front window. Then the rear one. And Dorian walking now across the driveway, looking into the same window and seeing him in the back. Omar. Who had called him the name and hit him in the stomach and then held him while Karim hit him in the face and later apologized via e-mail. Slumped now in the far corner of the seat. Eyes closed. To all appearances: Dead. "Not dead," Jon-David assures them. Standing now between the brothers. "Here, I'll show you." Opening the door, still holding the air rifle. Now pointing the gun at the body. Now pulling the trigger. "See." (The body twitching once, then shifting position.) "Not dead. Just extremely asleep."

By which time Mitch has not even found Kate, much less confirmed her condition. More than an hour gone and he told the boys he'd be back by now but he hasn't even found her yet. Having gone to the hospital and waited a half hour for his number (87) to be called, so he could approach the station where a woman with a tablet sat behind a barrier of clear plastic sheeting, so he could say Kate's name, then spell it, only to be told that she was not in the system . . . "What does that mean?" "It means she hasn't been admitted," the woman said. "So let's get her admitted." "She isn't here. If she's not in the system—" "She has to be here." "Mister—" "Wakefield. I just gave you the goddamn name. The ambulance took her a half hour ago. How can she not be here yet?" "What were her symptoms?" (Paralyzed momentarily by the question): "She was vomiting blood." "She might be in Wilton. The most critical ambulance calls are being diverted to Wilton for triage." "It wasn't critical. I mean, they said they were coming here." "That was before they got her vitals . . ." With the end result of being back in the car, driving to the other hospital, though not knowing for sure if Kate is even there ("I don't have access to that database" had been the woman's last words) and thinking: She won't be there. I'll get there and she won't be in that system either because her vitals were all right though of course she was sick (*is* sick, I'm

241

not denying that), just not critically—and the second hospital *will* have access to the information of the first and confirm that Kate is in fact there, where he just was, admitted and in stable condition, and Mitch will turn around and drive back, strangely grateful for the confusion and the scare put into him, since the resultant clarity and sense of hope will be, by contrast, sharper and more intense. While simultaneously (on a parallel plane of thought): I'll get to Wilton and her name will come right up, all data entered into the proper fields like words chiseled in stone: KATHRYN WAKEFIELD: CONDITION CRITICAL: QUARANTINED 9:04 P.M. And also (on a third plane): that she will be as absent at the second hospital as she was at the first, her name entered nowhere, her body not to be found in space, and I perhaps to travel for the semblance of all time the road between two hospitals (signifying the interstice between two possibilities), remembering how I loved her at the age of twenty-four like someone under a spell, loved her more than he whose name will not be uttered, more than he ever did or could have. And now, the almost thirty years since then (describable as the period of celestial coloration after the setting of a hot sun, which is the bending of the light of love: in other words, the *effort to love* in spite of anger and regret and an implacable yearning for a path we didn't go down), I can feel those thirty years of emotion being compacted suddenly now, like the matter of a dying star, into a mass so dense that a hole opens in my heart, and I falling into it and through its feeling-time even as I park the car and run across the pavement to the doors of the hospital, already thinking-as-saying: *I'm trying to find someone. Her name is Kathryn . . .*

While you, in the driveway of your home of the last eight years, stand with two right-wing supremacists alongside a car in the back of which sleeps a kidnapped eleven-year-old of Arab descent. No parents to help. Only a brother who is saying, "You better get lost, our father is inside." And the response of the man (to whom, a week ago, you told the name of the boy now lying unconscious in the car) is: "No he's not. He's at the hospital." (Then, looking at you): "Your mother is in my prayers, Dorian." (Knowing things he can't possibly know, as if he is something he can't possibly be—until he reminds you that your father posted on the community page at 8:02, explaining about the ambulance and that he was leaving to check on her and the boys were staying.)

Cliff: "Who is he?"

"Omar Mahfouz," Jon-David says. "But his name doesn't matter. Does your mother's name matter to them?"

"You said you have drugs."

"Did I?"

"Antibiotics."

"Not with me. I'll tell you what. Help me get this fucker in . . ."

"In?"

"You help me move him into the house and Justin will go for the meds. Be back in ten, fifteen minutes."

"No way."

"Big brother," Jon-David says. "Think ahead. What do you think's going to happen next? A nice orderly federal response to this shitstorm? Three successful biological attacks, maybe more coming, every day another wave of infection. Even if there *are* enough drugs in the stockpile, who says you'll ever see them. The drugs are the next target. How do they get them? Think. Some fuck like this kid walks into a clinic and blows himself into a thousand stinking pieces of raw meat. Think. Think like someone whose country is under attack. Think like someone fighting a goddamn war."

Say: "Can I have the gun now."

"Hm?"

"The gun."

"This isn't a gun, Dorian. This is a toy."

"I know."

He will go to the trunk of the car and open it and unzip a duffel. Then return to you holding a handgun.

"Do you know how to load?"

"No."

"Here," he says. (Handing you the weapon. In his other hand a rectangular rod. The ammunition.) "Push that in. Yep, right there. Now rack the slide. On top. Pull it back. Harder. There. Good. Now a round is chambered."

"Is the safety on?"

"Yes"—and as he shows you, you are thinking: *Now. Release the safety and shoot him. Not chest or stomach. Low. In the leg. Then what. What about the other one . . .* Holding the weapon two-handed but your hands still trembling as they trembled all through the lesson. Think. Think. He knows. Knows what you're thinking. Yet he will go down on one knee and fold his hands around yours, and you allowing him to hold your hands, holding the gun together until the shaking stops.

After which he takes back his gun and returns to Dorian the pump rifle. Saying: "Where'd you get this museum piece, anyway?" And requesting that Cliff assist the other man in carrying the drugged boy. Dorian holding the rifle. Expecting from his older brother a look of damnation, but getting only a blank expression suggesting not only the absence of any option other than compliance, but the irrelevance of any other option. Cliff's eyes saying: *What does it matter now, the end all but here and the context for all behavior being eliminated by its imminence, so what is the picking up of this kid and the taking of him into the house but the movement of a body from one point in space to another*. By which time the guy named Justin is opening the door of the car, grasping Omar by the wrists, and hauling him out of the backseat, saying, "Forget it, I got him," the boy's legs and feet (which are bare) knocking against the rocker panel of the car and then the asphalt of the driveway, the man dragging him over the driveway and into the garage, while Jon-David, as he circles to the driver's side, is saying, "Basement if they've got one," and Dorian realizing, as Jon-David cuts the engine, that the car has been idling all this time with nightbugs orgying in the glow of the headlights, and now everything, all at once, gone very quiet, still, and dark. Watching Jon-David go to the open trunk. Listening to him saying: "What's going to happen now is, we're going to have a sort of interrogation." And thinking (insofar as a knowing at one's core that one will soon have to act in one way or another is a form of thought): *But that isn't what his eyes should have meant at all. What he should have meant in that moment of looking is that with the coming of the end, a new context is created for our behavior, and every thing we do now, in these final moments, is not less important for its proximity to the end, but more so . . .*

"Mitch, is that you?"

A voice from behind them, from the lawn. Recognized by Dorian despite a distortion of the voice.

(Turning): "Mr. N. It's me—Dorian."

"Dorian."

Seeing him now. Wearing a nuke-bio-chem mask with giant eye windows and a metallic proboscis. Carrying a baseball bat.

"Is that your father?"

"No."

"What are you holding? Is that a shotgun?"

"It's just an air rifle."

"Dorian, you should be sheltering."

245

"Thanks for your concern," Jon-David says. "His parents are at the hospital—"

"Who are you?"

"With all due respect, I might ask you the same thing."

"He's our neighbor," Dorian says.

"Well, okay, neighbor. I'm Dorian's cousin. I'm taking care of things until their dad gets back. I guess you saw the post . . ."

And Moses Nkondo breathing. Taking breaths through the filter of the mask: creature from a world where humans, insects, and robots have interbred. And Dorian listening to him breathing. Thinking: *Go, Mr. N. Go.* Even while saying aloud: "It's all right, Mr. N. We're going up to the safe room now." Even while imagining (trying to inoculate reality against the event by a mental prediction of it): the gun firing, his neighbor spinning and falling, *struck by a bullet loaded by me*, while his neighbor is actually nodding slowly, saying: "All right but get in the house now, don't stand around out here; and stay strong, okay, your mother'll be all right, you'll see; you need anything, you text me . . ." Imagining the sound that will cut the speech short: loud enough to take hearing away: the neighbor set spinning, though in reality he is turning slowly, turning away now and walking back whence he'd come, his shoes crushing the dead shells of cicadas—*shp, shp, shp*—and his breathing almost like the sound of waves to a deafened ear. Listening and thinking of waves *a thing I won't ever hear or see again, for I won't ever stand barefoot on an ocean shore, I'll never go back to California, nor see the sun set over the Pacific, never will* while Jon-David turns back to the trunk of the car and lifts out and hands to Dorian what appears to be a toolbox, though it isn't that (not a collection of small objects but one dense thing), carrying it with one hand, with some difficulty, through the garage while holding the rifle in the other, knowing the time is coming, *the thing you can't know is the shape of the time and the way you will shape it,* but feeling certain, as he leads the

246

way to the basement, that a moment is coming to be shaped in part by him.

Cliff (as they enter the basement): "Okay, so you'll go get the pills now?"

"Big brother, chill."

The other man: "He's waking up, JD."

"Good."

Two flashlight beams, one showing the boy on the floor, the other casting around for a sense of setting.

"He's trying to get away, JD."

"So, impede him."

Planting a foot on Omar's spine and Omar going: "Umph!" While to Dorian Jon-David says, "There" (and Dorian putting it, whatever it is, on the card table on top of an unfinished Monopoly game), and then, having found a chair, says to the other man, "There" (while unzipping the duffel and removing a roll of duct tape), "let's bind him right there." And Omar saying as if coming out of a dream: "Wherem'I?" And Dorian thinking *it will take both of them to do it, one to keep him in the chair while the other tears off the tape.* And watching: Jon-David pulling tape from the roll and saying, "Hold him now," while the other is muscling the boy into the chair, and your brother (as ordered) holding the flashlights. You watching all of this and knowing at your core that there is an act for you to perform *one of the last things I'll ever do and maybe the last thing that'll mean anything* though still unsure about the shape of it and not yet aware of the means. "Dorian, open the case." There's a snap button. The top flips over. Inside: an old military telephone with a hand crank and a pair of cables ending in metal clamps (like what you use to jump-start a car) *which they will attach to him, one to his bare foot and the other—* And then both shape and means come clearer, as Jon-David removes the gun from his pants and places it on the table. Then goes back to taping the feet. "Will you fucking hold him." And the means within your reach, and you about to reach for it, when the shape suddenly changes. Because Omar is about to wake up. When it happens, you will be staring at the gun, about to reach, so you won't see his body jackknife into motion—elbow to the solar plexus of one captor, knee to the chin of the other—but you will see him on one foot (the other taped to the chair) trying to run and crashing into the table, sending everything on its surface—board game, torture device, nine-millimeter pistol—to the concrete floor across which the gun is now skating. Loaded and chambered. Skating and spinning. Omar screaming. You, on your hands and knees. Feeling on the floor. And finding it. The means in your hands, but your hands so tremulous, how are you going to create the desired end? You might hit anyone. Or nothing. One flashlight showing a spot of ceiling, then illuminating a part of a body, then veering off again. The other fallen to the floor. Then picked up by your brother, shouting your name and waving the beam around, showing enough of the scene that you understand who is where. Now: the safety. On the back of the grip. Feel it? Under your thumb. Push the switch forward, the trigger will untense. One hand around the grip and two fingers on the trigger and your other hand on the barrel trying to stop the shaking. Jon-David has him. About a yard away. A knee on his spine and choking him by pulling his shirt back against his neck, and Omar hacking for air. Go closer. Cliff capturing your movement in the beam. Jon-David seeing you and saying, "Put it to his head." And when your brother says "Dorian," it will be like a calling from a fog at a time of perfect stillness, like a loon calling from the heart of a still lake through the fog of dawn when you've woken up before the others and gone down to the dock, and there you stand, alone and hearing it: the haunted call of a loon *which sound I shall never hear again, never to stand again on that dock, waiting to hear it again, listening until suddenly: a stroke of wings on water from the heart of the fog and from the cabin the voice of my grandfather* whose boyhood toy of a gun you have shot many times (gust of compressed air, soft pop of a pellet), but which could not have prepared you for the use of this weapon, your grip is all wrong, not firm, and when you do pull the trigger, having pressed the barrel into his body and he saying sharply, "That's not him, that's me," the weapon—as you close your eyes and turn your head away—will nearly jump out of your hands. For a moment, you won't be certain what you've done. What you have done is this: You have done the best you could. On the darkest of pathways, you have managed to stay true to the better angel of your nature.

•

For millennia, RS subcommittees have been issuing reports claiming that all pathways are predetermined and all actions performed therealong inevitable and unchangeable: that the notion of a choice between two (or more) possible actions is an illusion; that a choice-not-chosen, though available to the mind as *idea*, can never be converted by the brain into the electrical impulses necessary for the enactment of the choice.

We do not believe this to be true. We believe, to the contrary, that every pathway is *created by choice*, by the energy which moves (like electrons between a negative and a positive pole) between two actions, either of which *may or may not* be selected; and that the grid is an open system (like a brain either organic or artificial), which responds to every single choice being made across its infinitude of axes, and through which the energy of choices is carried along those axes, from one set of coordinates to another, as information in a brain is carried from one neuron to another along a synapse.

Example: Karim Hassad, who, in $B_{39} - R^{61}$, is currently in the backseat of a moving car in the Province of New York, clothed in a vest containing enough explosive liquid to blow his body into uncountable pieces and propel ten pounds of small metallic objects in a

249

cycloramic arc at a speed of five-hundred feet per second. At which very same moment, on another path ($X_4 - H^{18}$), he is in a different car, wearing not a suicide vest but a school uniform: white Oxford shirt, navy blue sweater, gray trousers, loafers, a patch on the breast of the sweater: ÉCOLE INTERNATIONALE DE GENÈVE . . . He is being driven through the American night, in a city robbed of power, along streets devoid of light. *He is being driven through the European morning, through a city aglow with sun, along a lake of sheer blue.* It is nearly time to die. *It is nearly time for school.*

"Habibi."

"Mm."

"Look at the fountain."

She is pointing at the white column of the Jet d'Eau, shedding in the breeze a curtain of mist rainbowed by the morning sun. She asks him to say something about it in French. He says: "C'est tres bon." She gives him, via the rearview mirror, a look of disapproval. He has studied the language since the age of three, almost fluent now with a straight A in the subject last quarter, but he hates to speak it because the pronunciation makes his voice sound silly. (He likes English best, then Arabic.)

While in the rear of the other car, he is thinking of his mother. Holding the eyeglasses somehow not lost for more than a year now.

"You still have them," Yassim whispers.

"Mm."

(Nodding; a strange set to his jaw): "She's waiting. They're all waiting for us . . ."

And Karim thinking: No, they're not. They're not there, because that place is nowhere; they aren't anywhere *even as he sits in the backseat of the other car looking at her eyes in the mirror as they cross the bridge over the Rhône* and drive through Washington Park where the homeless of the capital live in makeshift shelters not unlike the one we built together, Yassim, and survived in for all those months and maybe better for you and me if things had just stayed as they were and no one had tried to right the wrong, because what does it mean to be set free only to find that one has no choice—*though next week vacation at last and they gave him two options about how to spend it; he could go back to that place in the Alps or there's a camp in the States, in the Northeast, in the Adirondacks* and he remembers that it isn't true: there *is* a choice, a choice of *when.* You can sit idly with these eyeglasses in your hands until the car arrives at its destination, then get out, then walk in, and then—at the appointed time, in obedience to orders given—pull the cord. Or you can pull it now. *And so in a week he'll be on a plane to New York and his Uncle Da'ud and Aunt Mai will meet him and drive him to the camp* by which time you will be dead, and a hundred people more because of you unless you pull the cord now: the energy of the choice-to-be-made moving at the speed of an angel (faster even than the nails and screws and ball bearings will be moving after the pulling of the cord) traveling over the synapses of the grid as along the rungs of a celestial ladder and *reaching him in the backseat of the car as an anxiety he can't source or define, as if there is something about his life that frightens him—but what?*

A whisper: "Karim . . ."

"Mm."

"What are you thinking?"

Turning now to Yassim and wanting to answer him but unable to tell the truth and unable to lie—and so saying nothing, though if he were to speak truly (and in words that would express his thoughts truly), he would say: I am thinking of pulling the cord. Which I almost already did, back in that place, and I would have—but for the baby; and now, despite having nearly done it an hour ago and there being now and here no baby to harm, I can't seem to do it, Yassim. Because right now there is still time. Air to breathe; things to see; a friend to sit beside for a while longer. The less time left to me, the more precious to me the rapidly diminishing time that remains. So that with every passing moment (which is another moment

251

subtracted from the remainder), it seems harder to do what I know I should—

"*Karim . . .*"

"*Mm.*"

"*We're here, habibi.*"

And yet, try to understand me, Yassim: To cling to this remainder of time—which is no more than a scrap of paper burning—at the expense of the futures we would destroy, the lives we would sadden, is to renounce something even more valuable than breath, sight, companionship . . . *Picking up his backpack, opening the door, going to the front passenger window which his mother is opening* while reaching across the seat and taking Yassim's right hand in his left; a gesture not rejected, but augmented by a firmness of grip that feels to Karim like a response to everything he would have said, a holding of the hand meant to mean: Yes, I do understand: of course: now. *His mother reaching out, touching his cheek on a new morning.* His friend holding his hand at the end of days. *And he almost tearful at the separation. Thinking: Maybe I'm scared about next week, flying across the ocean alone—well, it's too late now because everything has been arranged.* Though it is not too late. Despite all the arrangements of the men in the front. Pull the cord now and all their arrangements shall come apart on a deserted and darkened city block. It will seem, as you place her broken eyeglasses in your lap, that you can feel her hand on your cheek *as it is touching his*; and as you reach for the cord on the vest *he will be shaking off the weird squall of emotions because it isn't too late because he hasn't left yet. She says: "See you soon, Karim."* And despite your wavering faith, you can't help but believe her: envisioning her—as you close your eyes and pull the cord—in a place where a fountain streams skyward pure white water, and all is shrouded in a mist faintly falling, a rainbow in the mist made of sun and water, the colors of which are the true colors of light.

EPILOGUE

Later that night, in the Province of New York—on the pathway which, until this time, has been our focus—a boy named Dorian Wakefield will succumb to the early symptoms of a weaponized strain of hemorrhagic fever which will take his life by the following day (as it has already taken his mother's) . . . But on another path, at a parallel point on the grid, a boy named Dorian Wakefield will be in his home above the Russian River Valley in California, at the dinner table: brother next to him; parents directly across; sister at the head. All five of them holding their phones—they all have the photo up, the one Kathryn e-mailed them yesterday from the beach—and laughing together.

"It's not just the glasses on Mom," Cliff is saying. "It's that thing on Dad's—under his lip."

"It was called a soul patch," Mitch says.

"Ha! Oh, and the two of you think you're so cool—"

"We do not," Kathryn says.

"Yeah, you think you're such hipsters. And then look at me, your son and heir, fat as a blimp."

"You're not *fat.*"

"I'm like a baby that got delivered in a Denny's in West Virginia."

"That's offensive," Kathryn says.

"It is," Mitch says. "But it's true. He was a goddamn embarrassment."

And Dorian laughing, too, though he feels weirdly left out, having

253

not been envisaged much less born at the time his sister transformed his parents and brother via imaging software into a jigsaw puzzle of pixels which, at a certain degree of magnification, shows them exactly as they were one day on Goat Rock Beach in what must have been 2020 or 2021.

"I just don't remember this at all," Skyler says. "Are you sure I took it?"

"You must've," Mitch says.

Kathryn (pouring wine): "Sky, I remember, specifically. You dug this hole in front of us . . ."

And his mother repeating herself now, which she tends to do when she's drinking and happy. Happy because everyone is home: Skyler staying the weekend, in the bedroom that hasn't undergone a change since she moved out completely five years ago at the age of twenty-one. Evening meal long over. Everyone drunk but him (even Cliff, who has downed his one special-occasion glass of wine and negotiated a second); and Dorian feeling tempted to sneak away and smoke a green, but knowing if he does they'll know he did it and they really will be angry (his parents, that is), and he will have done damage to what in a way has been a perfect night.

"Doesn't matter who took it," Cliff says. "The point is, the two of you think you're so cool . . ."

And Dorian does leave the table, though not to do anything delinquent. Just going outside. Where the sun went down some time ago. Making now just the faintest light over the western horizon: as when, in a crystal ball, future images spark and swirl. And he thinking, *like the glow from a crystal ball*. And wondering if his sister, the aspiring fictionist, would appreciate that simile, maybe even use it in the book she's working on at school. *If she were out here with me, I'd tell it to her*. Or maybe he wouldn't. Because for some time now, a few months, maybe more than a few, he has been feeling . . . How? He can't say. Can't pin the emotion down with any adjective. Except:

254

Different. Different than he always has. As if something is changing (has changed already) and the old (or only) ways of feeling about and acting toward his sister are broken links: words and gestures pointing toward a relationship that has become forever unavailable.

The door slides open.

It's Skyler. Coming out of the house, onto the patio; and closing the door behind her, muffling again the laughter and the shouting, though Dorian can still hear it as he watches her fall onto a lounge chair.

"Our brother is sauced," she says.

"I know."

"I have to admit, I'm a little tipsy. Mom is completely trashed. Dad. Dad I think has a bionic liver. I hope you're looking forward to your future as an alcoholic."

"I guess I am."

"So," she says, "when are you leaving?"

"For camp?"

"Mm."

"Next Thursday."

(On her back, looking up at the sky): "You nervous?"

"Nah."

"No? So, what is it then? What's up with you?"

Silence while night seems suddenly to crest over them: a wave of darkness flotsammed with stars. And Dorian thinking of the night Skyler called him, a few weeks ago, late, to ask the same question (though her tone that night had not been casual), and he had told her there was nothing wrong, which is to say he answered her untruthfully; and remembering how, when his ringtone sounded, he had been dreaming, standing on the lawn of a house that was theirs but wasn't, with a car wrecked against a tree and the driver dead by gunshot. Her phone call shocked him out of the illusion, though he then had the feeling, for just a moment or two, that he had only traded one dream for another. In another instant: fully awake—and, in a way, lying to her (to whom he never lies, cannot lie), saying I am in no trouble, when in fact he'd been troubled for months, struggling to understand why everything seemed to be coming apart when everything was perfectly fine and still is now and yet even on a perfect night like this—*my family together and happy and I am even alone with my sister under the stars*—it seeming to him that something is being lost.

He finally says: "I dunno."

"Dodo."

"I'm serious, Sky. I can't explain it."

Something moves out by the eucalyptus trees, a swift passing of hooves or paws (deer or fox); then nothing again.

"Maybe you're in love with someone," she says.

"I doubt it."

"Maybe you're in denial about being in love with someone."

"Are *you*?" he says.

"What. In love?" Still supine. Staring up at what some see as Heaven: "I think so. Yes."

And Dorian thinking of the boy (strange to say: man) whom he has met more than once. Doesn't like him, doesn't dislike him. He who just is. Who might as well be a principle of physics.

"Things aren't like they used to be," she says. "Are they?"

"No."

"I feel it, too. I have this dream sometimes, I don't even know if I should tell you."

"What."

She sits up and sits on the edge of the chair. "Something happens in the city. An explosion, a meteor or a bomb. It hits the bridge and whole neighborhoods are burning, and you're really hurt, except you're not really you. You belong to someone else and—I can't really save you. I can't even stay with you."

"Sky," he says. "WTF."

"I know, but my point is, that would never really happen. Same with you and me. We'll never grow apart. No matter how much things change. We're just afraid we might. That's all it is. It's just fear."

And he thinking later (too late to still be awake and thinking, but he can't stop his thoughts): She's right. It's the same way people have always felt. Since the days we lived in caves and feared the violence of nature and then dreamed up the idea of gods and feared their anger and then joined together in groups and came to fear each other. Yet even after the passing (no, the slaying, as of dragons) of those primal superstitions and prejudices—despite the agreements, accords, and treaties of the New Enlightenment—a fear is still in us: haunting ghost of a time when we said it was already too late, the ice caps are melting, the oil is running out, the civilizations are clashing . . . (Falling asleep now, though still thinking, and the thoughts being bent by the curvature of sleep): *But we saved everything, we saved it all in the clouds {{examples}} all our memories and dreams and that's where we live now {{where}} in the cloud {{disambiguation needed}}* . . .

The next week, despite everything she said and the good sense it made to you, getting on a jet plane to fly across the continent will feel like embarkation on a spaceflight to another galaxy, during which trip you will sleep and dream for a century, to realize, upon awakening, that everything you once knew—everything you *were*—is dead and gone. Calm down. This is just how it *feels*. Say to yourself—after making it through the security check, putting your shoes and belt back on, slipping your backpack over your shoulder—as you stand blinking at the departures on the monitor, looking for **DETROIT PAN A.M. 343**, say: *It's fear, that's all.* And keep thinking, as you make your way to the gate: *Just a fear of what **might** happen.* Because you will take off from San Francisco and land in Detroit as safe as can be—and you'll make your connection in plenty of time, video-calling and texting and posting photos all along the way, aware of how lonely it would've been, once upon a time, to make a trip like this by yourself and have no real connectivity to anyone you'd left behind, no more contact than an analog phone call in a booth, a few minutes with only a voice: to your mind, the saddest form of communication. At the airport in Albany, by the luggage carousel, there will be someone waiting with a placard. **DORIAN WAKEFIELD**. The person holding it, a man (about the age of your sister's boyfriend, but with long hair held back by a bandanna), gives you a smile a moment before you even move toward him, and says (reaching out in a handshake that is more than a welcome; it's like an assurance that you've arrived at a place destined for you):

"You Dorian?"

The drive to the camp is two hours. This guy in the bandanna, it turns out, is the counselor in charge of your cabin, which houses twelve campers for the two-week session: four boys from each of the major religious backgrounds (three from overseas: Israel, Switzerland, and the Islamic Republic of Palestine). "If I remember correctly," he says, "you're a not-practicing Christian." Which leads into a conversation about your belief (or lack thereof) in God, and from there to a series of topics, including: organized religion, family, weather in Upstate New York, Major League Baseball, and the space-time continuum. Before you know it, you are in the mountain range, the peaks—those liftings of ancient rock (which had first appeared as blue ghosts in the far distance)—high around you now, green and bouldered, and the road curling through the gaps and saddles, no intersecting routes, only unpaved turn-offs into the forest, one of which will be the one that climbs about five hundred feet through the lowland conifers to a lake carved by a glacier, blue sky copy-merged onto the surface of the water, and a sign arching over the dirt road:

CAMP DAKOTA

So, now here you are—in a place where you will raft and rock climb, hike into the backcountry and pitch tents, build a fire and listen to the wolves (who, once endangered, thrive again in these mountains) howling from deeper in the wilderness; and, more than all this, where you will come to know children who share your ideals, with whom you will coexist and cooperate for a time, and later stay connected to via social media, creating a kind of intelligence able to span oceans and continents. The van stops in a pool of evergreen shadow, under crashing waves of insect sound.

"Loud, ain't it?"

"Cicadas."

He nods and leads you up the steps of the main lodge. "The Great Eastern Brood of 2038."

After you have checked in and made your last call home and surrendered your phone, proceed to a little settlement of log cabins with the names of native peoples written above the doorways: Cherokee, Cayuga, Oneida. Inside the one named Poospatuck is where you will find him . . .

"Excuse me."

A boy so absorbed in reading, he didn't even notice your approach. But he sets the book down now and looks at you through eyes with brows slanted like accent marks, and says: "Are you my bunkmate?"

"I think so. This is three, right?"

"Three, yeah." Sliding down from the top. "My name is Karim."

"Dorian."

"You cool with the bottom? We can switch if you want."

"No, I'm good."

While you unpack your duffel—clothes for a week, toiletries, a journal and a pen, a paper book, which he picks up and leafs through (*A Swiftly Tilting Planet*)—he explains that fire circle is in an hour and you'll meet everyone else and tell them where you're from and vice versa, though there isn't any prohibition (he claims) against revealing the information ahead of time, so you say California and he says Geneva. Well, I'm not *from* Switzerland. I was born in America. He has an older sister. Me, too. Here, I brought real pictures. Isn't it kind of cool, to hold them like this. And so on. The two of you finding it strangely and surprisingly easy to talk to one another, as it can be easy to talk once again to a friend from a long time ago, despite having gone down different paths.

•

Nature, like time, is a constant. Which is to say that, at every ($x = 0$) coordinate on the grid—in the geographical region defined on many pathways (though by no means a majority) as the Northeastern United States—the Great Eastern Brood of 2038, also known as Brood X, also known as *magicicada septendecim*, is nearing the end of its lifecycle. The females, with knife-like ovipositors, have scored the bark of thick branches and laid their eggs in the slits, from which will come, two weeks hence, the nymphs. Born into a world without adults, without mothers or fathers (who by then will be dead), and perhaps this is why the children fall from the trees by the millions and burrow underground and don't emerge for seventeen years: What they're doing down there is mourning. As millions of people across the infinitude of the grid shall always be mourning, coping with every imaginable variation of loss. Every loss deserves a telling. What we have presented here is a fraction of a whole, no more representative of the total narrative than a single cell is representative of the living body of a person, just as every person described herein is, in like manner, a fraction of a greater whole of selves. And yet, even this limited picture provides us with a working equation describing the relationship between widely separated coordinates and their interconnectivity, including possible trans-path causalities. It has been posited that, in the near future (c. $x = 500$), an algorithm will be devised, complex enough to generate a full report of *all* diversifications: in other words, that infinity itself will be captured in its entirety. For the time being, this imperfect story of one family's experience will have to suffice.

ACKNOWLEDGMENTS

Thanks to the following people and organizations: Dede Hill, Melora Wolff, and Linda Simon, for generous help with many drafts; everyone at Melville House, in particular Taylor Sperry (editor), Dennis Johnson (publisher), and Adly Elewa (artist); the Steering Committee of the Ledig-Rowohlt Foundation, and everyone associated with the Château de Lavigny International Writers' Residence; and Kathryn Davis, whose fiction showed me a better way forward and whose faith in this book was essential to its completion.

A NOTE ABOUT THE AUTHOR

Greg Hrbek won the James Jones First Novel award for his book *The Hindenburg Crashes Nightly*. His short fiction has appeared in *Harper's* magazine and numerous literary journals, and in *The Best American Short Stories* anthology. He is writer in residence at Skidmore College.